Source

Source

A Fast-Paced Financial Crime Thriller

Zach Abrams

Copyright (C) 2013 Zach Abrams
Layout design and Copyright (C) 2021 by Next Chapter
Published 2021 by Next Chapter
Cover art by http://www.thecovercollection.com/
Back cover texture by David M. Schrader, used under license from Shutterstock.com
Edited by D.S. Williams
Large Print Edition
This book is a work of fiction. Names, characters, places, and incidents are the product of the author's imagination or are used fictitiously. Any resemblance to actual events, locales, or persons, living or dead, is purely coincidental.
All rights reserved. No part of this book may be reproduced or transmitted in any form or by any means, electronic or mechanical, including photocopying, recording, or by any information storage and retrieval system, without the author's permission.

My thanks go to Jason for being a sounding block while the concept was being developed also to Karen and friends for technical advice. Special thanks to authors Elly Grant, Pamela Duncan and Simone Beaudelaire for ideas and corrections.

Prologue

There was a loud 'pop' and Tom ducked when the cork flew from the bottle, bounced off the ceiling and ricocheted in his direction. He heard Sally giggle and turned to see the foamy liquid spewing out from the top of the bottle and running down over her hand. He proffered a glass to avoid further waste.

"Don't you think it's a bit premature for a celebration? True, we've made a breakthrough, but we still don't know what it means."

"Don't be such a bore! We've worked intensely for more than a week and we deserve a reward. Maybe it isn't a major breakthrough, but you can't deny we've made real progress. Besides, I haven't gone overboard; it's only Freixenet. It's a decent enough cava, but it's not 'Bolly' – I'd have gone for real champagne if it was a proper celebration."

Froth was climbing over the lip of the first glass and Tom replaced it with a second one. Sally's enthusiasm was contagious; her grey eyes sparkled and tears of joy had moistened her cheeks. Her smile was so broad, arguing against her wasn't imaginable.

"Not for me," Ahmed said, when he saw Tom lifting a third glass, "Have you forgotten that I don't drink alcohol? But I'll happily toast our success with a glass of spring water. I'm sure there must be a bottle in the mini bar."

"With the amount this hotel charges, it'll probably cost more than the wine I picked up at the supermarket. Never mind, I suppose we can claim it on expenses," Sally replied.

"What's with the abstinence?" Tom questioned. "I didn't realise you were religious."

"I'm not," Ahmed answered. "I was born a Moslem, but I don't practice religion – I'm actually agnostic. I'm not an immigrant, I'm a third generation Scotsman. My grandfather came from Karachi and arrived in Glasgow in the nineteen sixties. We were the archetypal Packy family."

Ahmed caught Sally and Tom's stunned looks and defended himself. "Packy's only a bad word when it's directed as an insult by outsiders. I can say it because I'm talking about myself. It's like Jewish comedians talking about the holocaust, they can be poignant and side-splittingly funny, but the same words spoken by a gentile would be in bad taste and considered offensive. Anyway, like I was saying, Grandad worked as a bus conductor. His son – my father – opened a corner shop and ended up owning three, including a post office. I didn't want any part of the business though, so I studied English and Media. I'm about as westernised as it's possible to be. None of my family drink alcohol because of being Moslem, but for me it's more of a health choice. I don't drink tea, coffee or fizzy drinks because I cut caffeine from my diet, and I work out at the gym four times a week, when I'm home."

"Sorry Ahmed, we didn't mean to cause any offence," Sally said. "You and I have got something in common – my father worked for a bus company, but none of the family has ever opened a shop."

"It would take a hell of a lot more than that to offend me." Ahmed grinned. "Besides, I've got a thick skin, you don't survive long in Glasgow without one. Ferguson's a Scottish name – is that where your family come from?"

"I think my grandfather came from somewhere near Stirling," Sally replied, "but like you, I'm third generation, although in my case it's English. I was born in Manchester."

"The name Ferguson will make you popular in Manchester with Sir Alex's past achievements," Ahmed suggested.

"You might think so, but it's not really the case. Most Mancunians support City; United draws its fans from the rest of the country. And besides, I've been away from Manchester for years now.

"Well at least one of us is a pure-bred Englishman," Tom interrupted. "My family can trace its roots back to the seventeenth century."

His outburst was met with guffaws from the other two. " 'Pure-bred' and 'English' don't belong in the same sentence," Ahmed announced. "It's an oxymoron. With the possible exception of Americans, the English must be the most bas-

4

tardised race on the planet – and you can interpret that any way you like."

Chapter 1

Tom made his way through the fog. It wasn't real fog – at least, it hadn't been in recent years – but the cloying atmosphere in Stephan's office had never truly cleared after the ban. Prior to smoking being prohibited, you literally had to part the colloidal-imbued air to see your way to a chair. Now there was greater transparency, but no matter how often or how well the office was cleaned or decorated, it still felt the same. The smell of stale nicotine and whisky was immoveable and whether real or imagined, the smoke was still there.

A career journalist, Stephan Presley fulfilled every cliché associated with the industry. Now aged fifty, he frequently drank to excess and he'd been smoking sixty a day for over thirty-five years. More than three quarters of a million cigarettes in aggregate and his complexion and aroma bore testimony to it. Some years back, Stephan had tried to cost how much he'd spent on tobacco and alcohol in an effort to justify cutting his consumption down or out. His shock at the number of figures in front of the decimal point made him reach for a glass, and he didn't feel comfortable drinking without a fag in his hand. So the effect was minimal; a temporary, slight decrease in cigarette intake before resuming his normal levels.

When company regulations prohibited him from smoking in his office, he took to using the roof garden for breaks, but it was suspected he more often simply closed his door and opened the window to reduce the evidence of succumbing to his addiction. The smell wasn't too much of a giveaway, as the air was already contaminated by the noxious fumes diffusing from his skin and clothes.

It was rare for anyone to volunteer to visit Stephan's office, any guests he did have usually arrived as a result of a summons. But there was no doubting he was good at his job – very good, one of the most respected editors in the business. He had first class instincts and an excellent knack of sniffing out a good story, even if his nose was too damaged to detect his own odour.

Stephan's yellow-stained forefinger pointed to a chair and Tom reluctantly descended to perch on its edge, praying the fabric's smell wouldn't permeate his favourite Hilfiger chinos. Tom's attention had been focused on Stephan and he only spotted the attractive young lady on the adjacent chair at the last moment. His attention was immediately distracted by her curvaceous shape and his eyes were drawn to her shapely legs. She was wearing open-toed sandals. He saw with clarity that her toenails were brightly and perfectly varnished, confirming his suspicion that her legs were bare and the deeply tanned colour was her natural skin, not an illusion created by tights or stockings.

Tom's eyes lingered a moment too long, before letting his appraisal move northwards to take in her tight waist, shapely bosom and the flowing curls which framed a disarmingly pretty face.

"'Yes' is the answer to your question," she said, staring pointedly at him.

Tom lifted an eyebrow. "Yes? What do you mean? I didn't ask anything."

"Yes, it is an all-over tan and I'm only telling you because there's no other way you'd find out. And trust me; you didn't need to open your mouth to ask the question." The girl's eyes were slate grey in colour, but alive with mirth which spread to the rest of her face. The sparkling whiteness of her perfect teeth lit up the otherwise dingy office.

"Www— No, it was only—" Tom stammered. The room's temperature seemed to be rising, heat radiating from his embarrassment.

"Don't bother trying to deny it, Tom. You've been caught red-handed; well, red-cheeked to be precise. Just accept it and move on. You're starting this game one-nil down." The craggy, nicotine-stained teeth in Stephan's mouth formed a hideous smile, and although it was nowhere near as appealing as Sally's, it betrayed no less amusement.

Tom sank resignedly back into the chair, his eyes focused on the carpet. "Okay, what's this about?" he asked. He wanted to change the subject and try to regain some of his self-esteem.

"I suppose I'd better introduce you two first," Stephan suggested. "Tom Bishop, this is Sally

Ferguson and vice versa. You've probably already heard of each other. I'd be surprised if either of you weren't aware of the other's by-line."

This time, Tom was careful to keep has gaze above shoulder height and he wasn't disappointed. Sally's face was still aflame with cheerful amusement. Her smooth, even complexion was tanned to the same shade as her legs and complemented by the lightest application of cosmetics, which showed her almond-shaped eyes and full mouth to their best effect.

By contrast, Sally seized the opportunity to take a long, appraising look at Tom, studying his clean-cut image and powerful form, and the cropped, sandy hair topping his slim, angular face. "You don't scrub up too badly, a lot better than the photo on your column. You appear younger, too. What are you, thirty? Thirty-two perhaps?"

Tom was taken aback by her bluntness, but quickly reassessed his reaction. After all, what could he expect from a fellow journalist? He couldn't remember ever being attracted to someone in his profession before. "You don't look so bad yourself and I'm thirty-four actually, so thanks for the compliment. Maybe I'm not wearing as badly as I'd thought – but more likely, you're in need of seeing an optician."

"Isn't that a contradiction of terms? If I couldn't see clearly, I wouldn't be able to see an optician."

Stephan cut in. "Okay, children, enough of the word games. Let's get down to business." He sank into his chair and picked up a pencil, holding it between his fingers and sucking on it as if it was a surrogate cigarette. "I can see I'm going to have my work cut out, trying to control you two. As if Tom hasn't been a big enough pain in the ass for the past five years, now I've got both of you to deal with." He eyed them for a moment. "Sally, I'm sure you already know Tom's been our lead features writer at the London office for some time now. Tom, I know you'll have heard of Sally, but you might not know she took over the lead in Sydney a few months back."

Tom stared at Sally. "So the tan's real then, and I know you're not meant to ask a lady's age – but as you don't qualify, I'll ask anyway."

Sally shrugged. "Cheap shot. I'd expected better than that, but I've got nothing to hide. I'll turn thirty-one next-week and to save you asking the other questions; I'm single, heterosexual and no, I don't want to go out with you for a drink, dinner and certainly not breakfast."

"That's two-nil, I reckon," Stephan broke in.

"Oh, and my IQ's one hundred and seventy, so don't be misled by the blonde curls."

"Bloody hell! One-seventy – that's more than Carol Vordeman or Rachel Riley," Tom announced.

"That's more than Einstein, but thanks for confirming you keep the few brains you do have in your pants."

Stephan interceded again. "Three-nil, but much as I'd like to sit and listen to you some more, it won't create any copy and we've got column inches to fill, so we need to get some work done." He inhaled deeply and looked at each of them in turn before continuing. "Tom, you've been asking for a free rein to carry out research into Royal National, to see what's been happening with their share movements and I've been holding you back. Sally's been making similar requests Down Under. So here we are. I'm taking a chance on putting the two of you together; a dream team." Stephan laughed, but immediately started to cough and it took him several seconds to regain his breath and his composure. "Just as I expected, it was love at first sight – I reckoned there'd be a bit of rivalry, but I want you to put that aside and cooperate. I want results and I want them fast. I'm putting my ass on the line here, so don't let me down. Unless you can show me something developing in the next few days, that will be it, and I'll have to cover for the extra expenses. I don't want to be doing that, so I need you to deliver."

Bouncing up from his seat, Tom protested. "Wait a minute, I always work alone."

"Well, 'always' has come to an end. You either work together, or you don't work on this project at all," Stephan asserted.

"Why can't we each do our own thing?" Sally asked.

"Because I make the rules. I think there might be something worth chasing and I reckon it could be big. I wouldn't have dreamed of putting you together otherwise. You either collaborate, or you're off the case and I'll have you working on nothing more interesting than obits for the rest of the year."

"You can't be serious!" They both responded in unison.

"Too bloody right I'm serious. You've got the rest of this afternoon to talk things through, then I want you both on the first shuttle up to Glasgow. It's the best place to start, as that seems to be where the last leak came from and it was one of our associates there who scooped it. I've been able to second one of the local boys from the associate to help out, give you introductions and act as interpreter. His name's Ahmed Akbar and I can get him to meet you at the airport—"

"Ww— Wait a minute, I can't fly," Sally interrupted, her voice losing its confident tone. "How about we get the first train instead?"

"What do you mean, you 'can't fly'? Big-time reporter wannabe, and you're too scared to get on a plane?" Tom detected the first sign of weakness in his competitor and he wasn't going to let the opportunity go. He already had too much ground to make up, to show any compassion.

"Yeah, Sally. What's this about?" Stephan asked.

"I'm not scared," Sally argued. "I've only just flown back in from Oz, but I have an inner-ear infection and the pressure of flying would be excruciating. I'd be useless for hours afterwards. How about I take the train? I could even take tonight's sleeper and I'd be able to meet Tom in Glasgow in the morning."

"No, I want the pair of you travelling together. There's a Virgin train leaving at about 5.30am from Euston; I'll get you both booked on it."

"I'm not much of a morning person—" Tom began.

"That's too bad. You won't have to be up any earlier than you would for a 7.15 flight; probably later, in fact. You won't need to be at Heathrow in time to clear security before the flight and you'll arrive in Glasgow city centre around the same time. That's settled then," Stephan added with finality.

Sally got to her feet. It was only when she stood that he noticed her diminutive stature; she couldn't be more than five feet tall. The shapely legs he'd been caught admiring were no less alluring, but in height terms, the top of Sally's head was level with his chest.

Seeing his jaw drop in surprise she winked. "Don't you know all the best surprises come in smallest packages?"

Tom was still shaking his head when he and Sally left Stephan's office.

"Let's get out of here for a while, I need fresh air," Sally suggested. "Let's go and grab a coffee somewhere and discuss our plans."

"Maybe there is some hope; that's the first thing you've said that I've agreed with," Tom replied. "There's a good Italian bistro a five minute walk away. The coffee's excellent – much better than the mega chains."

Sally's eyes twinkled when she responded. "Sounds good to me, but remember a five minute walk for you might take ten for a short-ass like me."

Once settled at their table, Tom began, "I'm really not comfortable sharing; I've always worked alone and this is my story."

Sally shook her head slowly. "Play another record, Tom. I don't like this either. I can make the same claim. I've been tracking what's been happening with RNB for four months now, starting from the shock when their shares dropped twenty percent in a day following the fraud revelation. I've followed every announcement and each blip since. I've every right to be leading this."

"But-"

"No buts, Tom. Stephan's made it pretty clear what he's looking for. Neither of us like it, but we'll just have to live with it. What's the old bugger like to work for anyway? I've only heard rumours."

"I don't know what you've heard, but I suspect it won't be close. He has a reputation as a total bastard, but don't believe it. True he can be a cantankerous old sod but his bark's worse than his bite. I'll admit I've had my own run-ins with him, but he's brilliant at his job; he supports his team and if you can stand to be close to him you'll realise he has a heart of gold."

They both ordered Americano's with sweet pastries, and they spent the next two hours comparing notes regarding their suspicions while formulating an intended approach to their enquiries.

As time passed, the patronage drinking coffees and whiling away the afternoon made way for the early evening customers who were seeking a drink or a bite to eat before going home, or partaking of the pre-theatre menu. The restaurant swiftly filled up.

Aldo, the bistro's proprietor, approached their table. "Good evening, Tom. It's good to see you, and thank you for introducing more custom to me," he said, inclining his head toward Sally. "Can I offer you a glass of Prosecco? Or perhaps you'd like something to eat?"

"Mmm, sounds like a good idea," Tom replied. "I am rather peckish. How about a plate of mixed hors d'oeuvres?" he asked Sally.

She nodded enthusiastically. "I could probably eat a horse, never mind hors d'oeuvres."

"Sorry, but you won't find any horsemeat in my food," Aldo quipped, "but you might want something more substantial. I'll get you the menu."

In the spirit of her earlier words, Sally polished off a bowl of minestrone followed by a large serving of penne arrabiata. Tom picked at some stuffed mushrooms accompanied by focaccia.

"I don't want anything too heavy," he explained. "My wife will have prepared dinner."

"Wife? So you've found someone stupid enough to marry you." Sally joked.

"There's nothing stupid about Anne," Tom countered. He flipped open his wallet to show a photo. The picture was a classic family portrait; Tom was cradling a baby in his arms while an attractive blonde lady held one arm around Tom's shoulder while the other hugged a toddler.

Sally smiled. "You look the perfect happy family."

When that photo was taken, maybe, Tom thought, *but that was more than two years ago. God only knows what I'll be going home to tonight.* He smiled wryly but didn't reply.

They swilled down Sangiovese and were half way through a second bottle before Tom realised the time.

Chapter 2

"What do you mean, you'll miss another concert? You promised after the last time that it wouldn't happen again." Anne was livid, her face flushed, her cheeks so bright he suspected the tears streaming down them risked evaporating on contact.

That's what the expression 'steam rising' must mean, Tom mused, but he swiftly pushed the thought away; this discussion was serious and he should concentrate. "It's work, I can't help it. It might be really big. I've got a hunch it could be the biggest story I've ever worked on. It could be the making of us," Tom blurted, his defences uttered as a staccato rant. "Much as I want to be at Jenny's concert, it really isn't possible. Besides, she'll be so excited, she won't even notice. After all she's only seven. There'll be plenty of chance for me to make it up to her."

"That's where you're wrong! I told you last time I wouldn't stand this any longer. I do love you Tom, but I can't live like this. I *won't* live like this. This is the last straw. It's not just this concert; it's all the missed events and broken appointments and cancelled holidays. This might be your idea of family life, but it's not mine. You've come home late again tonight and you stink of garlic and cheap wine. You've missed the kids' bedtime and you're planning to leave first thing tomorrow without seeing them, and what's more, you're going to miss Jenny's concert tomorrow! If this is how you want it, then don't bother with your overnight bag, take the big case instead. Fill it up and don't come back."

"You can't really mean that," Tom pleaded. He wanted to smooth things over and belatedly realised his insensitivity. This argument had been brewing for some time. Now wasn't a good time for it to explode.

"I do; collect all the stuff you need and get out."

Tom held out his hands, trying to placate his wife. "No, wait a minute. Be reasonable, just calm down." Under the circumstances, he realised his words couldn't have been more inflammatory.

"Don't tell me to calm down – you… you insensitive bastard! Be reasonable?" she spluttered, fury glowing in her eyes. Anne's hand thrashed about, seeking something to pick up, a weapon to throw or wield. Her fingers chanced upon a soup spoon from the dinner table and she held it up menacingly in front of her.

Tom couldn't help giggling, the image of Anne standing there, red faced and holding the spoon as a bayonet amused him. He reached for her, wanting to draw her into an affectionate embrace but he'd clearly underestimated her anger. She slashed the silverware aggressively. Tom jumped backward, but the slice of her down-swing caught his thumb painfully and drew blood.

"For Christ's sake, woman, what's wrong with you?" he yelled.

"I thought we'd already established that," Anne replied, her voice calmer. "I told you to pack up and get out, and don't try to come near me again."

Tom began to realise the extent of her fury. "Wait a minute – this is my house, too! You can't throw me out."

"I can and I will. I am doing, in fact! This is my house and the children's house. If you don't like that, then you can get a lawyer to contest it. I've already checked with mine."

Tom's eyes widened. "You've already spoken to a lawyer? You've had this all planned?"

She shook her head sadly. "No, it wasn't planned. I've been telling you for months that things had to change, but you wouldn't listen, so yes – I went to get advice. I've told you before, this was your last chance. This wasn't planned, but I was prepared."

Tom was shocked. He stared at Anne, unable to comprehend his predicament. When he'd arrived home, his thinking might have been slightly blurred from the wine, but he wasn't drunk and the confrontation had quickly wiped away any residual fuzziness. He felt totally sober, but no less confused. "How about I sleep in the spare room and we talk about this when I get back from the trip?"

Anne settled her hands on her hips, the spoon still tucked in her fingers. "No, I've told you how it's going to be, there's nothing more to talk about. You're not going to win me around; I won't let you smooth-talk me again. You've done it too often before, but no more. Now that I've decided, there's no reason to put off making this happen. You can pack a case now and get out. I'll let you back in to collect the rest of your things at the weekend. I'll arrange for my father to let you in, so I don't need to be here, but you're not staying tonight and you're not going to wake the kids. You've caused them enough upset already."

Tears welled in Tom's eyes, his emotions in turmoil. He was angry, contrite and miserable all at the same time. Words of fury – hateful, spiteful words – flashed through his mind, but he had the self-control to bite his tongue. He hoped and prayed there would be a way back for him. Once Anne had calmed down, he'd be better able to talk to her, try to convince her to take him back – but here and now, he had to let her have her way. If he dared utter the thoughts crowding his head, if he was to counter attack or even offer further defence of his behaviour, it would make coming back so much more difficult.

Tom slowly made his way to their bedroom. He needed to pack for his trip to Glasgow so he quickly located a spare pair of chinos, a couple of fresh shirts and clean underwear, then placed them together with his sports kit, shaver and toiletries bag into a holdall.

"Take one of the big cases, they're on top of the wardrobe." Anne's instruction came from the doorway, her voice steady and emotionless, her arms folded across her chest.

Reluctantly, Tom stretched up and pulled down a suitcase. It was one of a pair of ultra-lightweight, hard-bodied cases they'd chosen together only a month before, thinking they would be ideal for family holidays. The light weight enabled optimum use of the restricted allowances when flying, and the hard top provided good protection for the contents along with easy manoeuvrability – at least until you had to traverse a staircase, as they'd found out on their way home.

Tom half smiled at the recollection, but quickly sobered, gritting his teeth as he flipped the case open. He carelessly threw in an assortment of clothes and footwear, not bothering to straighten the items or pack properly. Normally Anne did their packing, but even so, Tom was being deliberately slob-like. Although not consciously thought through, he wanted her to feel obliged to assist him, to recreate some bond.

"You're only hurting yourself if you ruin your things," Anne spat. "Take your CD collection as well. I can't stand listening to any of it."

Tom almost rose to the defence of his rock heroes. How could Anne be so dismissive? They'd attended many concerts together and she'd enjoyed them as much as he had. He fought back the urge, realising he was being deliberately baited. Instead, he trudged through to the lounge and collected a few of his favourite CD's adding them to his case and being considerably gentler with their handling. "I'll get the rest at the weekend," he muttered.

Tom slung the holdall over his shoulder, zipped the case and rolled it through to the lounge. Only then did it dawn on him – there was nowhere for him to go. "Please, let me stay tonight," he begged.

"Not a chance."

"I've nowhere else to go."

"That's your problem; you should have thought about that before now, you should have thought about that a long time ago," Anne said wistfully.

Tom thought for a moment, resigned to his situation. "I'll try Archie. See if he'll give me a bed for tonight."

"It's up to you. I really don't want to know any more."

Tom went over to the drinks cabinet and lifted a half full bottle of Glenlivet. "I'm taking this with me, to smooth the way."

"Take it. I told you I don't care. Just leave."

Tom struggled out the door, his laptop carrier and holdall straps balanced on one shoulder, and wheeling the case and holding the bottle of whisky in the other hand. The door slammed behind him and he heard the key turn in the lock. He stopped to adjust his burden and through the closed door, he heard the unmistakeable sound of Anne weeping. He thought about opening the door and letting himself back in, but realised it would be a mistake. Tom slid the bottle inside the holdall to make his load easier to handle, before he trudged to the end of the driveway. He pulled the remote from his pocket and opened the boot of the Astra Sports, then loaded his case and bag before slipping through the driver's door and taking a seat. He was breathless from the exertion of the short trip. Tom discarded the idea of driving, realising he'd consumed considerably more wine than the legal limit. Thinking he would call a cab, he decided he'd better check with Archie before arriving unannounced. He lifted his Samsung phone and scrolled through to his brother's number.

The phone rang repeatedly, and he was about to give up when the call was answered. "Hi Tom, what's your problem?"

"What makes you think there's a problem?"

"Tom, whenever you call me, I know there's a problem. Perhaps on a weekend I could be lured into believing it was a social call, but after nine o'clock on a weeknight, I know something's wrong."

"Okay, Archie, you've got me. I'm phoning for help."

"If you're going to ask me for a favour, perhaps you ought to use my real name. It's Arthur, remember? Everyone else manages to get it right." Arthur was clearly irritated. "It wasn't funny when we were kids and you called me Arch, or

Archie or the Arch-*bishop...* or the Cardinal, or the Monk. It was even less funny when you got other kids to do the same. The joke's worn thin now, don't you think?"

"I'm sorry Arch— Arthur. I wasn't trying to up-set you. I really didn't mean it. It's, well, it's a force of habit, I suppose." Tom couldn't help him-self, he burst into a fit of giggles when he realised he'd made an unintended pun.

"So what's the reason for the call?" Arthur snapped, sounding as though he didn't know whether to be amused, or even more outraged.

"I'm in trouble. I hoped you would help me out."

"Go on," Arthur offered begrudgingly.

"I've had an argument with Anne and I need to leave her with some space to calm down. I'm booked on an early train to Scotland tomorrow and I wondered if you might give me a bed for the night?"

"I can't blame her for losing the rag with you – you treat her like shit."

"That's not fair!" Tom protested. "You've got no idea what this is about, yet you're already taking her side."

"I'm not taking anyone's side, but I do know what you can be like – after all, I've known you all my life. Anne's a lovely girl and you don't deserve her, or these two fabulous kids you've got. I've seen what you put them through. So while I'm not taking sides, I'm aware of your past form."

"So you're not going to help?"

"I never said that. Of course I want to help, but I'm not home now and I won't get back until well after midnight. You can come over then."

Tom shook his head. "That's not much use. I need to be up about five, but thanks all the same."

"Will you be back tomorrow to sort things out?"

"Not possible, I'm afraid. I've been assigned to a new story and I'm likely to be in Scotland for two days at least. I'll try to call Anne tomorrow to smooth things out, but I don't think it's going to be easy. She told me to pack my case and get out and said she doesn't want me back."

Arthur cursed. "Christ, Tom, I didn't realise it was so serious. From what you said, I thought you were just giving Anne time to cool off. You didn't tell me she'd chucked you out! What the Hell's happened? Have you been playing around?"

Tom rubbed his fingers over his temples. "No, it's nothing like that! In the nine years we've been married, I've never been unfaithful. It's all to do with the job. She doesn't understand the hours I have to put in."

"While she's left at home, bored to death, with two youngsters to take care of?" Arthur added sarcastically.

"Yes, that's about it. I try to make it up to her – to them – when I'm home, but it's never enough. And yes, I'll admit it's true; there are some times when I've been a bit insensitive."

Arthur's voice dripped with cynicism. "A bit?"

"Alright, sometimes a lot. Tonight was one of those nights. I came home late because I went for a snack with a colleague to discuss the new project. When I got home, I told Anne I needed to be up and out early and because I'd be away, I'd miss Jenny's concert tomorrow."

"And you wonder why she's upset? I think you need your head examined. And this colleague, is it a female by any chance?"

"Yes, but that makes no difference. Besides I didn't mention that."

"Because you didn't tell her, doesn't mean she doesn't know. And is this female colleague going to Glasgow with you?"

"Yes, but it's business, there's nothing else to it," Tom defended.

"Who are you trying to convince – me or yourself? Listen, since it's important, I'll get away now, I can be home in an hour or so and you can sleep on the couch if you'd like. This new flat doesn't have a spare bed, but you're welcome to stay anyway. I'll see if we can get you sorted out."

Tom quickly considered his options. The prospect of spending the night with Arthur and potentially suffering further berating for his behaviour didn't appeal and he begged off. "No thanks, Arthur. You stay where you are, I can arrange something else and maybe we'll get together at the weekend. Would you do me a favour though? As I'm going to be away, I'd appreciate it if you'd give Anne a call tomorrow and check if she's okay? You might even put in a good word for me, if you get a chance."

"Sure, no problem. Are you sure you'll be okay? It's no trouble to come home right now."

"No, I'll be fine. Talk to you later." Tom disconnected the call and mentally ran through the list of his friends and acquaintances living in the surrounding area, discarding all of them. He considered hotels which were either close to the house or the railway station and again discarded them all for one impracticality or another. In the end, he decided he'd sleep in the car. He rescued the whisky and a handful of CD's from the boot and settled back behind the wheel. He inserted Metallica's Black Album, shut his eyes and took a long, slow draw from the bottle. The whisky had a warming effect, but burned his throat and made him cough. When the fourth track started, Tom thought better of listening to 'The Unforgiven' and switched the CD, opting for Adele. He sat back again with his eyes closed, trying to relax while his fingers drummed on the wheel and he took occasional slugs from the bottle.

Tom's mind drifted, thinking about his current situation and how it had come about. He and Anne had met midway through their English literature degrees and swiftly become inseparable. After graduation, they'd shared a flat while they sought to develop their careers. Anne became a librarian and Tom commenced his career in journalism, taking a junior position with a local rag. They made a comfortable living from their joint incomes and when Anne unexpectedly became pregnant, marriage seemed a natural progression. Their joint decision was for her to give up work when Jenny was born. Around this time, Tom had secured a salaried position with a national. They chose to move out of the city, but maintained their lifestyle, able to afford the mortgage to buy a small terraced house near Reading. For Tom, the travel was a bind, but it had been worth it to afford them the much-maligned 'yuppie' standard of living. Life was good and they lived it to the fullest. Everything changed though, after Colin was born. Much as it had been an easy pregnancy and delivery, and Colin was a delightful child, Anne had suffered from post-natal depression. Tom did everything he could think of to help, but it had been of little avail. He eventually took a sabbatical from work, which only succeeded in accumulating bigger debts, giving Anne further reason for distress. Tom sought help from Anne's parents, but they'd refused to acknowledge that anything was less than perfect. Anne's GP prescribed anti-depressants, but did little else. Forced by their eroding financial situation, Tom had returned to work, although he was fearful of what he might return to each evening. Sometimes he would come home to find Anne vibrant and en-thusiastic, but more often than not she was de-pressed and withdrawn. For a while, she would binge eat and then become depressed about her weight and body shape and would practically starve herself for weeks on end. Her yo-yo eating regime no doubt placed further strain on her sta-bility and gradually Anne had grown more with-drawn. She was moody and felt unattractive and rebuffed any physical advances from Tom. He in turn grew more resentful of her rejection and increasingly lost himself in his work, using the need for financial stability and career advance-ment as an excuse for increasing levels of ab-sence. Colin was now thirty months old and Tom couldn't remember the last time he and Anne had been intimate.

He was shaken from his reverie by loud knocking on the windscreen.

"This is ridiculous; you can't go out driving in the state you're in! I'm going to phone the police, have them arrest you for drunk driving. You won't get away with this!"

Tom's eyes sprang open, and he tried to focus in the half light. He made out the shape and voice of Mrs. Gilmour, his next door neighbour, who was also acclaimed as the local busybody. All Tom's pent up fury, which he's been unable to release at Anne, came to the surface. "Mind your own business, you stupid, stuck-up cow! In case you hadn't noticed, the engine isn't switched on and even if it was, the gate's closed. I've no intention of driving and the only reason the key's in the ignition is so that I can listen to some music. Why don't you climb back on your broomstick, and fuck off!"

Mrs. Gilmour spun in the opposite direction, tut tutting as she went. "I've never been so insulted."

"Oh, I'm sure you must have been," Tom replied, before acknowledging that he really didn't want to make his current predicament any worse. Climbing from the car, he called after her. "Mrs. Gilmour, I'm sorry, I shouldn't have said those things; you took me by surprise, that's all."

Mrs. Gilmour didn't turn back; her only response was the slam of the front door once she'd reached the sanctuary of her own home.

Tom turned back to the car and hammered his fist on the roof in frustration. As he climbed back into the driver's seat, he thought he saw a glimmer of light escape through the parted curtains from the bedroom of his house. He imagined Anne peering out to see what was going on, but still too angry, disinterested, or frightened, to come out and check.

"Perfect end to the perfect fucking day," Tom muttered. "Why is it that when one thing goes wrong, everything goes wrong?"

He silently listed his irritations. *First I received the garage's bill for servicing the car, and it was twice what it should have been because of the extra work they claimed needed to be done on the brakes. I wasted another hour arguing about it, to no avail. Then I tainted my clothes with the stink of nicotine from Stephan's office. And he forced me to share my project, the one I'd been crying out to do. Now he wants me to do all the work and give credit to it being a team effort.*

Worse still, all the problems with my family and even my neighbour. As an afterthought, Tom amused himself with a thought *—at least Sally will provide some eye candy; she might be small, but she's certainly a looker and feisty, too."*

Tom set the alarm on his Samsung; he didn't want to risk missing the train. He placed a CD of Rodrigo Y Gabriela in the player and set it to continuous play with a low volume. Although the music was exciting and passionate, Tom found it created a soothing background. He reclined his seat and closed his eyes, hoping to get some sleep. A street light some twenty metres away had a fault and went through unpredictable phases of working normally then arcing. The result was an intermittent strobe effect accompanied by crackling, and Tom couldn't settle into any pattern of rest. He turned up the volume on the stereo to try to drown out the background noise, and grabbed snatches of sleep lasting only a few minutes at a time. In a sleepy haze, he pondered disjointedly over what he really wanted from life. Arthur had been right when he'd said that Tom had two fabulous kids, and he didn't want to lose his family. Yet, when he thought about it, his relationship with Anne had become increasingly strained. If he was honest with himself, he considered her high maintenance and he'd been growing increasingly resentful over the emotional cost of her depression. On consideration, perhaps that was why he was being less than generous with his own commitment to their relationship. Would it be such a bad thing for them to have a break apart?

Chapter 3

Alighting from the mini-cab, Tom was grateful it was a mild spring morning as he hadn't thought to bring a coat. He'd left his suitcase in the car's boot at home, but had his computer case and holdall as he walked along Euston Road to enter the station.

He found Sally waiting as they'd arranged, in front of WH Smith. Attracting admiring glances from the scattering of early morning commuters, she was as pretty as a picture. She was wearing a tight-fitting, short-sleeved yellow top, complementing her sunny disposition and her matching mini-skirt was little more than a belt, which again treated Tom to a view of her shapely legs. She had a cabin-bag-sized version of Tom's suitcase and she grasped a cup carrier holding two cardboard beakers of carry-out coffee.

Tom's enjoyment of the view was quickly cut short by her admonishment, "You sure weren't joking when you said you weren't a morning person. You look like shit warmed up. Did you sleep in those clothes?"

"Yes, actually; it's a long story. We've only got a few minutes to get to our seats, so I'll fill you in later."

"Relax, we've got plenty of time, there's a twenty-minute delay."

"In that case, take a seat and excuse me for a few minutes. I'll go to the gents and have a quick shower and a shave. The station has much better facilities than the train. It would have been better still if the first class lounge was open, but for some inexplicable reason they start the trains at the back of five, but don't open the lounge until 7.30. It takes away the point don't you think? Anyway, I'll be back in a mo'."

"What about your coffee? It'll get cold. Do you want to take it with you?"

Tom thought for a second then nodded. "Thanks," he mouthed, grabbed one of the cups and disappeared around the corner.

Tom felt better, but the strain of racing to get back in time for the train left him stressed. Whether he hadn't dried properly, or he was perspiring from racing about he wasn't sure, but his skin and clothing felt damp as he returned to where Sally was sitting in a waiting area, a few yards from where he'd left her. She appeared calm and relaxed, but walked towards him as soon as she saw him approach.

"I didn't know if you'd make it on time, I was about to go ahead and find our seats. It would have taken quite some explanation if I'd arrived in Glasgow alone." Sally scanned Tom's appearance critically. "You're a bit more presentable than before, but nobody's going to mistake the creased clothing effect for Armani and you still look pretty awful. Your skin's really grey except for the dark rings around your eyes – in fact, the only colour you've got is the red in your bloodshot eyes. I can't wait to hear the whole story."

They fished out their tickets, fed them through the turnstile and walked towards the train. Their first class seats were reserved for carriage 'A', which was at the far end of what appeared to be a very long train. They'd only covered half the distance when they decided it prudent to climb into the closest carriage and walk the rest of the way on board.

It proved to be a good decision as they'd barely travelled a few yards further before the doors closed and the train started to move. It was a Virgin Pendolino, a high speed train, and it was modern, clean and bright with smooth contours.

Even for such an early departure time, the train was busy, many passengers were still settling in and rearranging their luggage. Tom and Sally's passage was slow and cumbersome as Sally regularly had to lift her case over discarded items still blocking the aisle. Tom wore both the holdall and laptop carrier over his shoulder, but had to manoeuvre carefully to avoid colliding with passengers who were leaning out into the aisle while preparing for their journey.

Some minutes later they arrived – relieved, exhausted, hot, and more than a little bothered – at the entrance to the front carriage. Sally pressed the button to part the electric doors and Tom heaved his bag and then Sally's case onto an already burdened luggage rack. Tom kept his laptop with him and Sally had her iPad, and they shuffled forward to find their seats.

Alarm bells were ringing in Tom's head when he scanned the full carriage, but they reached an earth-shaking crescendo when he neared their seats to discover two heavily-built young men already occupying them. Each was dressed in a singlet, cut-off denims and heavy leather boots. The vests carried the logo of Chelsea Football Club and had the name 'Terry' emblazoned on them, but they were clearly knock offs. The clincher – 'Terry' was spelt with only one 'R'. Tom suspected they'd probably purchased them from somewhere like Black Bush market at two for a fiver – which might explain their twin-like dress. Their heads were shaved and their arms and shoulders, together with what he was able to see of their legs, were covered in tattoos. The letters of the words 'LOVE' and 'HATE' were in-scribed on their knuckles. Each was swilling from a can of lager, with four more cans and an un-opened six-pack sitting on the table in front of them. Judging from the size of their matching beer bellies, this was not an unusual level of con-sumption.

Tom glanced at Sally to see her reaction and she merely raised her eyebrows. He suspected she was waiting for him to do something. "Excuse me; I think you've accidentally taken our seats. We have a booking for them." Tom held up his ticket, to support his argument.

One of the men responded, his tone belligerent. "We've bought our tickets too, and we're here now – so piss off."

Tom experienced a mixture of fear and anger in equal measure, but not wanting to appear too wimpish in front of Sally, he tried again. "I'm not saying you don't have tickets, but they won't be for these seats. These are our seats and I'm politely asking you to vacate them and go and find your own."

The man straightened up, his eyes narrowing. "Listen mate, we were booked on the other train going to Preston, and when it was cancelled, we were told to find seats on this one instead. We've found seats, like we were told to do, and we're not moving. So what are you going to do about it?"

"I'm sorry, but if you won't move I'll call the guard to get you put off the train."

"Ho, ho, ho." The man guffawed, but despite his size and shape, there wasn't anything Santa-like in his delivery. He dragged himself out of the seat. Although Tom was big, this man was enormous, dwarfing Tom. "You sure you want to take me on?" he threatened.

With the reserve English people are famed for, every other passenger in the carriage found something compelling to stare at through the windows or found particularly interesting passages in their books, all the while risking furtive glances to see what was going on.

"He doesn't, but I do," Sally challenged. "And you might be interested to know I received my military training from the S.A.S." She dropped her iPad onto the table, kicked off her heels and adopted a martial arts stance, as if she was ready to attack.

The two louts exchanged uncertain glances before the second man stood and grabbed his associate's arm. "C'mon Billy, it's not worth the effort." They scooped up their belongings and scampered out of the carriage, collecting a couple of sports bags from the doorway.

A spontaneous round of applause broke out and Sally recovered her shoes, if not her composure, before cautiously sliding behind the table. She was smiling but her hands were visibly trembling.

"Are you okay?" Tom asked. "You handled that brilliantly."

Sally nodded in response and she swallowed a couple of times to generate some saliva in her dry throat.

"Have you really had military training?" Tom added.

Sally smiled weakly. "I suppose I have, in a manner of speaking. About two years ago, I did a feature on army training and spent a couple of weeks at Aldershot barracks. I'm sure some of the squaddies I met must have been in the S.A.S."

"You're incorrigible," Tom said, grinning broadly.

"I have taken a couple of self-defence classes. You know the sort of thing – protection, so a girl can feel safer walking down the street at night, but it was nothing sophisticated and certainly wasn't intense." Sally swallowed again before continuing. "I'd have had a real problem with those two. It wasn't so bad when they were sitting down, I could easily have reached soft targets, but when the first one stood up, he towered over me. I wouldn't have been able to stretch to reach for his throat or face, so the best target would have been between his legs and probably that wouldn't have worked either, because judging by his reaction, he didn't have any balls."

"I'm glad you're on my side," Tom smirked.

"You say that now, but perhaps you'll think differently later. Anyway, back to a more important subject. You were going to tell me how you got yourself into such a state. Come on, spill the beans."

Tom knew he couldn't escape without offering some explanation, but he was reluctant to say too much. He liked being the one asking the questions and was uncomfortable when the tables were turned. He considered trying to dismiss Sally's enquiry with a joke, but knew he wouldn't get away with it under Sally's keen scrutiny. At the same time, he didn't want to be airing his personal washing in public. He'd only known Sally for a few hours and a confession of his and Anne's failings would hardly be appropriate. A 'my wife doesn't understand me' would sound pathetic. In the end he chose a compromise strategy, admitting some of his own faults and insensitivities and hinting there'd been an overreaction by his wife. He put it down to everything being blown out of proportion, a storm in a teacup, and hoped he sounded more convincing to Sally than he did to himself. As a distraction, he made a joke out of the experience with his neighbour and the faulty light.

Sally huffed out an annoyed breath. "Why didn't you call me? You had my number. It would have been a better alternative than sleeping in the car overnight."

Tom raised his eyebrows in response.

"I wasn't inviting you into my bed!" Sally rolled her eyes. "I'd have got you a room in my hotel or found you a chair to sleep on."

"Yeah, but much as that would have helped," Tom replied. "think how it would have looked to my wife. Thanks for the offer, though."

The train attendant arrived to offer them coffees and a cooked breakfast. Sally opted for fruit juice and croissants with marmalade, but Tom was ravenous. He'd only snacked the previous evening at the restaurant and hadn't eaten since. The whisky hadn't helped his situation either. He devoured a plate stacked with bacon, sausage and eggs accompanied by toast, and washed it down with two mugs of coffee.

Tom used a slice of toast to mop up the last of the egg yolk then stuffed it in his mouth. He looked up from his plate, revived and ready to renew their conversation. "Now it's your turn."

Sally's gaze flew up to meet his. "What do you mean?"

"To tell me your secrets."

"Why would I do that?"

"I've opened up to you, told you about private things and exposed my weaknesses."

"So what do you want? Are you expecting me to tell you I was sexually abused by my uncle, or that I've indulged in lesbian relationships ever since as a consequence?"

Tom's mouth dropped open and his eyes grew wide. "Rrr— really?" he stammered.

"No, not really," she shot back. "My, my – for a journalist, you really are gullible. Or are you using a lack of sleep as an excuse? You only told me what you did because you were forced into it.

You didn't volunteer a thing, but you needed to explain the state you were in when you arrived. Besides, just because you shared something, it doesn't mean I have to reciprocate."

"Come on, be fair. Tell me a little bit about yourself. If we're going to work together, wouldn't it be better to be friends and know we're able to trust one another?"

"It's not a convincing argument," Sally replied, "but okay, I'll give you some background. I was born and brought up in Manchester. My father was a bus driver and a senior shop steward with the T&G. My mother worked as a dinner lady at a local school. We were a good, working class family with solid socialist values. I did well at school and became the first member of my extended family to go to university. Mum and Dad scrimped and saved to make it possible. I studied English and got a gig working on the student newspaper. Bus deregulation and privatisation had taken place not too long before and because of my father's contacts, I managed to get some inside information. I wrote it up for the student press; articles about the chaotic process involved, and some of the mad things that were going on back then; bus wars and property exploitation and the likes. I managed to get information about employee-owned businesses and what was happening behind the scenes and the big companies which were swallowing them up. Some of my articles were picked up by the nationals and I ended up getting lots of freelance work as a result. I was only in my teens and enjoyed making some real money. In fact, I got so much work, I nearly dropped out of Uni. My family was really upset about that idea though, and talked me into knuckling down. In the end I scraped an honours pass."

"What happened then?"

"After I graduated, I couldn't get a proper job at first. Anything I got offered was really junior and paid considerably less than what I'd been getting for freelancing, so I kept on with what I'd been doing and then started writing a novel in my spare time."

Tom was impressed. "You've written a book?"

"Not exactly. At the time, I had all the ambition and idealism of a young student. I thought I might be the next Hemingway or a Faulkner. I wanted to write the perfect book, full of life and characters, exposing all the social injustice of Thatcherism and New Labour."

"And how did you get on?"

"The first chapter was brilliant, but not brilliant enough, so I re-wrote it. It took me at least twenty attempts before I realised I was going nowhere and the first attempt had probably been the best, but by then it was long lost."

Tom was intrigued. "So you gave up?"

"I suppose. I always intended to go back to it, but it never happened. I continued working freelance until I met my ex. He's Australian and in media; he was over here on a project. We hit it off and he asked me to go back with him and offered me a job in Sydney, and after a while we shacked up. The job didn't turn out to be anything like it had been described and he really only wanted me as a showpiece, no interest in what was in my mind. The relationship didn't last, but while I was there, I managed to get a reporting job at Global and after a while I was promoted to regional lead."

"Sounds impressive," Tom agreed. "You've not been out of your relationship for long then?"

"About eight months now, but I was well over him before that, a long time ago in fact," Sally announced.

Tom studied her astutely. "You may think so, but I think he's left scars. That's why you've been so aggressive and given me such a hard time."

She crossed her arms over her chest. "And when did you qualify as a psychoanalyst? No, you're completely wrong. I wasn't being aggressive, it's just my way. I've always been like that. It's certainly not as a result of being involved with Randy. I just don't suffer fools and I never have. I've had to work for everything I've achieved and—"

"His name was really Randy?" Tom questioned in mock disbelief.

"Yes, and—" Sally stopped abruptly, stared at Tom for a moment and then they both burst into fits of giggles. "So is that us even, now?" Sally enquired when she'd managed to control her amusement.

"Well, I probably could have gotten most of what you've told me from your Wiki page and your LinkedIn and Facebook accounts, but you've shown a willingness to be open, so yeah, we can call it quits." Tom offered her his hand.

Sally accepted the gesture and returned his handshake with a firm and confident grip. "For good measure, I'll offer you another of my secrets. I have a sweet tooth and could fall for just about any man who can afford to keep me supplied in quality chocolates."

"I'll bear that in mind." Tom's grin was broad and unreserved.

Noticing the time, he reached for his phone. "It's nearly eight o'clock. Anne should be up, getting the kids ready. I'll try to get her now and see if I can have a word with Jenny too, before her big concert."

The phone rang six times before the answering machine tripped in. Tom left a message, then dialled again to Anne's mobile. This time it rang twice before going dead – she'd obviously rejected the call.

"Shit, she's not taking my calls," Tom muttered, more to himself than to Sally. His earlier good humour evaporated and deep frown lines furrowed his brow when he glanced at the screen. "Oh bugger, my battery's nearly flat." He fished in the laptop bag for his phone charger, but it wasn't there. Retrieving his holdall, he all but emptied it without success.

"You can try mine, but I don't think it will fit," Sally offered.

Tom checked, but it was no use. "Does anyone have a charger for a Samsung Galaxy Ace that I might borrow for half an hour?" Tom announced to the carriage, but unsurprisingly, there was no response. "I'll pay," he added. "I only want to recharge my phone, enough to get me as far as Glasgow." Again, there was no response and Tom threw himself back into his seat despondently and leaned his head against the window.

"Why don't you text her, or send an email," Sally suggested.

Tom grumbled. "I hate texting, but I suppose she's more likely to see it. My fingers are too large for the keys and the stylus isn't much better." He keyed in an apology to Anne, along with a special message for Jenny and finished by saying he'd call later.

The train slowed to a halt at Preston station. Tom almost jumped out of his skin when there was a loud hammering against the window, not far from his head. He spun around to see the two louts, shouting and making 'V' signs with both of their hands. They still had their sports bags strapped over their shoulders, but there was no sign of the beer. Tom suspected they'd probably finished it.

A few second later, the louts ran off, staggering against the tide through a surge of passengers up the exit ramp towards the taxi rank and pick-up area. It quickly became obvious they were being chased by two railway police.

Having recovered from his shock, Tom glanced at Sally and viewing the comic scene, they both burst out laughing.

Chapter 4

They arrived at Glasgow Central a little after 10.40; only a few minutes behind schedule. Tom collected their luggage and they alighted onto Platform One, then weaved their way to the main concourse.

"Where are we meant to meet this Ahmed?" Sally asked.

A blank expression fell over Tom's face. "I don't know, Stephan only said that he'd meet us on arrival."

They both searched the surrounding crowds for any likely suspects, walking towards an exhibition displaying a Ferrari, situated in the centre of the station. "Stephan gave me the impression Ahmed was young and the name sounds Asian, but I don't see any obvious candidates, nobody wearing the proverbial yellow carnation or holding up a name board," Tom said, this his eyes brightened. "Wait – Stephan gave me his mobile number, let me check." Tom reached for his phone, but rolled his eyes. "Oh shit, I can't access it with a dead battery and if he's given Ahmed my number, he won't have gotten through."

"How about I give Stephan a call and get his number?" Sally suggested.

"Yeah, that makes sense."

Sally punched in Stephan's number and put the phone to her ear. "Hello Stephan, we've arrived in Glasgow, but we haven't found Ahmed yet. Can you give me his number?"

Sally held the phone away from her ear to minimise the pain from Stephan's booming response and Tom could clearly hear his boss's voice. "Where the hell's Tom? I gave him Ahmed's number. Is he not there with you?"

"Yes, Tom's here but—"

"For fuck sake, can't I trust him to get anything right? It's not that difficult; he doesn't have to pole vault over mouse turds."

Sally spoke quickly. "His phone's not working, the battery's dead."

"Have I got to hold his fucking dick for him to have a pee?" Stephan demanded.

"It wasn't Tom's fault. He's had some problems and—"

"Christ! You're not going soft are you? Or are you going soft on him? I'll not stand for you two sleeping on the job – not together anyway – at least not on my time. What you choose to do in your private life is up to yourselves, provided you get my story first and before print deadline."

Sally's eyes blazed with annoyance. "Now you hold on a minute. You can't talk to me like—"

"I'll talk to you any way I like. You're in the fucking news business and if you've been working in Oz, you're bound to have heard much worse, so don't you go getting all prissy. Get me my story and then I'll talk nice to you, okay?"

"Can you tell me how I can recognise Ahmed? Or give me his number?" Sally insisted.

"I don't know what he fucking looks like, I've never met him! How many Ahmed's are there likely to be in a Glasgow train station? Why not bare your tits and yell out 'Ahmed' at the top of your voice; I'm sure he'll come running."

"Can you please give me his number?" Sally replied through pursed lips. "Better still, text it to me," she snapped, then rang off before Stephan had a chance to berate her further.

"I'm sorry about that," Tom offered sheepishly. "He's probably having a bad morning. He's really an okay guy, but when he smells blood, he goes in for the kill, it's his instinct. He doesn't mean anything by it."

"Don't worry. It'll take more than that foul-mouthed, foul-smelling old hack to put me off my stride."

"Hack? You sound as if you've been watching too many 1950s movies."

"Sorry, I should have been able to come up with something better—" Their conversation was interrupted by a chime from Sally's phone. She pressed the 'accept' button and read the message; **'Feisty, I like it'**, which was followed by the eleven digits of a mobile number.

Sally had her finger poised to link to the number when they heard a voice and glanced up to see an approaching figure. "Mr. Bishop? Miss Ferguson? I'm Ahmed Akbar."

"Yes, that's us," Tom replied. "We were trying to contact you."

Ahmed seemed surprised. "Didn't you get my text? I had another job to get cleared this morning and wasn't sure I'd be in early enough, so I suggested we meet at Burger King. I knew it was right next to the platform you'd come in on and would be easy to find. When I got here and saw the train was in and you weren't there, I came looking for you."

Tom studied the young man; he looked to be no older than fifteen. He was immaculately dressed in a dark brown, three-piece suit, matched with a white shirt which appeared to be so starched, it would stand up by itself, and a complementary plain tie. He was bright faced and his skin was pale, at odds with the colouring Tom had expected from his name. Ahmed's eyes matched his suit and he had straight, mid-length hair. His skin was smooth and even, and Tom suspected he never had to shave.

He offered Tom his hand. "Mr. Bishop, I'm so honoured to meet you. I've been a fan of your writing for quite some time. I really liked the article you did last month, on aggressive tax avoidance. You have the marvellous ability to take on any subject, even one as dry as taxation, and make it interesting and amusing. I loved the quote from that Chancellor from the sixties – Denis Healey, wasn't it? The one about the difference between avoidance and evasion being the thickness of a prison wall. Classic."

Tom was beaming with pride and jumped on the opportunity to demonstrate his knowledge. "It was somewhat historic though. It was accurate for its time, but attitudes have changed now. Although avoidance is technically legal, there are moves afoot to change it, for some types at least. There's an outcry because some of the biggest and most successful companies can make billions and yet pay very little tax because of careful international structuring and transfer pricing. The real difficulty about legislating for it is – where do you draw the line?"

Sally, anticipating the potential for a long debate decided to interrupt. "Okay guys, can we save the back patting for later? We still have a job to do."

"Spoilsport. You had your moment of glory back on the train and now you want to cut mine short," Tom mocked.

"It's not me, Tom. You heard Stephan as well as I did, and unless we deliver, it might not just be your glory he'll be wanting to cut short – unless you've already been circumcised?"

Tom smirked. "Yeah, actually, since you asked. Do you want to check?"

Ahmed stood staring at them both, dumbfounded, but clearly enjoying himself, his eyes darting back and forward as he followed the repartee.

Tom glanced at his watch and realised the day was running away from them and they hadn't even started. "Before we do anything else, I need to buy a battery charger for my phone. Is there some place close-by?"

"There are lots of phone shops on Argyle Street. You're bound to get what you need there and it's only a short walk. You've been booked into the Radisson, that's on Argyle Street too, so we can kill two birds with one stone; get you checked in so you can drop your bags and pick up a charger. I know you're in the big league compared to me, but someone must really like you to book the Radisson. The only time I've been sent away on business I was told to book the Premier Inn."

"The plan sounds good to me, but perhaps we could save some time. If you could point me in the direction of a phone shop and give me directions to the hotel, you and Sally could get us checked in and we'd be able to meet up in Reception."

Ahmed pursed his lips. "Good in theory, but you might prefer to have me with you, as one of my jobs is to be your 'Weegie' translator."

"Weegie?" Tom questioned, and Sally looked equally puzzled.

"Glaswegian, that is. I'm sure generally you'll get along fine, but with some of the locals, you might have a problem with the dialect. Walk this way and I'll keep you right."

Tom and Sally scoffed at the suggestion, but as they exited down the steps and onto Union Street, snatches of conversations overheard from some locals made them quickly realise they might have a requirement for Ahmed's skills.

There was a moderate breeze, but the day was warm and a bright blue sky was interspersed by occasional clouds. They walked quickly, arriving at the first phone shop they came to, where Tom purchased a charger together with a new pre-charged battery. He paid his bill using his personal MasterCard without even checking the amount. He installed the battery and paused to check his voicemails and texts. There were two messages from Ahmed and a number of other business and personal ones, but to his disappointment, nothing from Anne.

Tom tried both his home and Anne's mobile again, with the same result as before. He tried Arthur's number, hoping to find out if he'd made contact with Anne as asked, but his phone rang out unanswered and Tom gave up.

Urged on by Sally not to waste any more time, the three walked westerly along Argyle Street, under 'The Hielanman's Umbrella' – a famous landmark in the centre of Glasgow, it was a glass-walled railway bridge which carried the platforms of Glasgow Central station across Argyle Street. Before emerging from the other side, they saw the impressive glass-fronted structure of the Radisson Blu hotel.

"This part of town used to be quite downmarket until the hotel was built. It's fairly recently opened and it's given the area a real lift. From red light area to blue, you might say," Ahmed said, pleased to be able to make his own humorous contribution to their conversation. "Let's get you checked in, then we'll go on to my office. It's only a few minutes' walk, or we could take a cab if you prefer."

The lobby was busy due to the overspill from a corporate event on the first floor. A coffee break was in progress and delegates were sprinkled all around, some in small huddles discussing the presentations, while others had sought out private corners for more discrete conversations and negotiations. Tom and Sally were all too aware of how such events often provided ideal cover for meetings of executives who would not normally be seen together. On occasions, it was an opportunity for deal negotiation, dispute resolution or headhunting; sometimes even the early stages of a takeover, merger or joint venture was delivered in innocuous surroundings, affording neither party the home advantage.

The reception staff processed their reservations quickly and efficiently, but Tom and Sally were advised that their rooms wouldn't be ready until 1.00pm. They were able to deposit their bags in a secure room and once ready, their luggage would be sent upstairs to await their arrival.

The walk to the newspaper office took less than five minutes and was conducted at a brisk pace. In the short time they'd been in the hotel, the wind had strengthened and held a distinct chill, while the skies had darkened with heavy, grey, threatening clouds. More than a few gentle spits of rain spotted their clothes as they climbed the steps of the entranceway, but no sooner were they through the door when they turned to see a fully-fledged downpour in progress.

Overcompensating for the day's earlier warmth, cold air from the building's not-so-sophisticated climate management system hit them as they made their way through the lobby. All three shivered from the effect, chilling them through already damp clothing. Ahmed led them to a private room which he'd pre-arranged as their work area. Settling down around a large, square table, Ahmed advised them there was a free-vend beverage machine in the corridor of the hallway outside and sandwiches had been ordered and would arrive by twelve thirty.

"Okay, Ahmed, let's get some coffees in and then we can make a start. According to my information, this paper had the scoop last week, revealing that Royal National had been playing silly buggers with customer complaints about insurance mis-selling. This is a tabloid and not in the habit of picking up major leads on business news, so I want to know how you got the information?" Tom began.

"I knew that's where you'd want to go, and I've arranged for you to speak to the reporter who fronted the story. He'll be here at twelve, but I warn you, he won't be prepared to tell you his sources. It's not the done thing."

"You're preaching to the converted. I'll only be interested in sources if it's key to my investigations," Tom agreed

"*Our* investigations," Sally corrected.

"Yes, 'our'. You're right Sally. Sorry about that, I'm so used to working on my own."

"Keep that up and you won't be working at all," she replied with menace, but followed it up by playfully punching his arm.

"You've probably already seen it, but I have a copy of the paper it was printed in," Ahmed offered.

"Thanks, that's good," Sally replied. "I haven't seen the original, I only read it off the 'net and of course I've seen what's been happening with all the other press picking up on it."

"Me too," Tom agreed.

While they pored over the article and other items of interest, noon came and went. At twelve fifteen, there was a quick rap on the door and it opened before they had a chance to respond.

The figure standing in the doorway was the embodiment of untidiness and bad taste. He was slight in stature, hardly any taller than Sally, but this was more pronounced because of his stoop and puny, rounded shoulders. His narrow, pinched face was disguised behind two or three days of growth and his upper head was shrouded by greasy, straggly, straight hair, which at the back, extended to his shoulders. To say he was 'dressed' would be misleading, but his body was certainly covered by clothing. A green chequered shirt struggled to contain his large belly and it was tucked into maroon jeans at one side only, the other side flapping freely when he moved. His apparel still bore evidence of the runny egg he'd had for breakfast – hopefully from that same morning. "I'm Charlie McMillan, you wanted to see me?"

Speak to you maybe, but I'd have sooner not seen you, was Sally's immediate thought, but in the interests of making progress, she restrained herself from vocalising it. The contrast to Ahmed's pristine appearance couldn't have been more pronounced and even Tom's dishevelled arrival at Euston had been immaculate in comparison. Sally had often heard of tabloids being referred to as 'gutter press' and she thought the term must have been coined with Charlie in mind.

"Grab a coffee and join us," Tom said.

"I'll pass on the coffee, can't stand the sludge out of that machine. You need to go to the café across the road if you want something drinkable. I've brought my own with me." He produced a bottle of Highland Spring.

Sally wrestled with the concept of Charlie being a coffee connoisseur and suspected the bottled water contained some alcoholic additive.

"I gather you're up from the smoke to follow up on some work I've done. What's this all about?" Charlie continued. There were no pleasantries or introductions.

"Well, not exactly," Tom replied. "We're working some research on large and unusual stock market movements, trying to see if we might have the basis for a story."

"Good for you – you get the luxury of being able to take your time to research your stories. We're at the sharp end here. We pick up on something, check its authenticity and then either print it or drop it. We don't have the time to chew things over."

"It's no picnic for us either," Tom said. "True, we may have a bit more time, but we're expected to produce results and we have to meet deadlines too."

Looking at Charlie's food-stained clothing, Sally stifled a giggle at the picnic analogy.

"So what do you want me for? I've not much time and I need to make deadlines on a daily basis." Charlie's hostility was almost tangible.

"Okay, we've all got the same problems, the same objectives and the same bosses, so we'd really appreciate any help and cooperation you can give us. We've been looking into some odd things happening at Royal National and your story last week on the insurance claims contributed to it. We need to learn more about the background," Tom explained.

Charlie shrugged. "What background? I learned about what was happening there, I checked it out and cleared it with legal department and then it ran. That's all there was to it."

"Come on, you're doing yourself a disservice there. I know this is only a regional tabloid, but—"

Charlie crossed his arms. "You can get off your high horse right now. We're not a regional tabloid, we're a national. Scotland is its own country and besides, we have a worldwide readership with online subscribers. Our circulation is higher than many of the broadsheets. The last time I checked, it was double what your rag gets and we're a daily when your mag is a weekly – so go do the maths. And yeah, our articles may not be too high-brow, our reporting on Europe, on immigration and on the English for that matter may be a whisker within the anti-racial discrimination laws. We might concentrate on celebrities and royals and football. We may alternate medical headlines between telling our readers that alcohol or cigarettes or the latest super-food either kills you with cancer and heart disease or is the latest wonder cure for it, but we give the punters what they want. That's why they shell out their dosh six days a week." Charlie paused only long enough to draw breath. "I chose this line of work; it was a lifestyle choice. I used to do what you do. I have my Fleet Street credentials, I have a first-class honours degree to go with it and I read at Oxford, but I couldn't stand the backstabbing and the travel and the pretension, so I moved back to Glasgow and now I've got quite a cushy number. I earn well, I live the way I like and so what if I have to wear this uniform?" Charlie took a moment to run his hand over his chest, smoothing out some of the creases on his shirt. "Dressed like this, I can walk into any pub and pick up on the latest gossip. I can always change first if I have a more important meeting, so I don't get chucked out of the Hilton. Mind you, they know me well enough in there anyhow.

So what makes you so big and important? Where did you study?"

"I took English literature at Cambridge," Tom replied, almost in a whisper.

"Ah, Fens Polytechnic," Charlie scoffed. "So now that we've set the ground rules, what do you want to know?"

Ahmed barely managed to contain a snigger and Sally fought to keep from gaping in amazement. Charlie's slight frame seemed to take on a new stature.

Tom's facial reaction was less controlled as he struggled to find words. "I'm sorry. I didn't mean to offend you or your newspaper. My mind's been so focussed on what I'm trying to do that I didn't think through what I was saying. I suppose it must have come across that I was really up myself. Can we turn the clock back and start again please?"

There followed a long pause, while Charlie's intense glare all but bored a hole through Tom, then he howled with laughter and blurted, "Christ, you Sassenachs are really easy to wind up. It's the best sport I've had for some time," before offering his hand.

Ahmed immediately joined in, but it took a few seconds before Tom recovered enough to participate and even then he seemed shaken and unsettled.

"Now what can I do for you?"

"Well, as I was saying before, we're hoping to find any information which can help explain the problems Royal National have been having. From what I've seen, every time they start to recover from one problem or revelation, they're hit with another. It's all too much of a coincidence and we want to see if there's any pattern."

"So you're hoping I can give you my source, so you can follow it up?"

"Exactly," Sally intervened. Now that hostilities seemed to be over, she was eager to participate in the dialogue.

"No can do. It's not that I'm unwilling to help, but I don't have a source – at least, not one that I know."

"What do you mean?" Sally asked.

"I never spoke to anyone. The information was sent to me anonymously. It came by post with no message; a copy of an email sent from a senior manager of RNB addressed to the call centre managers, telling them to crack down on any compensation claimants. I was suspicious right away. I thought it was probably a fake, someone trying to create a stir. But the correspondence had authentic logos and references and the names and phone numbers checked out. I tried calling RNB and they didn't deny it. I only got 'no comments' in reply to my enquiries. I ran it past legal and they gave me clearance to publish, although as you've already seen, what I said was carefully worded to guard against any libel claims. Some of the other papers weren't so careful when they picked up on it and some of the web reporting was positively abusive."

"No offence intended, but why you?" Sally asked. "Do you think it was sent by someone you'd had previous dealings with?"

"I've asked myself the same question, but truly, I haven't a clue. As you said before, we're a tabloid, financial reporting isn't our forte. Sure, we record exchange and interest rates and we talk about house price and stock market movements, but we don't go in for serious analysis, there are too many others who do it better than we could possible manage, yourselves included.

So why send it to me? The only angle for me to take was attack it from the punters point of view – all the poor account holders who've been cheated in the first place and are now being given short shrift if they try to complain. If it was some sort of sabotage, I would have thought it would have done more damage if tackled by the financial specialists."

"Maybe yes, maybe no," Tom replied. "Coming through you, the first reaction was to mobilise public opinion. That would lead to the Financial Services Authorities stepping in and of course, the serious financial press would jump in as soon as you'd revealed the issue."

"Yeah, I suppose. I wasn't complaining anyway, as it did my street cred no end of good."

"Do you still have the email and the envelope?" Tom asked.

"Yes, of course."

"Could we see it? Better still, would you let me borrow it?"

"Yeah, I suppose it's the least I can do after upsetting you so much before. If you can hang on a minute, I'll get them for you."

"What's happened to those sannies? I'm fam-ished," Sally said. "If we can track them down will you join us for a bite?"

"Sure, I'll go and find the email while you sort it out."

Chapter 5

Charlie returned within ten minutes to find the others had already made significant inroads into the food which had arrived, and had plates in front of them littered with crumbs and debris from what they'd already devoured. Currently, Sally was daintily nibbling on a chicken tikka wrap while Ahmed was crunching into an apple. Tom was apparently on a refuelling mission, stuffing well-laden sandwiches into his mouth in quick succession.

Charlie laid a folder on the table and reached for a plate. "Thanks for waiting, very courteous of you."

"You really are a sneaky, manipulative bastard, aren't you?" Sally said, and Charlie noticed her iPad screen open in front of her.

Tom was aghast, concerned they'd only just gained Charlie's confidence and fearful that Sally was blowing it.

Charlie shrugged off the insult. "Goes with the territory, did you have anything particular in mind?"

"I've checked you out online. You do have a first class degree, but it's from Aberdeen. You may have read at Oxford, but it wasn't for your degree, it was when you were doing a book launch and you were marketing it by being interviewed and reading excerpts at the student union!"

"Did I tell a lie?"

"Precisely my point – you're a sneaky, manipulative bastard."

"Now that's unfair. If I can look it out, I'm sure I have a birth certificate somewhere, although it could be difficult to trace as my filing system's got somewhat overloaded. Anyway, you have to remember the first law of journalism."

"What's that?" Ahmed enquired eagerly.

"Never let the truth stand in the way of a good story, well, not the whole truth anyway. You have to have some standards."

Tom chuckled and shook his head. "You may have set some ground rules, but from the sound of it, the earth keeps moving."

Charlie leered at Sally. "I'd be quite happy for the earth to move a bit, if you know what I mean; nudge, nudge, wink, wink."

"Okay, some decorum please," Tom said, wanting to re-establish some control. "You've brought the papers. Can we see what you have?"

Charlie slid open a cardboard file and lifted out and unfolded an A4 sheet of paper and a used envelope. He then produced some further A4 sheets. "This is what I received," he said, pointing to the first two items. "You can examine them as much as you like, but I want to keep custody. Here are some photocopies you can take away."

They all studied the documents carefully.

"Pretty damning stuff, I can understand you must have been orgasmic when you received it. What did you do?" Sally asked.

"You mean after I cleaned myself off?" Charlie answered, giving her a lewd smile. "Like I said before, I checked out its authenticity as best I could. I confirmed the email addresses it came from and went to, and the phone number at the bottom was the private line of the sender, at least, via her secretary. Her name's Catherine Farnham and she's a senior hitter in the Financial Services Division at their head office; works immediately under the director. I tried calling her but she wouldn't take my calls, even when I threatened to run the story. The only reply from either her or the press department was 'no comment', so I ran the story. Of course, it's gathered arms and legs since then, with other media picking it up and speculating on the value, both of the bank's policy and the implications of being found out. The bank's denied that it was ever their policy and said they're making enquiries. Farnham's been suspended while that's going on."

"Have you done anything to trace who sent it to you?" Tom asked.

"No, not really, it was sent anonymously. The envelope was franked, so there wasn't even a postmark. I was grateful to receive it, but I didn't think there was any way to find out who sent it. I'm sure the bank would like to know, but the sender ought to be protected anyway under whistle-blower legislation."

"Hmm, I'd like to speak to RNB directly, but it's a question of knowing who to ask and the right place to look," Tom said. He lifted a magnifying glass from his pocket so he could closely examine the original papers.

"Hey Sherlock, have you got a deerstalker, pipe and violin to go with that?" Charlie scoffed.

"Mock all you like, but if you carefully examine a printed frank, there's often an identification code. We might be able to check where it's been sent from. It may not track it down too closely, but we should know whether it was local, or from the other side of the country. Then again, if we're lucky, it might even pinpoint the sender. I want to have a closer study of the email too, but first, let's check where this was posted."

Armed with an internet connection and a telephone, it took Tom less than an hour to confirm the letter had been posted from RNB's Glasgow call centre.

"Imagine the nerve; the whistle-blower actually used RNB's own postal system to send the letter at their cost," Sally said, then continued, making eye contact with Charlie, "as it came from Glasgow, it might well be someone you've had previous contact with."

"It might be the case, or it may have only come here because we're the local paper," Charlie replied.

"Yeah, but it was addressed to you personally," Sally continued, pointing to the address label on the envelope. "Also, it was printed, not handwritten."

"I wouldn't put too much meaning on that. I'm well known in these parts and anyone could pick my name off credits from articles I've written. If you don't believe me, you can take a look at my daily mailbag."

"Fair comment," Tom replied. "Okay, moving forward, do you have any contacts at RNB, preferably in the call centre building?"

"I do," Ahmed chirped up. "I used to work there."

All eyes turned to him.

"After I graduated, I was trying to get work. I applied to all the papers as well as TV and radio and not only in Glasgow."

"So we weren't your first choice after all," Charlie said, making a theatrical gesture of pretending to be wounded.

Ahmed glanced at him, shook his head, then continued. "I was desperate to be doing something and earning, so I had an excuse not to be dragged into the family business. I registered with all the agencies, willing to try any sort of work, temp or permanent. Most didn't offer me much hope, but a couple of them seemed quite on the ball and Headcount actually delivered the goods. They arranged an interview with RNB and it went well and I was offered the job. That was only last June. I got on fine and made some good mates. It's where I met my girlfriend, actually."

Charlie rolled his eyes then rotated his arm in a 'get on with it' gesture.

"Anyway, I worked there for about six months before this job came up and I still know quite a few folk there."

"Are they all operatives, or is there anyone more senior?" Tom asked.

"I know two or three of the team leaders and one of the department managers."

"Can you give the manager a ring and see if he'll talk to us?" Tom questioned.

"Sure, give me a few minutes. I keep the number upstairs in my desk. I'll call from there if you don't mind and let you know how I get on. It should only take a few minutes."

Ahmed left to make his call, returning after about a quarter of an hour.

"Mixed news; the manager wasn't in but I spoke to Angela, one of the team leaders. I had to explain what we were trying to do and she said she'd be happy to help, but she'd need to get permission and it would all need to be off the record as well. She said she'd speak to a manager to see if it would be okay and then come back to us. I stressed the urgency because you wouldn't be here for long, and she promised to come back this afternoon."

"I wouldn't hold out too much hope," Charlie began. "RNB are hurting because of press coverage and worse still, coverage that they consider I'm to blame for. So they're unlikely to be willing to do us any favours."

"We'll see," Sally answered. "I've got a good feeling about this and I don't know why."

The conversation was disturbed by the ring-tone from Ahmed's phone, playing the Superman theme. He quickly answered.

"They'll do it," he cried, his whole face lighting up when he disconnected the call. "Angela explained they've been upset by bad press and they want to build some bridges and create a better rapport. They've set some conditions though. They'll meet with us tomorrow morning for confidential discussions; they want anything said to be off the record unless they give us express permission to quote them. Angela will be there, but only to do introductions. There'll be a regional manager and one of their press specialists. It's set up for tomorrow morning at nine thirty. Did I do okay?"

"Absolutely perfect," Tom replied, displaying a matching smile.

"Well, what do we do now?" Ahmed asked.

"Don't know about you lot, but I've got some work to do. I'm going down the pub. I should have been there ages ago," Charlie replied.

"Would you like to meet up later for a meal or a drink?" Tom offered.

"Thanks, but no thanks," came the reply. "I've got other plans, but please keep me informed about how you get on and give me a mention if it turns into something big."

"Will do, thanks for your help."

Charlie picked up his file then left the other three.

"Well, where to now?" Ahmed asked again. "What else can we do?"

Tom checked his watch and noted it was almost 4.00 pm, Jenny should be home from school, snacking and resting before her concert.

"There isn't much more we can do on this to-day. I've got some calls to make and then I'm go-ing back to the hotel. I've got some editing to do on a draft of a diary column for next week's publication. If I can keep my eyes open long enough, I'll take a glance over it and then have a swim before getting ready for dinner. What about you two? Shall we meet up for dinner? Can you recommend somewhere, Ahmed? Per-haps you'd like to bring your significant other, if she'd like to join us?"

"If you promise not to tell anyone, I think I'll have an early night and sneak off home. I can lead you back to the hotel first, so you don't get lost. Much as I enjoy the work, if I go back to the newsroom now, there won't be anything meaningful for me to do, but someone's bound to want to use me as a gofer." Ahmed thought for a second before continuing. "In answer to your question, there are loads of great restaurants in Glasgow. You could probably eat in a different one every night for a year, so if you tell me what type of food you like best, I can make a shortlist. And yeah, I don't know about significant other, but I'd like to bring my girlfriend, I'm sure she'd love to meet you both and it would be nice to make up a foursome."

"Whoa there," Sally cut in. "Don't go making any assumptions about foursomes. We're not a couple; we're only working together and even that's under sufferance." The lightness of Sally's tone betrayed her words were spoken in jest.

Tom raised his eyebrows in response.

"What about eating style?" Ahmed asked. "There are loads of Italian, French, Spanish, Greek, Turkish, Chinese, and Indian restaurants but if you want something different, we can offer Russian, Mongolian or Afghani."

"How about going traditionally Scottish?" Tom suggested, glancing at Sally. "Since we're here, we ought to try something more local? What do you think?"

"I'm game," Sally replied.

"Maybe so, but what would you like to eat?" It was too good an opportunity for Tom to resist and he had plenty of ground to make up on the verbal sparring.

"Touché. All right, I'd be more than happy to experiment with traditional Scottish cuisine," Sally corrected.

"You say that now, but you may change your mind after a night with your head down a toilet. No, I'm only joking," Ahmed added. "There are some very good Scottish restaurants; it's not all about deep fried Mars bars."

"Is that real? I'd heard of it, but thought it was an urban myth," Sally asked.

"No, it's actually real, although it's not traditional. After all, Mars is an American company, but it's been hyped up for the tourist industry. There's a chippie at Glasgow Cross I can take you to, if you'd like to try it."

"No, I think I'll pass," Tom replied holding his hands up defensively.

"Me too," Sally added.

"Okay, I think I know an ideal place," Ahmed suggested. "I'll make a booking for eight o'clock if that's okay. I'll come by at seven-thirty to take you there."

Tom tried phoning home, Anne's mobile and Arthur's home and mobile, but he only received outgoing recorded answer messages in return.

Fortunately, the rain had passed by the time they left the building. All three walked back to the Radisson, where Ahmed deposited Tom and Sally to collect their keys before he set off for his own home.

"Are you away to do some work now?" Sally asked "I'll try out the fitness centre and get some exercise. I've been sitting about and snacking all day, I need to burn off a few calories before we go out for dinner."

"I don't know if I can concentrate, I think I'll do the same. I'll go freshen up and see you there in what, fifteen minutes?" Tom replied.

"Sounds okay to me."

Chapter 6

Twenty minutes later, Sally arrived at the gym and spotted Tom setting a reasonable pace, jogging on a treadmill. She took a second to admire his powerful frame and smooth elegant movement before opening the door and approaching him with a welcoming, "Hi."

Seeing the image of her approach, attired in body-hugging Lycra which accentuated every curve, Tom's heart skipped a beat, but worse, because of the distraction he misjudged his footing and almost collapsed off the machine. After the stumble, he quickly recovered enough, with the help of the support frame, to reach out and reduce the speed to something less challenging, "Glad you could make it," he panted.

Sally suppressed a giggle, not convinced if Tom had tripped or was merely clowning. They both undertook a fairly rigorous routine on cardio-vascular equipment, matching each other's pace to enable conversation while they tested adjacent rowing machines, cross trainers and bikes. They casually continued to converse, their voices husky from their exertions. Each exercised and demonstrated their fitness without overstraining, staying well within their limits, to avoid embarrassment. The conversation came easy and was light and uncomplicated. It occurred to Tom that it been a long time since he'd enjoyed himself so much. Recently, his existence comprised of a mixture of work alternating with a strained home life. He had little opportunity to unwind and what there was, he normally spent worrying about some problem or other. The time passed quickly and by the end of their routine their skins glowed with perspiration from the workout.

"Have we time for a quick swim?" Sally asked.

"Good idea," Tom replied. It'll give us a chance to cool off before we get ready to go out. I'll see you through there."

Tom quickly showered and changed into his Speedos and was lowering himself into the water when Sally returned. If he'd been attracted by her gym outfit, he was positively enraptured by the sight of her wearing a bikini. He thought Sally's lingering assessment of him was an appreciative one as well, but feared it may have been his imagination. As it was, he was grateful to see a small tattoo of hearts protruding from her top and he decided to comment on it, thereby permitting himself an excuse, if accosted, for paying too much attention to her breasts. He'd learned from his berating yesterday.

Albeit the view was marginally short of complete, Tom could see that Sally's claim of an all over tan had been justified. Yesterday, it occurred to him; it was only yesterday. It seems so much longer; so much had happened, yesterday seemed a lifetime ago.

Over the years, and often as a result of his profession, Tom had met and known many beautiful women and on the sheer beauty stakes, Sally fell short of some of them. It was not just her height, if he was honest, her nose had a slight kink and she had an uneven smile. There was no questioning her attractiveness, but there was something else, something Tom couldn't put his finger on.

Something Tom *mustn't* put his finger on, he corrected himself.

Sally came close and touched Tom's hand in greeting. It was the lightest of touches, but Tom experienced a jolt, as if shocked by a lightning bolt. Feeling her touch and seeing her almost naked body, Tom detected the beginnings of arousal, a stirring in his loins. Expediency being the better part of valour, he thought it best to lower himself further into the water and swim to avoid any evidence of his approval showing. In hindsight, his trunks had been a bad idea – he'd have been safer wearing swimming shorts. However, the cool water and the distraction of swimming provided the solution.

Being a quiet time of day, they had the pool to themselves and as both were competent swimmers they glided through the water with ease and grace, losing count of the number of lengths.

After a while, Tom noticed Sally check the time. "Do we need to go and get ready?"

"You can stay longer if you like, but I'll need to go. As I didn't bring a bathing cap, I'll need to get my hair dried before I can think about getting changed."

Returning to his room, Tom had his first opportunity to check and appreciate the quality of his accommodation. It was spacious and comfortable, with solid wood furniture and flooring. Light shone through the large windows overlooking Argyle Street. Now feeling relaxed, he dressed in shirt and trousers, taking an unusually long time to preen to ensure he looked his best.

A vision of Jenny at her concert entered Tom's mind and his thoughts rambled. He checked his watch. She'd be there now, nervous and preparing to perform. She'd been practising for weeks and of course she'd be fine. Tom believed he knew the words of her solo almost as well as she did, he'd heard her rehearse so often. He really wanted to be there in person to cheer her on and give her confidence. Perhaps he could have been there, if he'd fought harder with Stephan to reschedule, but in reality he knew it wouldn't have helped. He consoled himself, reasoning that it really hadn't been possible. As for Anne's overreaction, that was totally out of the park. *Okay, admittedly, I might have been more considerate and gotten home earlier last night,* he thought, *but I didn't deserve the treatment I got. Anne's becoming more and more unreasonable and I don't know how much more I can tolerate. Last night was bad enough, but to ignore my calls all day today and not even let me talk to Jenny and wish her well was cruel to Jenny, not just me.* Once the concert was over, Anne would come back down to earth, he hoped. If he came back from dinner early enough he could try again; then again, he might be better waiting until morning so he'd be able to talk to Jenny too. He wondered if Arthur had managed to speak to Anne – Tom hadn't been able to get hold of him all day either. It was strange, but then Arthur was often a bit strange. He decided to give him another try before going out.

Following another unsuccessful attempt, Tom closed his door and made his way to reception to find Sally and Ahmed already waiting. Sally was fresh and radiant. She was wearing a flowery cotton print dress. Ahmed had changed, but his attire was almost as formal as his daywear had been. He'd discarded his suit but was dressed in smart trousers with a shirt and tie.

"I don't know. Why do women always get a bad name for taking so long to get ready, when it's the men who always turn up late?" Sally announced.

Tom checked the time and realised it was seven minutes after their planned rendezvous. "Whoops, sorry," he mouthed unconvincingly. "What's the plan? Will I need a coat?"

"No, you should be okay," Ahmed replied. "It's a bit of a hike and the weather is forecast to remain unsettled, so I brought the car. Provided I can pull into a space close by, there's little risk you'll get wet. I've parked right outside the door, on the double yellow lines. I've left Morag in the car so I don't get booked.

"When I got home, I had a look on 5pm.co.uk for offers. I've booked us into the Ingram Wynd and, because I used the promotion website, I've got us a 20% discount from the a la carte menu, and I've earned loyalty points for myself as well," Ahmed added with pride.

"A good demonstration of the famed Scottish frugality there. It's a business dinner, so I'll be able to charge it, but it'll save the company some money."

"Morag's not part of the team, so should I pay you for her share?"

"Not necessary. I'll be able to include her on the claim. Besides, you told us earlier that you met while you both worked at RNB so I can ask her a question or two about it then it will be a legitimate claim for the costs associated with an interview," Tom explained, his smug appearance betrayed how pleased he was with his own reasoning.

"I've no complaints and I'm sure she'll be happy too."

They walked through the doorway. Seeing them approach, Morag slid from the car to be introduced. She appeared to be about thirty, tall and slender with a round, cheerful face. She had pale skin, but her most pronounced feature was her hair. It was bright ginger in colour, styled fairly short in gelled spikes, which stuck up into the air like corkscrews. To accompany the effect, she had piercings, sporting multiple small gold rings through her ears, nose and upper lip.

Ahmed carried out the introductions and Tom and Sally tried not to stare. Morag appeared a most unlikely partner for the very conservative Ahmed.

"It might be a crush," Morag began, beckoning them towards the door of the three-door Toyota Aygo. "I'll travel in the back with Sally, so the men can have more legroom in the front." She reached inside to unclip the lever, moving the front seat forward and allowing access into the back. Tom suppressed an appreciative sigh watching Sally as she climbed in and slid across behind the driver's seat. She was followed by Morag, who yanked the front seat upright, allowing Tom access the passenger seat. Ahmed walked around the car and slipped into the driver's side.

"It's not far, but because of the one-way system, I'll have to go around in a big circle to get us there," Ahmed said.

"The same as the rest of my life; always going around in circles," Tom replied. It was meant as a humorous aside, but it seemed tinged with sadness and resignation and no-one wanted to comment.

A few minutes later, Ahmed drew up in front of the restaurant. "If you'd like to get out here, I know somewhere I can park around the corner. The restaurant has a garden area off to the side, but I think we'd be better indoors. Those clouds are looking really threatening."

The three piled out and Ahmed shot off to park the car. Morag advised the waitress of their booking and they were shown straight to what was the only vacant table, situated next to the window. A cacophony of sound assaulted them as enthusiastic diners tucked into their meals and talked loudly in a babble of languages and accents.

"My name's Becky and I'll be your waitress this evening. I'll bring your menus in a moment, but can I get you a drink in the meantime?"

"I could murder a G&T," Sally said.

"Same for me and Ahmed will want a pint of soda water and lime," Morag added.

"Three G&T's," Tom said.

"All for you? Or does that include ours?" Sally probed. Tom pursed his lips and shook his head.

Ahmed arrived back at the table at the same time as the menus.

"If you want to try something tradition-ally Scottish, you'll need to have some haggis," he suggested. "They have it here as a starter, see there – 'grilled haggis, black pudding and mashed potato' or else there's 'pan fried, breaded haggis'. Or would you prefer something safer?"

"Safer? What is haggis, anyway?" Tom asked.

"Let me explain," Morag offered, relishing the opportunity. "It's sheep's pluck, that's the heart, liver and lungs, and it's mixed with oatmeal, suet and spices. In its traditional form, it's all put together and then encased in a sheep's stomach and cooked."

Tom looked incredulous. "You're having me on, aren't you? They've put you up to seeing how gullible I am, haven't they?"

Morag broke into a laugh before replying. "Do you prefer the explanation that it's a small furry animal that runs about on the banks and braes? They always run anti-clockwise around the hills and as a result, their right side legs are longer than the left. The best way to catch them is to meet them going the other way, so that when they turn to escape, they fall over and then you can scoop them up. I can take you to a shop in

Queen Street. It's called Tam Shepherd and you can buy a haggis hunting licence there."

Before the others had a chance to react, a stout lady with an American accent tapped Morag on the shoulder. "Excuse me, young lady, I hope you don't mind me intruding, but I thought I over-heard you saying you knew a place where you were able to buy a haggis hunting licence. My husband and I are on holiday from Houston and we'd dearly love to be able to take one of those licences home. Can you please tell me where to get it?"

Morag struggled to keep a straight face. She couldn't fathom whether the woman had been taken in by her story and really wanted to buy a hunting licence, or whether she understood the joke and was playing along to be a part of it. Not wishing to risk offending her, she gave directions to where the trick shop was located.

Returning to the conversation at their table, Sally confided, "I've eaten haggis once before, when I was attending a Burns Night, but I never knew what was actually in it. I remember it tasted okay, but I may not have thought so if I'd known."

"If that's what haggis is, I'm rather frightened to ask about this. What's Cullen skink?" Tom asked.

"Oh, I think you might like that. It's a traditional fish soup made from smoked haddock."

The conversation flowed and the four enjoyed a delicious meal washed down with a couple of bottles of Pinot Grigio, and to maintain the Scottish theme, Tom and Sally each ordered a malt whisky to go along with their coffees.

"Now this is meant to be a business dinner, so for me to fulfil my obligations, I need to ask you about RNB." Tom addressed Morag in a voice only slightly slurred by the alcohol he'd imbibed.

"What would you like to know?"

"Well, to begin with, what do you do there? Are you involved with the insurance call centre?"

"Yes and no. I've got no operating involvement there, but I work in I.T. I'm called when there's equipment breakdowns, or when there's upgrades taking place. Sometimes, although it's less often, I get involved in software problems."

"Oh, I see," It was hardly noticeable, but Tom's shoulders slumped. He hadn't expected to get anywhere, but even so, he was slightly disappointed.

"Wait a minute," Sally interrupted. "Do you have anything to do with the email system?"

"A little bit, I suppose."

"Then you must already know about the leaked information. What all the media have been jumping on. The actual source was a copy of an email instruction, from the head office to the call centre managers. Can you tell us anything about how that works?" Sally asked.

"I'd need to see the email to know for sure, but internal instructions shouldn't come through normal email channels. The bank has its own intranet to handle internal communications. It's much more secure, because it doesn't travel through third party networks."

"Can you tell by checking a copy of the email whether it's internal or external?" Tom enthusiasm was restored.

"Yes, the layout would be totally different."

"If a message comes through the intranet, can it only come from an internal source?" Sally probed.

"It's almost certain, but I can't guarantee that it's not possible to hack in. After all, even NATO and the FBI have been hacked, but it'd be a hell of a job to do it."

"Thank you very much, that's been really helpful," Tom said. "You've earned your dinner tonight."

"You're most welcome," Morag replied. "Now if we've finished here, we can either drop you two back at your hotel, or if you like, we'll invite you back to my flat for a nightcap. We don't live far away. It's around the corner from here; one of the new flats in Parsonage Square. It's only a short walk to the other side of High Street and the Collegelands development."

"If you don't mind me prying, you said 'my' flat but 'we' live. What's the story?" Sally asked.

"Why are journalists always searching for a story?" Morag answered. "Ahmed's the same. But we've got nothing to hide, so I'll tell you. It's my flat because my parents bought it for me. They have a property business and technically, it's part of their inventory, but they let me live in it for free. They understand I love living in the city centre, well, the Merchant City to be more precise. Ahmed and I have been together for a good few months now and it's suited us both, it's worked well. I'm sure you've noticed that I'm a little older than Ahmed, about five years, so he's my toy-boy."

"I'm not a kept man. I earn for myself and pay my own way," Ahmed defended himself.

Morag patted his arm. "It's okay, I was only joking. I didn't mean anything by it."

"I really appreciate the invite, but I'm dog tired. We had an early start this morning so I think we should call it a night and go back to the hotel," Tom replied.

"Before you make a final decision, I can tell you that I have a good selection of vintage whiskies you might like to sample," Morag suggested.

"Tempting, but I'm afraid no. I'd be too tired to appreciate it. Can I take a rain-check?" Tom suggested. "Talking of checks, I'll get the bill."

He signalled across the room and Becky responded. Tom fished in his pocket and handed over the first card out without thinking; it was his personal MasterCard. Becky inserted the card and keyed the necessary data into the hand-held, chip and pin machine before handing it to Tom for the authorisation code.

"I'm sorry, Sir. It's been rejected. Would you like to try again?"

Tom had her repeat the exercise with exactly the same result.

"That's really odd because I used the same card this morning with no problem and I know there's plenty of headroom on the credit. I'll need to check what's happened. Never mind, put it on this one instead. I should have used it in the first place." He handed over his company credit card, but was feeling distinctly embarrassed.

A moderate shower was falling outside and Tom and Sally were grateful they didn't have to walk. Ahmed left to collect the car. Having partaken of a fair quantity of alcohol, Sally and Morag were still in the party spirit, but Tom had sobered up almost instantly because of the problem with his card.

On the journey back to the hotel, he sat silently, brow furrowed, trying to imagine what the problem might be. It may only be a simple error which could be quickly identified and rectified. But, alternatively, he was worried that the phone store may have put through a wrong charge that morning. He remembered an occasion, some years before when he'd hired a car in Florida, when the hire company had insisted on a five-hundred-dollar deposit. Despite giving him a receipt for the five hundred, they'd processed a charge for five thousand dollars and Tom had only realised when he'd tried using his card later. He'd managed to recover the money, but not before incurring a lot of anguish and wasting a day of his holiday. Despite complaints to his bank, the car hire company and the Florida Tourist Board, he hadn't received so much as an apology in compensation.

Tom feared this might be a repetition, or worse still, it could be identity fraud. Someone, somewhere in the world may have used his name fraudulently and drawn money or purchased goods against his card.

It suddenly occurred to him that it might not be an error; it could be genuinely maxed out. Anne had a card on the same account. Perhaps she'd gone out today and spent enough money to max out the card limit. He knew she was angry with him, but it wouldn't be like her to act so rashly. Right now, he had no way to be sure. All these thoughts and worries perturbed him as the journey proceeded and he was anxious to phone the bank and try to solve the mystery.

"Tom? Tom, are you okay? We're back at the hotel, and you need to get out, because I'm stuck behind you and I'm dying for the loo. You don't want to take too long about it, or Ahmed would never forgive either of us," Sally joked.

"What? Oh sorry, I was in another world." Tom quickly got out of the car and the four exchanged parting comments, promising to meet up again sometime soon. Ahmed agreed to call for and collect Tom and Sally at eight forty-five the following morning.

Tom and Sally made their way through the lobby and took the lift to their floor. Alighting from the elevator, Tom realised their rooms were in opposite directions.

"I really enjoyed myself today and that was a lovely evening. Thanks Tom." Sally leaned forward and stretched upwards towards him.

"I enjoyed it too," Tom lowered his head for the customary peck on the cheek, but was surprised as Sally's hand caressed his face and her lips met his, her tongue gently brushing across his teeth. Then she turned and was gone.

Tom stood on the spot, dumbfounded. The incident had been brief, a couple of seconds at most, but the effect had been profound. The aroma of her fresh, fruity perfume lingered on his nostrils and he could still taste the whisky from her breath.

He didn't know what to do. He was tempted to go after her. He wanted to recreate the moment, to extend it, even to take it much further. But where? How far would he want to go? In his nine years of marriage, Tom had no shortage of opportunities to stray, but he'd never been interested – not until now. He and Anne were going through a bad patch, but surely they'd come through it? He wanted them to come through it. He *thought* he wanted them to come through it. Tom was confused and the prospect of an extramarital relationship would only confuse matters more. What was he thinking? Wasn't he getting ahead of himself? He'd shared one brief embrace with Sally and he was now contemplating a relationship. *Who's to say whether it's what she wants anyway? She's probably only flirting.* She'd been teasing him one way or the other since they'd first met and this was just a further stage. She'd had lots to drink tonight, too, so even if she had seemed a little amorous, it might only be the drink talking.

Tom plodded back to his room, scanned his door card and opened the door. There was a folded sheet of paper on the floor. He lifted it, saw a chequered logo at the top and, thinking it was an advertising flyer, placed it on the table.

First things first, he thought, *I need to call my bank and see what's happened to my card.* He lifted his phone and noticed there'd been a text. With all the background noise in the restaurant he hadn't heard it come in. He flicked to the in-box and saw that Arthur had contacted him. *Shit,* he thought, *I was going to try calling him again.* Tom opened the text first and read: – **We need to talk, but better face to face. How about at weekend once you're back? Don't call until then.**

"Now what the fuck's that about?" Tom murmured aloud. *I can do without any more hassle and I need to concentrate.* He dismissed it from his mind for the present while he called the bank.

Twenty minutes later, Tom was a stage further forward, but nevertheless unsure about the cause and possible consequences of the problem. He'd eliminated the phone shop from culpability and he knew there had been four transactions of five hundred pounds each through his account, but he was unable to determine what they were. He'd arranged for the transactions to be disputed and his account put on hold until it was investigated further. He then called the fraud protection departments for each of his other personal cards and put them on hold too, to avoid the risk of further misuse.

Tom felt totally drained. It was then he saw the paper he'd picked up at the door when he'd come in to the room. He distractedly flicked it open and his eyes widened in horror as the contents grabbed his attention.

He read the page a second and then a third time, trying to fathom out the meaning.

The note was an A4 page of copy paper, folded in three. At the top, what he'd mistaken earlier for a logo was a depiction of a chess board, a large square comprising a black and white chequered pattern of sixty-four smaller squares in an eight by eight matrix. Alongside, in large font, the same size as the large square was the word 'CHECK!' Below was printed the message.

'Bishop has moved into unknown territory and is attacking White King.
Bishop is being threatened by Knight.
Bishop needs to take better care if he doesn't want to be trampled on.
You have been warned.
Either resign now or take your chances.'

Chapter 7

As tired as Tom was, sleep eluded him. His head was buzzing and it had settled into a dull ache. There was so much happening in his life – too much – and he was finding it difficult to reconcile himself with any of it. Every time he closed his eyes, the buzzing grew louder and he visualised one or the other of his current dilemmas.

The night dragged by. Glancing at the clock, thinking hours had passed, Tom was dismayed to see the hands had hardly moved. He wasn't convinced he'd come any closer to finding solutions.

Trying to blank out his problems and clear his mind proved ineffective as his imagination and night demons took over. Instead, he thought he'd take the opposite route. He detailed all his issues on a sheet of paper. It wouldn't solve anything, but the effort of systematically listing would give him something to work from when he was fresher. He wanted to purge his mind and enable some restful sleep.

On the personal front, he listed his issues with Anne and Jenny and placed a question mark over whatever was happening with Arthur, together with the complication of his feelings for Sally.

On a financial footing, he was concerned about the problem with his credit card, but for good measure he listed all his mortgage and loan accounts.

For work considerations he identified various thoughts and lines of enquiry he had with the RNB investigation, but then there was the sheet of paper slipped under his door tonight. Tom didn't truly understand what it meant, but knew it must connect somehow with his current investigations.

The process did work and for a few minutes he drifted into a slumber; at least, he imagined he must have been asleep as dream-like visions flitted through his brain. It became almost surreal. He imagined looking down from the ceiling and seeing himself next to Sally. She was dressed in her bikini and he was standing close to her, as he had been when they'd exited the lift. He inhaled her perfume and it was intoxicating – his head grew cloudy. He raised his fingers to trace the shape of her tattoo, then lowered his hand to slip into the bra cup, touching and then kneading her soft flesh. Tom took pleasure from hearing her passionate responses. He became aroused, and sensing a hardness twitching between his legs, he lowered his hand to release his trousers and free his now-rigid penis. He lowered his head to kiss her, but then what he was seeing started to change. The face grew longer and became paler and gaunt. It was no longer Sally; it had metamorphosed into Anne. He jumped back in shock, but then, from above, he saw his hand move forward again to grasp her breast – only it wasn't his hand. He wasn't standing with Sally any more – it was Anne with Arthur.

Tom's eyes jerked open and he felt sick. He was still exhausted, but he was wide awake. He sat up in bed then switched on the television to provide a distraction. He had no idea what he was watching, but he needed the pictures and the sound to replace the images replaying through his troubled mind. He made tea and sat watching the screen blankly.

Filled with apprehension, at seven thirty Tom picked up his phone and called home, predicting the usual result. To his surprise, it was picked up on the third ring and he heard Jenny's voice say, "Hello?"

"Daddy," she shrieked when she recognised his voice.

"I called to talk to you about your concert." In the background, music was playing from the radio. It was country and western, not the sort of thing he or Anne or Jenny often listened to, more like Arthur's taste. A bad omen, his apprehension grew. He thought he recognised Dolly Parton's voice spelling out the letters 'D.I.V.O.R.C.E.'. Already fearful about making the call, he was considerably more so on hearing the music. With dread, he suspected what might be coming.

"Daddy, it was wonderful. Everyone was there and they said I did great. They all stood up and clapped when I finished."

"That's wonderful, darling. You know I wanted to be there too, but I had to go away for work. I'll make it up to you when I get back. I'll take you out somewhere special to celebrate."

"That's okay, Daddy. Everyone else was there. All my friends and their families. Grandma and Papa, even Uncle Arthur was there."

"Oh, that's good." Tom's heart lurched, the first of his suspicions confirmed and bile rose in his throat.

"After the concert, Uncle Arthur took me and Mummy for an ice cream before we came home, and he said he'd stay here until you came back, so Mummy and me wouldn't be lonely."

And there it was. Tom tried speaking, but at first, the words wouldn't come. He breathed in deeply and tried again.

"Is Mummy there?"

"Hold on a second."

There was a clunk and then a pause until Jenny lifted the phone again. "Mummy says she can't talk now, and I've to go and get ready. See you soon, kiss, kiss, kiss." Then the line went dead.

Tom remained seated for several seconds, holding the disconnected phone to his ear, tears streaming down his cheeks.

After some minutes, he laboriously moved to the bathroom and splashed some water over his face. He climbed under the shower and let the warm jet wash over him, hoping it would do something to invigorate him and cleanse his troubles. Next, he threw on some clothes and made his way to the restaurant.

He wasn't hungry, but felt he ought to eat something. Unable to face anything cooked, he filled a bowl with fresh fruit cocktail and returned to the table. He sat playing with the food, prodding it with a fork, but unable to lift any to his mouth, let alone swallow. The restaurant was busy with a mixture of tourists and conventioneers, passing him on all sides with plates heavily laden from the buffet. He had vague thoughts of the circus being in town, with willing participants challenging to devour a small African nation's annual production at one sitting. Tom of course, was being ridiculously unfair; he wanted a target as an escape for his hurt. On any normal day, he'd have been one of the challengers. Instead, he sat people-watching the carnival, thinking cruel and malicious thoughts.

Tom was so pre-occupied, he didn't see Sally approach until she edged out a chair and sat down opposite him. She lowered a plate with a modest helping of bacon and scrambled eggs onto the table, along with a second holding two croissants. "What gives? Yesterday you had an excuse; it was five thirty in the morning and you'd slept in a car overnight. You look even more like shit this morning. So what the hell were you doing after I left you? And who with, for that matter?"

Tom stared at her morosely. "Thanks. That's how you know who your friends are. Go on then, hit a man when he's down."

"Sorry for breathing."

He shook his head. "No, I'm sorry. I shouldn't be taking it out on you. I had a bad night."

"You seemed fine when I left you, what happened?"

"A long story, but for me, on a personal level, everything's going pear-shaped at the moment."

"Had another fight with your wife then?"

"Nope, it wouldn't be so bad if I had. I've not even spoken to her yet or rather, she's not been prepared to talk to me. There have been other things going on and I really can't talk about it." Tom was fighting back tears as he spoke.

"You might want to take some time out. I can handle things here and you can go and get yourself sorted."

"No, I'm not ready to do that."

Sally leaned back in her chair, regarding him seriously. "Well, I'm no shrink, but unless you're able to do something about it now, I reckon your best course of action is to immerse yourself in your work."

"I might have a problem there, too. When I got to my room last night, I had the strangest message waiting for me."

"What do you mean, strange?"

"It was weird. It was cryptic, a message written as if it was describing a chess game. I found it threatening – as if it was a warning to back off."

"Can I see it?"

"It's up in my room."

Tom's fruit salad remained untouched, but Sally had swallowed several mouthfuls of food. She lifted a croissant and looked expectantly at Tom. "What are we waiting for?"

Travelling back up to their floor, the lift was crowded with bodies huddled close together. Tom could feel the warmth from Sally's back pressed against his chest. His nostrils twitched, inhaling the aroma from her fragrant shampoo emanating from her hair. He closed his eyes – it was so comforting. He had an overwhelming desire to hold her, to embrace the back of her neck, to…

"Our floor, Tom. Wakey, wakey."

Tom jumped, his eyelids springing open and he wearily exited the lift and followed Sally along the corridor. He'd never brought a young lady back to a hotel bedroom before. He'd never brought anyone back to his bedroom before – besides Anne. Tom tried to recall how untidy he'd left it, but he couldn't remember. There was nothing he was able to do at this point anyway. Tom opened the door and Sally followed him inside.

To his surprise, it wasn't too bad. The one exception was the bed where the quilt had been left in a rumpled heap, seemingly tied around the pillows. The sheet was untucked, lying creased, crumpled and hanging askew off one side.

Wanting to distract Sally's attention away from the bed, Tom quickly located the page and handed it to her. "Here, tell me what you think."

Sally scanned the contents. "This must be some sort of joke; don't you think? Have you any idea who it might be from?" she asked.

"No and no. I don't see anything funny about it, and I haven't a clue who sent it or how it got there. Who even knew where I was staying or what I was working on? I'm completely mystified."

"It does sound somewhat threatening. Maybe we should take it to the police?" Sally suggested.

"Probably a waste of time."

"There's no harm in trying. Listen, if you're insisting on working today, you need to get cleaned up and have a shave. How about you do that and I'll call the police and see if they can help?"

"Sounds like a plan." Tom followed Sally's instruction. He wasn't used to being led in this way, but he experienced a small thrill from the idea of getting ready in the en-suite bathroom, while Sally was only a few feet away.

Tom went through to the bathroom to wash and shave. His thoughts flitted between the attractive woman he had sitting in his room to his situation at home. He was incensed by the idea of Anne having a relationship behind his back and worse still, with his own brother. But as he pondered what he actually knew, he decided he could be jumping to the wrong conclusions. Maybe it was all totally innocent and Arthur was merely offering Anne some comfort and company while he was away. Tom had actually asked Arthur to help, and possibly, that's all there was to it and everything else was in his own sordid imagination. Perhaps he was being paranoid. But if that was the case, then why would neither of them speak to him? He knew Arthur had always had a soft spot for Anne. No, Tom thought he was being too polite. Arthur'd lusted over her, more like. So, knowing that, why had he been stupid enough to ask Arthur to contact Anne, knowing she was already vulnerable? Tom grew pensive. For that matter, what would Anne think of him if she could see him now, half dressed, with Sally sitting in his bedroom, first thing in the morning? The more Tom thought, the more confused he became.

* * *

Sally used the room phone to call down to Reception, asking them to place a call to the local police station. When she was connected, she spoke into the phone. "Hello, I'd like to speak to someone to report a threatening letter."

"Hold on, Madam, I'll find an officer to take your call."

Sally tapped her fingers on the table while she waited.

A minute or two later, she heard a different voice. "Hello, DC McAvoy, how can I help you?"

"My name's Sally Ferguson and I'm calling to report a threatening letter that my friend's received."

"I'm sorry, Madam, but it's your friend who needs to make the report and he'll need to come into the office to file it. Do you know the location of your nearest police station?"

Sally's hackles went up right away, hearing the tired, uncooperative voice of a seasoned officer and obviously a jobsworth. "My friend has been traumatised by the letter and I'm trying to help him by seeing what can be done. Will you help me?"

"Okay," McAvoy sighed. "Let's hear about it."

Sally was no happier with his response, he was obviously going through the motions, but having come this far, she proceeded to read him the contents of the letter.

"I don't understand," McAvoy responded when she'd finished. "Where's the threat? Who's Bishop and who are Knight and King?"

Sally huffed out an impatient breath. "Don't you see? It's a chess analogy. My friend's name is Bishop, Tom Bishop."

"A what?"

"A chess analogy, it's referring to terminology in the game of chess."

"This is the police. We're here to uphold the law. We don't have time for people playing games."

Sally tried to hide her exasperation. "This isn't a game. It's someone making a threat, but they're making reference to a game."

"So, what's the threat and who's making it?"

"We don't know who's making it, that's why we want to report it! Can't you do something? Can't you check the letter for prints, or DNA?"

McAvoy barely hid a derisive snort. "I think you've been watching too much television. We don't have the resources to go running tests and checking out every piece of paper, and certainly not when there hasn't even been a crime committed. I think you should come back after you've got something more to go on."

"You mean wait until he's been murdered and then bring you the body?" Sally's sarcasm was palpable.

"Now Madam, there's no need to take that attitude."

"What attitude do you expect me to take? This isn't a crank call. My friend and I aren't idiots. We're investigative reporters for an international publication."

"Well in that case, you hardly need us. You can investigate it all by yourselves."

"I want to speak to your superior officer."

"I'm afraid that won't be possible. You've been put through to the serious crimes unit and I'm the only one here just now. All the other officers are out investigating a murder which was reported this morning. You see what I mean? They've been called to an actual serious crime? If you require to speak to a senior officer, I can transfer you back to the switchboard."

Sally was incensed and couldn't hold down her temper. "Doesn't it tell you something that they're out investigating crimes and you're the one left in the office to man the phones?" She slammed down the receiver in frustration. "Arrogant, supercilious, bastard!"

"Whoa, and I haven't even said anything yet," Tom said when he came back into the room.

"Sorry Tom, you were right. Fucking stupid policeman didn't want to know. Anyway, you look considerably better now." She cast an appraising scan over him. "Too much eyeshadow, but otherwise fine."

"I'm not wearing— Oh. Right, very funny. Let's make a move." Tom scooped all his belongings into his case and left the room.

"I'll get my stuff, too."

Tom followed Sally along the corridor and into her room. On reflection, he needn't have worried about the tidiness of his own. It was quite the reverse, in fact – as the surfaces were all covered in scraps of paper, discarded clothes or other sundry items, but the bed was immaculate. The quilt was drawn across and folded almost exactly in half. In the uncovered area, the sheet was flat and even, except for a perfect impression of her petite body showing exactly where she'd been lying. As Sally gathered up her belongings, Tom stared at the outline. He found the image erotic and he was suddenly uncomfortable knowing, he was alone with a young woman in her room.

"Let's get moving," he blurted.

"I've still got to pack the last of my things, you go on down if you like. I won't be long. Wait a sec, there's something stuck in your hair, I think it's a feather," she replied.

Tom moved forward, turning to the mirror and reached up to check, but as he did, Sally launched herself onto a chair to give herself extra height and reached forward to help him. Their combined movements resulted in Tom's face being pressed against the softness of Sally's breast and his left hand was cupping it. He froze for a second, instinctively wanting to caress the skin he was touching , but instead he recoiled as though burned by an electric shock and fled out of the door, muttering apologies as he went.

Tom's heart was racing and he was hyperventilating. He half ran along the corridor, cursing his clumsiness and ineptitude as he went. Not wanting to stand waiting on a lift, he pushed open the door to the stairwell and descended to the half landing before he stopped, holding his head in his hands. While he couldn't deny his attraction to Sally, he hadn't intended to touch or fondle her. Indeed, had he planned such a move, he'd have hoped to have been more suave and manly instead of effecting an adolescent fumble. But running away, as he had, only added to the impression of culpability. It had been a genuine accident and the last thing he needed now was an accusation of sexual harassment of a work colleague. Sally was no shrinking violet and he knew how quick she'd been before with her accusations. This time he was innocent, but might easily be condemned by his own cowardice. Why had he run away, rather than stand his ground with a blasé apology? He had excuses of exhaustion from lack of sleep together with the multiple traumas he was facing, but would anyone believe him? Now what could he do? Should he go back to her room and try to explain? But what would he say? Panic was starting to overtake him and he thought he wanted to lie down and die. It wasn't in Tom's character to give up without a fight and he gradually regained his composure and his breathing returned to a reasonably normal pattern. Resignedly, he decided there was no point hiding any longer, he needed to face the music and try to tackle whatever was thrown at him. He slowly and miserably descended the rest of the stairs and shuffled out into the hotel lobby.

"Tom! What the hell's wrong with you?" Sally's voice immediately accosted him.

"I'm sorry, I'm sorry," Tom blurted his reply, fearing the worst. "It wasn't intentional."

"What are you talking about? I hope you're not having some sort of breakdown. You ran off for no reason, leaving your bag. I've had to lug everything downstairs myself. You didn't say anything, you just vanished." Sally appeared genuinely concerned and took his hand in hers. "Are you ill? Is there something wrong I don't know about?"

Tom was lost for words – he'd clearly overreacted. He could have kissed her he was so relieved, but then that would only add to his problems or create a new one. He wondered what he could say that wouldn't sound too puerile. Staring at the floor, he started to stammer an honest explanation. "I, I don't really know, I'm not coping well, I have too much to think about and with the lack of sleep, I guess it was some sort of panic attack."

"You need to calm down and pull yourself together. Otherwise you won't be able to handle anything," Sally pointed out.

"Yes, you're right of course. I think I must be getting paranoid."

"Well you know what they say – just because you're paranoid doesn't mean they're not out to get you."

Raising his eyes and seeing Sally's smile, Tom's spirits were lifted. "That's alright, as long as I can find out who 'THEY' are. Anyway, we'd better get checked out so we're ready for Ahmed."

"Already done," Sally replied. "I've charged both rooms on my company card. As for who

'THEY' are, isn't that what we get paid to find out?"

Chapter 8

Ahmed turned up exactly on time and they squeezed their cases into the boot of the Aygo then climbed on board. It was only when Sally was manoeuvring into the back seat that Tom noticed she was attired in a smart trouser suit. The realisation came as tangible disappointment when he missed seeing her shapely legs struggle into the confined area. His earlier preoccupation with his own real and imagined problems had dulled his sense of observation and he knew he needed to sharpen up if he was going to be effective in his work. When he re-appraised the three of them, both Ahmed and Sally were smartly dressed and business like, whereas he was barely presentable in crumpled casual wear. Still, they were where they were and he'd have to get on with it.

They detoured via Ahmed's office for him to check his correspondence before proceeding to the RNB call centre a few minutes ahead of their appointment. The building was new and modern; the eight storey glass and metal structure had been custom built only a few short years before to house the special facility. Ahmed was welcomed by the reception staff as an old friend and Tom and Sally took a seat and scanned through the morning's newspapers which had been provided for visitors. Meanwhile, Ahmed caught up on old times and new gossip with some of his former work colleagues.

At nine-twenty, they were instructed to take the elevator to the eighth floor where they were met by a young lady who introduced herself as an executive PA and they were directed towards a bright and airy meeting room. It was a corner room with external windows on two walls, affording a panoramic view across the city. The remaining two walls were built using opaque glass bricks which kept the room light while providing privacy from adjacent areas. A large, rectangular table made of beech filled most of the floor space and it was surrounded by eight padded leather executive chairs. A computer-enabled projector and a spaceship-shaped telephone device suitable for conference calls sat on the table. At one end of the room a camera hung from the ceiling, enabling video communication and at the other there was a pull-down screen for use with the projector. In front of each chair was a blotting pad and pen, both sporting the bank's logo, laid out like a place setting. A chilled water dispenser was in the corner and, incongruously for what was otherwise a modern room, there was an ancient flipchart stand, equipped with paper and marker pens

All three walked over to the windows to benefit from the view. It was a clear sunny morning and Ahmed was able to point out various places of interest in the city and beyond with the horizon stretching to the Campsie hills and the Clyde coast.

The door opened again. "Good morning, I'm Rachel Young, the Regional Communications Manager and this is Charles DuPont, one of our call centre managers. I'm pleased to meet you. If you would please take a seat." Introductions and business cards were exchanged and they all sat down. "We'll need to hold back a minute or two, as we're going to be joined by Mr. Matthews. He needs to finish a phone call with head office before he's free."

"Matthews, as in Oliver Matthews, the Operations Director? From the bank's main board?" Tom enquired.

"Yes, that's right. He's temporarily based in Glasgow."

"I've followed his career. He's held a number of senior roles in major companies where he's been responsible for major turnaround and growth. He only joined the bank's board about eighteen months ago, wasn't it?" Tom asked.

"Sort of, he was a non-exec for a year before he took up the full-time position."

"You said 'based' in Glasgow – not visiting?" Tom immediately sniffed something out of the ordinary.

"Yes, it's unfortunate really. He comes from Glasgow and much of his family are still here. His father has Alzheimer's and was recently taken into a nursing home, but his mother has a tumour and she doesn't have long to live. She's in a hospice. Mr. Matthews has set up office in the regional HQ, a few hundred yards from here, so he can be near her and visit regularly. With the internet and tele and video conferencing, he's able to handle most of his work from here, although he shuttles back and forward to London whenever required."

"That's very sad. It must put a great strain on him," Sally said.

"It hasn't affected his work performance at all, you'll be able to judge that for yourselves in a minute," Rachel added respectfully, almost in a fearful tone.

The words had barely escaped her mouth when the door flew open and Matthews strode in. Although several inches short of six feet in height, every fibre of his being exuded power. He was dressed in a brilliant white shirt and pale blue tie, paired with pinstriped suit trousers which were supported by scarlet coloured braces. His head was rounded and almost bald, save for thin, jet-black, curly locks at the back and sides. His long crooked nose and two cauliflower ears gave the impression of him having been a former boxer or rugby player, and his sharp, piercing, blue eyes had an intensity seeming capable of x-ray vision. There was no individual characteristic which inferred his status, but his whole confidence and demeanour conveyed the seniority of his position.

"Now what's this all about?" Matthews didn't wait for introductions. His gaze quickly took in the surroundings. After a quick, dismissive glance at Ahmed, his appraisal concentrated on Tom and Sally, but in different ways. He seemed to be sizing up Tom as if in preparation for a duel, while a lingering scan of Sally was more in the nature of undressing her and considering mating potential.

"I thought it had been explained when Ahmed set up the meeting?" Tom began.

"I know what was said, but why should we trust you? Why should we believe anything you say to us? Most of all, why should we tell you anything?" Matthews was answering Tom's comment but much of his attention remained on Sally.

Ordinarily, Tom would have wanted to court the attention of such an influential figure, but instead he took an instant dislike to the man. Perhaps it was the abrasiveness of his entrance, perhaps his aggressive challenge, but there was also the way he'd been leering at Sally. Although he had no justification, Tom almost felt aggrieved at this apparent infringement on his territory. Sally couldn't be considered his in any way, shape or form, but he thought of Matthews' attitude as an abuse of his own position.

Matthews attention wasn't lost on Sally either. She ground her teeth while glaring back at him. She remained silent, fearful that if she spoke, she wouldn't restrain her comments and might lose them any cooperation.

Tom didn't want competition for her attention and his initial reaction was to fight back. However, there was important business to be done and he couldn't allow the meeting to descend into two cocks fighting over a hen. Nevertheless, he felt the need to assert his position.

"If that's how you feel, let's not waste each other's time. I'm sure you have lots of important things to do and I know I have, but before we go let's set a few facts straight. One, we're serious journalists from Global Weekly. As you ought to know, it's one of the most prestigious business publications in the country. Two, we're not interested in any sensationalist articles, it's not our style. Three, we're carrying out a serious investigation because we think it's more than just a coincidence that RNB has been the focus of so much negative media attention. We believe you may have been targeted and we want to understand why, how, and who's behind it. We're going to continue with our research either with you or without you. It makes no difference. Obviously, if you're cooperating, it will make our task easier and is also more likely to give the Bank a more favourable treatment in any resultant report." Tom stood as if to leave. He had surprised himself by his own determination and assertiveness in such an imposing environment. Sally and Ahmed both seemed surprised and impressed by his performance.

"No, wait; sit down," Matthews replied. "I'm sorry. Perhaps I was hasty with my comments. We've been taking loads of stick from the media recently and I didn't want to volunteer for more." His whole attitude changed and his reply was solely focussed on Tom for the first time. "Let's take some time and see how we can help each other. First let's get some coffee. Rachel, ask Avril to bring us some refreshments."

Rachel left the room and returned two minutes later accompanied by two austere ladies. One was middle-aged and carrying two thermal jugs, one of tea, the other coffee. She was being directed by her younger colleague, the PA who'd shown them to the room when they'd arrived. She was holding a tray laden with crockery, which was quickly distributed, and a plate stacked with wrapped chocolate biscuits.

"Thank you for the hospitality," Tom acknowledged. "After your introduction, I wasn't sure whether we'd be leaving by the door or out of that window."

"But we're on the eighth floor," DuPont pointed out.

"Precisely," Tom replied.

"I did come on a bit strong," Matthews started." But I had to get a better feel for what your motives were. I've read some of your articles, and Sally's too. So I know the quality of your work. But we can't afford more bad press and I had to be sure you weren't simply looking for a cheap filler at our expense. Growing up and doing business in Glasgow, you learn to be tough. You have to test and be sure of anyone you're working with."

"I know the system," Tom replied, "Always best to get your retaliation in first."

"Yes, something like that. Now, tell me what you already know?"

Tom and Sally explained their understanding of what had been happening over the preceding few months, when a series of serious blunders at RNB had been revealed, each causing a significant wobble in its share price.

"You're absolutely correct. Every time we're on the verge of recovery from one problem, there's some new revelation which rocks us. One time might be carelessness, twice stupidity or negligence, but there have been five separate occasions now and I don't believe in coincidence. It seems to be some sort of campaign, as if we're being targeted, as you suggested."

"Have you any thoughts on who might be behind it?" Sally asked.

"We have no idea, there are too many possibilities. It could be a former customer, someone who considers the Bank has been at the root of their problems. Possibly a disgruntled employee or ex-employee more likely. It might be some sort of anarchist or anti-globalisation campaigner, or it could be totally random. Being a large international banking corporation, one of the largest in the world, means we're not short of enemies."

"Perhaps it's more commercially driven," Ahmed suggested, speaking out for the first time. "Perhaps it could be a bear trader."

All eyes turned to him, they all understood what he was suggesting, but allowed him to continue.

"If someone knew or expected a large drop in the Bank's share value, they could sell short, contracting at current price and they'd make a mint by buying the shares at the reduced price to fulfil the contract. Wasn't there a load of suspicions after 9/11, about the fortunes that were made that way?"

"Yes, that needs exploring, but I don't know how easy it will be. The Bank's shares are traded on every exchange and it's not easy to analyse who's behind the transactions," Matthews replied.

"On a personal note, it can't be doing much for the value of your share options." Sally was undaunted, staring him straight in the eye.

"Let's keep my personal finances out of this." Matthews spoke slowly, his attitude defiant.

"We may come back on that, but okay for now. In the meantime, I've got a few more questions about what action the Bank's taken?" Tom said, wanting to avoid any conflict at this point.

"I have a team of management auditors trying to investigate what's happened, but they've come up with nothing significant so far. Our problem is that in each case, there's been a news report which has some tenuous basis of truth, but is a misstatement or gross exaggeration. We can try to deny the content of the report, but we have to be careful how far we go. Because of the similarities to reality, it will be even worse for us if our denial is shown to be in any way incorrect. Whoever's behind this has a good understanding of the Bank's operations and of where there are weaknesses that can be exposed."

"Can you explain in more detail?" Sally asked.

"Okay, take the most recent example. The story broke stating the Bank had a policy to kick back any claims for insurance mis-selling. It's completely untrue and we've already paid out millions. We have four separate teams around the country dealing with cases. They've been pro-active searching for customers who have a genuine basis for grievance and contacting them to arrange a settlement. What is also true is we're being hit with shed-loads of false and spurious attempts. There's a whole industry of claims companies who've sprung up on the back of the problem. You can hardly switch on the radio these days and not hear an advert from one of them, soliciting for any customers who have bought insurance in the last ten years, alleging they'll be able to win the punter thousands in compensation. They charge them a percentage of the 'win' and get rich on the back of it. The biggest problem is that it costs us a fortune to process each claim, even the ones we reject – especially those, in fact – because of all the admin when claims companies are involved. Many banks have adopted the policy of offering a token settlement so as to close the case, but doing so only encourages false claims and claims companies, which in turn generates far more of them. It becomes a vicious circle." Matthews examined each of them to check for reactions before continuing. "RNB have had countless debates about this at top level. We want to pay all genuine claimants, but we want to discourage the spurious and fraudulent ones. We have not, in any way, been trying to avoid our responsibilities. The papers say they've got their hands on an internal memorandum, instructing the claims centres to knock back new applications from genuine claimants and because of the previous bad press we've had, it's been taken as the irrefutable truth."

"We already know about this one," Tom said. "The local rag which started it off has told us they asked RNB to comment, but no explanation was offered."

"From our investigations you're partially correct. The paper phoned the bank one hour before print deadline, saying they were running the story and asking if we wanted to comment. By the time the message filtered through to the right people, we were already too late and it became a damage limitation exercise."

"Did you see the memo?" Sally asked.

"No, I was told it was an email from one of our senior managers to the call centres, and the contents were implied, but I don't believe we've ever seen a copy."

"From what we've seen and been told, you're right – it was an email from Catherine Farnham to the call centres and the content is more damning than you've suggested," Tom replied.

"You've seen it?"

"Not only that, we have a photocopy." Tom opened his case and lifted a sheet of paper to show Matthews.

Matthews face paled as he read and reread the email, "Oh my God. No wonder they were so aggressive. We quizzed Catherine and she denied sending anything. Although we found some more innocuous comments on the subject, we never found anything like this on the mail system at either end. We put out statements asserting the Bank's true policy, and in order to quieten the baying wolves, Catherine has been suspended from her duties. She's been put on garden leave while the investigations are being carried out. We had to show we'd taken some action, and with a sufficiently senior executive. If this copy is of a genuine email, the suspension was justified and she's in much deeper trouble."

"Could someone else have sent the email from her address?" Sally asked.

"We'll need to check into that. They'd have needed to have access to her machine or her log in codes though."

"Check as well to see if your security could have been breached and the email hacked in from outside the company. Also, could you have a rogue employee in IT?" Tom suggested.

"It sounds unlikely but these are all possibilities we'll need to check into. They don't sound any more unlikely than Catherine actually being responsible and doing something so stupid."

"When we interviewed the reporter, he claimed he'd tried to call Catherine Farnham for a personal comment and she wouldn't take his calls and he'd tried the press department only to receive a 'no comment' in reply," Tom pursued.

"No, that's rubbish, according to Catherine, anyway. Your reporter's probably made it up."

"I don't think so," Tom replied. "I've no doubts he can embellish a story when he has to, but he doesn't strike me as the sort to make up something like this."

"Well, I know who my money would be on," Matthews declared.

"Not so fast. First, check if the phone number on the email is correct. Also if someone's been able to hack into the email system, they'd no doubt have the ability to reroute phone calls as well," Sally retorted

Matthews let out a low whistle, "Yes, that's credible. It's something else for us to check. Where do you go from here?"

Tom shook his head. "I don't think we can do much more here. I'd like to speak to Catherine Farnham. Can you set that up for us? Where is she based?"

"She works at our head office in the city, but I think she lives in Richmond."

"That's not far from my neck of the woods. Could you set up for me to meet her over the weekend, or perhaps on Monday?" Tom asked.

"I'm sorry, no. I'm happy to cooperate, but I want to be part of this. Besides, I don't think it's right that you should be seeing her without someone senior from the Bank present."

"Don't you go back down south at weekends?" Sally asked.

"No, I don't. I'm up here for family reasons and I particularly need to be here at weekends."

"Yes, we'd heard. We were sorry to hear about your problems," Sally said.

Although he seemed relieved that he didn't have to explain, Matthews was obviously uncomfortable knowing other people had been discussing his personal situation. He shot an accusatory glare at Rachel, from which she visibly shrank before he returned his attention to Sally. "My wife and children are in London, but they're coming up to spend Saturday and Sunday in Glasgow. It's the first time I've been able to see them for three weeks, so a London meeting is out. How about I arrange for Catherine to come here on Monday and we can meet again?"

"Okay, we can plan for that," Tom replied. "You set it up and let us know the time and place, and we'll be here."

"What are you planning to do next?" Matthews asked.

Tom checked his watch, "I don't know how practical it will be now, but I want to go to

Manchester; it's the location where the previous incident was exposed. It's already late morning, so it will be late afternoon by the time we can get there and it's Friday – POETS day."

"Pardon?" Matthews enquired.

"Piss off early, tomorrow's Saturday," a chorus replied.

Matthews nodded. "Who do you want to see?"

"Ideally, the same as we've done here. I want to speak to the reporter responsible for releasing the article and, if relevant, I'd like to speak to someone at the Bank who can attest to what the truth is."

"Try and call ahead and see if you can pin down the reporter, I can ensure the Regional Director of RNB will be there for you and have any relevant staff available too. His name's Hartson; I'll give you his number. Having said that, I'd like you to report to me directly, I want to be in control of what's happening."

"Okay, we'd appreciate your help, but let's get this straight, we don't work for you and we don't report to you. I don't mind keeping you informed of developments that affect you, where appropriate, but you have to understand we must retain total independence," Tom asserted.

"Okay, I can live with that, as long as you get to the bottom of this," Matthews replied.

"Fine, but there are no guarantees."

"Here's my private card, it has my mobile and a direct number to my private line at the bank. It already has a divert taking it to my office in Glasgow. I can give you my home land line here, as well. I want you to be able to reach me without delay if you have any news."

"Just one thing," Ahmed interrupted. "If this is a conspiracy being carried out by someone with the technical ability to hack emails and intercept Ms. Farnham's phone, then how safe are your phone connections?"

"You're right. It's not too likely, but it's not impossible for my calls to be monitored. I'll buy a separate mobile, maybe a cheap pay-as-you-go, so there won't be any records linking it to me and I'll text you the number. I won't use it for anything else," Matthews said.

Sally considered how quickly Matthews had been able to adapt to accommodate subterfuge tactics and couldn't help wondering how often he may have used them in the past, either for business or nefarious purposes.

Tom excused himself, stood and walked out to the corridor to phone the Manchester paper. It wasn't part of his company's group so he had no clout and had to beg and promise reciprocal credits in exchange for the cooperation he needed. The reporter who'd released the story was on vacation, but Tom arranged an appointment for late afternoon to see the news editor. He returned to the office and imparted his news.

Ahmed was staring at his mobile. "I've checked flights. Flybe are the only ones left doing the Glasgow to Manchester route. They have a flight at 14.40, arriving 15.50. By the time we clear the airport and get into the city, it will be half four to five o'clock."

"You might be better by train," Rachel suggested. "It takes a little over three hours, but you'll probably arrive in Manchester city centre about the same time."

"I've got the 'trainline' website open," Ahmed replied. "We can be in Piccadilly by four thirty."

"We'll go for that," Tom replied, glancing at Sally; he could see she was pleased. "Ahmed, while you're on the page, book us three first class singles; Sally will charge it on the company card." Knowing he'd suspended his personal cards, Tom's business card was the only one he had active and he didn't want to risk any problems with it, particularly not while in the present company.

"Three? You mean I get to come along?" Ahmed asked gleefully

"Yes, you're part of the team now, whether you like it or not," Tom replied.

"I like it. I like it. And I get to travel first class too!"

Chapter 9

Following their meeting with Matthews; Sally, Tom and Ahmed were all in high spirits. They hadn't discovered anything new, but they'd made a useful ally who was capable of opening doors to facilitate their enquiries. Nothing had changed though, Tom didn't like the man, but he was prepared to work with him if it would help achieve their objectives. Ahmed was thrilled to have been in his company, believing his life and career expectations were getting better by the minute. Sally was more blasé. She was aware of and quite flattered by his attention, but she held a similar view to Tom – seeing him only as a catalyst to help them progress their research.

Leaving the building, Sally accosted Tom. "I really appreciated how you handled that. I got the impression he wouldn't have tolerated the same sort of assertiveness from a woman, but what's all this about the Manchester trip? We'd talked about the sites of the various leaks, but we hadn't made any plans. We have the bookings to get there, but it's a late afternoon meeting or meetings, so what do we do then? We don't have plans for onward travel and we don't have hotel bookings."

"If we're staying over then I'll need to pop home to collect a bag and a change of clothes," Ahmed said, clearly relishing the prospect.

"To be honest, I hadn't thought that far ahead. I knew we were making progress and I didn't want us to lose momentum. I don't trust Matthews and I want us to keep him on the back foot. To do that we need to stay one step ahead and have him think we know more than we do. Manchester was next on the agenda and I said it. It just came out before I had a chance to think about the logistics. We have three hours on the train to plan what happens next. In the meantime, let's get some food."

Tom was ravenous and as they had some time before departure, he suggested a lunch. Tom and Sally went ahead while Ahmed detoured to collect some belongings to take with him and to pick up their tickets, then he quickly caught them up. They stopped at one of the pizza franchises close to Central Station and everyone over-indulged, eating from the buffet. It was treated very much as a refuelling stop, rather than a culinary experience.

They made their way through the station to the platform for the First TransPennine Express. Their carriage was at the far end and they walked toward it at a leisurely pace. Tom and Ahmed's bags fitted in the overhead rack, but Sally's case was too large and they had to leave it in the luggage rack at the end of the carriage.

Following two sleepless nights and the rigours of the morning's meeting, Tom was exhausted and looking forward to relaxing, and possibly even catching a nap during their journey.

Their allocated seating was positioned around a table and Tom collapsed into the nearest one

This section of the train was less than one third full, although most of the unoccupied seats had reservation cards showing they'd been booked for some section of the journey. All seats were scheduled to be taken by the time they left Carlisle. A few rows in front, there was a mother cradling a young baby in her arms and across the aisle from Tom was a young couple. They appeared to be aged in their late teens and only had eyes for each other as they snuggled together, kissing and whispering covert messages in each other's ear, holding hands with intertwining fingers and giggling. *Get a room,* was his immediate intolerant thought before remembering back to his own experiences of young love. He found it difficult to remember, but knew that he and Anne had once been the same way with each other. It seemed a long time ago and seeing the youngsters together reminded him that perhaps 'he and Anne' were a thing of the past. With the pressures of work and the RNB meeting, he hadn't given further thought to his own tenuous relationship with Anne since that morning. His feelings of anger, insecurity and despair returned and added to his tiredness; he felt leaden. He needed to try again to contact her. He lifted his phone in hope rather than expectation. He was only marginally disappointed when he received the expected voicemail recording asking for him to leave a message and he declined, believing he had nothing new to say, nothing he would want to leave as a recording at any rate. He sat deeply into his seat, trying to find more comfort and rested his hands on the table.

Tom jumped when Sally unexpectedly placed her hand affectionately on his. "Tom, sorry, I didn't mean to shock you. You look shattered. You need to get some rest. But first, we have to talk through the plans then Ahmed and I can check what arrangements can be made and you can try to get some shut-eye."

"Good idea," Tom replied wearily. "Let's think it all through. We're due into Manchester before four thirty. Provided we get there on time, we can take a cab to the Sentinel's office and should be there by five. It's not far from the station; I've been there before. Gilby, the editor, said he'd see us right away and if he does, I can't see it taking long, we'll be out by six. I can't see him wasting any time because he'll be wanting to get home too. I doubt we'll need to see the local RNB, so we can plan to go home ourselves. We can take any questions back to Matthews on Monday. But if something big and needing more immediate attention comes up, we can call Hartson and arrange to see him and whoever. If that happens we can rethink our plans at the time."

"Okay, but there's an awful lot of ifs in there. We can work on the basis you've outlined and see what travel plans are possible, but we need to keep them fluid in case of delays. What comes next though?" Sally pressed.

"There isn't any more we can do over the weekend and I have a few things I need to sort out at home," Tom gave a knowing look to Sally, indicating he didn't want to say too much more in front of Ahmed.

"What about next week?" Ahmed asked, inadvertently rescuing him.

With perfect timing to the question, Tom heard his ringtone, indicating a text had been received. He checked and saw an unfamiliar number. He pressed to open it and read the message: **nu no for ur use only. meet set up - same office 10 mon - OM**.

"That's Matthews confirmed for ten o'clock on Monday, so we all need to be back in Glasgow. I think our next move from there will be Barcelona."

"You can't be serious?" Ahmed was grinning from ear-to-ear. "And I get to go too?"

"Only if you can tone down the excitement," Tom replied, unable to share his enthusiasm.

"I've always wanted to go to Barcelona, but why are we going there?" Ahmed asked.

"It's where one of the other disclosures was revealed and it was to do with international trading," Sally replied before Tom was able.

"How long will we be there? Will there be time to take in a football match?"

"We're only there on business," Tom replied. "As soon as the work's done, we need to be away. But depending on flight and appointment times we might manage a tour of the Neu Camp."

"Really? Oh yes, please," Ahmed pleaded.

"I said might, and that's what I meant, so don't get too carried away."

"So what's the plan?" Sally asked.

"If we're seeing Matthews and Farnham on Monday morning, let's see if there are any flights from Glasgow to Barcelona in the afternoon. If not, check going via London or Paris or anywhere else."

"Flights?" Sally asked. A concerned frown spread over her face.

"Can you think of any better way of getting there? I understand if you're not able to travel, but we still need to check it out and we'll keep you up to date."

"There's not a chance of you doing this without me. I'll fly, although I might have to get a bit doped up first."

"Okay then, can you check travel possibilities for Monday, both to Glasgow and from Glasgow to Barcelona. Also, see how we can get home tonight. I'm travelling back to London, I take it you are too and Ahmed will need to get back to Glasgow. We might have to consider car hire if there isn't any other way," Tom said.

"I think I'll stay in Manchester over the weekend, I still have relatives there and I've not seen any of them since I came back from Oz."

"Yeah, sounds too good an opportunity to miss. Better phone them first to make sure they're at home," Tom said.

"Fine, we'll do all of that, you try to get some rest," Sally replied.

* * *

"Waaa! Waaa!" Tom's eyes sprang open in response to the piercing yell from the screaming baby. He blinked a few times trying to focus and reacquaint himself with his surroundings, but everything seemed befuddled and it took a few seconds for him to make sense of it. Unfamiliar faces ranged in front and to the side of him. It was only after hearing the repeated clickety-clack, when his eyes strayed to recognise Ahmed and then Sally, before he was truly sure where he was.

"Oh, you're back in the land of the living," Sally welcomed.

"Yes, sorry. I must have dropped off for a few seconds," Tom replied.

"A few seconds? You've been out for the count for more than an hour. We've already passed Penrith," Sally said. "You've been sleeping like a... like a..."

"Train?" Ahmed suggested.

"No, I don't think so Ahmed, but thanks for trying. A baby more like – mind you, Tom, you've been snoring like a train."

"I don't snore," Tom replied, affronted.

"No? Ask anyone in this carriage. It even managed to divert the attention of your neighbours across the aisle," Sally said.

Tom glanced to his side to see the young couple were still intimately engaged as they had been earlier. As he cast his eye along the carriage he saw it was now full. There was a young man sitting in the seat opposite him who hadn't been there before. He was dressed in the standard urban youth uniform of denims and T-shirt and he was wearing headphones connected to a small screen which he was following intently. Judging from the squeals escaping from the audio, he was watching an action film and had the volume set at an ear damaging level.

"Anyway, it wasn't the snoring that was so bad," Sally added, "it was when you were talking and arguing in your sleep. Who is Amanda, anyway?"

Tom was shocked, what could she be talking about? Indeed, what might he have been talking about? And who was Amanda? Tom's deliberations were interrupted by loud guffaws from both Ahmed and Sally. "You had me going there," he conceded.

"The food trolley came around while you were asleep," Sally continued. "The privilege of first class allows you free coffees and soft drinks, a sandwich, a biscuit and a packet of potato crisps. I didn't know if you'd be hungry after the lunch, nor what you'd like if you were, but I took a chance and got you a chicken salad wrap, a Coke and a packet of crisps. They're pickled onion flavour."

"That's great, thanks, as long as you don't mind my breath smelling of vinegar," Tom replied.

"Oh, I hadn't thought of that. Better do this now then." And before Tom realised what was happening Sally moved across and gently pecked him on the lips.

Having so recently awoken, Tom's mouth felt dry and rough. Much as he enjoyed the kiss, he was stunned by the gesture and too dumb-founded to react, not that he'd have known how to react. He licked his lips to taste the sweet-ness and fragrance from where Sally's lips had touched him and he suddenly felt self-conscious about how his own lips and breath might have tasted after his garlic-enhanced lunch followed by a sleep. He glanced at Sally and then at Ahmed – for different reasons – trying to gauge their reactions.

Mistaking the meaning of his quizzical appraisal, Ahmed replied. "Now don't look at me. You're not my type. I prefer my partner to have bulges in different places."

Then all three broke into laughter.

Tom stretched his arms, a pained expression on his face. "My back's killing me, it's really stiff from this seat, I'll need to get up and move about."

"Why not take a walk and ease your joints," Sally suggested.

Tom stood and reached his arms up to the luggage rack, using this as a support to strain and stretch his muscles, trying to bring them back to life. He then took a slow walk along the carriage and back. On the way, he passed the mother and baby. The lady was sitting with her blouse unbuttoned, her breast exposed to feed the infant. The baby was now silent, save for muted sucking noises as he devoured his mother's milk. Tom averted his gaze and walked by, but as he did, he couldn't avoid hearing the disdainful utterances from the next row on the opposite side of the aisle.

"Disgraceful, it shouldn't be permitted. It's awful how standards have dropped. Why can't she go to the toilet or to somewhere else at least, if she's going to expose herself like that." The words were being exchanged between two very prim-looking elderly ladies. They were dressed in conservative garb and were talking in a stage whisper, clearly wanting to be overheard by the offending party.

The young woman's face flushed and she turned her head away in embarrassment, protectively moving her child closer to the window, not wanting or prepared to face a confrontation.

"And as far as that couple further along are concerned, it's disgusting to behave like that in a public place. They're all over each other like a rash," the woman continued, even louder, seemingly gaining confidence as she went.

Tom re-examined the ladies and noted with amusement that they each had paperbacks open in front of them, both were of the historic romantic fiction genre and of the bodice ripping variety. Affronted by their narrow mindedness, and unable to hold his tongue, he said, "Ah ladies, you have a strong sense of propriety but not much interest in the real world. Clearly you prefer to get your excitement only from fiction," and before they had time to react, he walked along and resumed his seat.

He heard the "tut tuts" as he walked on, but spotted amused looks on other passengers' faces.

"Have you taken your brave pills, or something?" Sally asked once he was settled.

Tom shrugged, wondering whether to take a chance and return her earlier embrace and perhaps give the ladies something else to complain about, but by the time he'd thought it through his courage had waned.

"Where have you got to with travel plans and arrangements?" he asked, feeling safer talking about business.

"Well, let's start with tonight. The good news is there shouldn't be a problem getting out of Manchester. For Ahmed, even if he can't get away earlier, there's a train at eight forty-six which gets him back to Glasgow Central a few minutes after midnight. I'm staying with my sister so I'm okay and you should be fine too. The last realistic train to catch is at nine fifteen arriving before midnight. There's another fifteen minutes later, but it doesn't hit London until one fifteen in the morning. Have you somewhere to stay when you'll be arriving so late?"

A panicked look flashed over Tom's face. He hadn't thought so far ahead.

Sally's face morphed into sympathy. "I can give you my hotel room. It's paid for by the company anyway, and as I won't be there, it makes perfect sense. I'll only need to phone ahead to give them permission to hand you the key. They know me well enough, so it shouldn't be a problem."

Tom considered the offer. The simplicity was attractive and the idea of sleeping in what might be regarded as Sally's bed, surrounded by her personal belongings had a definite appeal – a somewhat erotic one – the more he thought about it. But he couldn't come to terms with it being correct, not when he was so unsure about his own domestic situation. "No thanks, it is a considerate and generous offer, but I'm sorry, I can't accept. I'm not going to take the chance of giving Anne any ammunition to throw at me until I know for sure what's going on. I will need a hotel though, probably for three nights and I don't want it to be the same one, even though you're not there."

"If you're sure," Sally replied.

Ahmed was staring, trying to piece together the meaning behind the conversation. "I can check the 'net and phone around to see if I can get you a good deal, just tell me what you're looking for and where."

"Thanks Ahmed, that will be a great help; be sure to advise them it will be a late check in."

"Okay, we shouldn't have a problem tonight, what about Monday?" Tom asked.

"Well that's a little more complicated. Ahmed will already be in Glasgow. If I take the first train at six thirty, then I'll get in shortly before ten. It's cutting it fine, but better than staying over or getting the sleeper and I don't want to be flying twice on the same day. The drugs won't last that long," she added. "As for you, you can get any of the early flights and be there in plenty of time. As for onward travel to Barcelona, here are the options. Jet 2 do a direct flight from Glasgow but not on a Monday. They fly Tuesday at eleven thirty, but that isn't much use. Ryanair are the only ones who fly direct and it's from Glasgow Prestwick. Their flight leaves at two fifteen in the afternoon and Prestwick has a direct and regular train link to Glasgow Central, so it's even easier to get there than to Glasgow International. We'll need to be clear of the meeting not too much later than eleven to make it on time. There are other options like flying BA to London, either Heathrow or Gatwick, and then onward BA or Iberia to Barcelona. There's also an option going KLM via Amsterdam, but much as Ahmed fancied that one, I'd opt for the direct flight. There are options through Edinburgh too, but they're not at all practical."

"It looks as if you've done a thorough job, good work."

"Less of the 'looks as if', if you don't mind. We have done a thorough job," Sally retorted.

"Whoa, a bit defensive there, aren't you? Yes, there's no doubt you've done a thorough job, magnificent, marvellous piece of work. Couldn't be bettered," Tom mocked.

"Enough already," Sally replied, "I think I preferred you when you were sleeping – snores and all."

"Ahmed, if I can take up your offer to find me a hotel. Try and get me somewhere near Euston, so I don't need to travel through London late on a Friday night. A single room will do, it doesn't need to be anything special, so long as it's clean and has an en-suite it'll do. As I'm paying for it myself, try to get me a good price. Sally can you book the Ryanair flights please, also the Monday morning travel to Glasgow for each of us? While you're both busy with that, I'd better call Stephan and bring him up to speed. Given what we've achieved so far as a team, I think he might be happy with me for a change. I'll go through to the corridor to call and if you don't hear his voice from here, then you can take it as a good sign."

Chapter 10

With what Tom considered at least partial recompense for his uncomfortable journey, the train arrived exactly on time. The three hurried through the station, being buffeted by the throng of commuters making their way home at the end of the week. The taxi queue was long but the frequent arrival of a sequence of cabs cleared it quickly and they were soon on their way to the newspaper.

Tom had already passed on the briefing he's received from Stephan. Gilby was an old acquaintance of his, they'd worked together on the same student periodical in a past life and they'd developed a mutual respect and distant friendship over the years. He described him as a good solid professional, whose only weakness was to concentrate on the presentation rather than the substance.

They reached the Sentinel ten minutes ahead of schedule and found the reception deserted. Using his mobile, Tom called Gilby's office and was directed to take the elevator to his floor, where they were met personally.

A tall elegant man approached them. Although late in his working day, he was fresh and precise. He was wearing a suit and tie, his shirt was crisp and the ironed-in crease of his trousers almost came out to meet them.

"Mr. Gilby?" Tom addressed the man, extending his hand in greeting.

Gilby's eyes scanned the visitors. "I didn't know you'd be coming mob-handed." It was stated as a matter of fact, not in any way aggressive, and Gilby's handshake was delicate and brief.

"I'm sorry, didn't I say? I'm Tom Bishop, this is Sally Ferguson and Ahmed Akbar."

Sally received a similar greeting, but Gilby held onto Ahmed's hand for noticeably longer.

"Better come through to my office. It's late in the day and most of the news staff has already left, leaving only the skeleton crew in case something breaks. There aren't any support staff either, so I had my girl set up the coffee filter before she left. I'm sorry I was only expecting one so there may not be enough to go around. There's a water cooler and then there's always the vending machine for an emergency."

"Why is it that every newspaper office in the UK is fitted with these dreadful machines? It's so strange for an industry that survives on caffeine. Why don't the proprietors realise they'd get much better results if they provided better coffee facilities? They seem to have it mastered in every other country," Sally said.

"Don't worry about me, I'm fine with water," Ahmed said.

"Dear boy," Gilby replied, resting his hand on Ahmed's shoulder as he guided them into his room.

The office was bright and clean, bearing no comparison to Stephan's at Global. There was a row of modern filing cabinets against one wall and a small conference table in front with six chairs. A large, padded leather seat was tucked behind Gilby's desk which held two widescreen monitors connected to a tower style computer. Three slim, cardboard folders sat stacked on the desk, but otherwise there were no documents, notepads or post-it notes on display. It was the closest approximation Tom had ever seen to a paperless office in the media business.

Gilby invited them to sit around the table and then fussily served the filter coffee, pouring it without any milk or cream into three dainty little cups. He then filled a fourth with water for Ahmed.

Gilby sat, inhaled the aroma, then gently sipped from his cup and sighed. "Original Arabica beans from Ethiopia. You don't know what you're missing."

Ahmed nodded. "I'm perfectly fine with this."

"So what's your big story?" Gilby asked.

"It's no big story. We're investigating some strange goings on at RNB," Tom replied

"Don't treat me like a fool. I've been about for a long time and you won't find it easy to pull the wool over my eyes. I'm a competitor. For you to ask for a favour and come and see me at all, means you're onto something. For there to be three of you on the project tells me it's big. If you're expecting cooperation, you at least need to tell me what you're on to and then we can consider what I'll want back."

Only then did Tom realise how naive he'd been bringing Sally and Ahmed into this meeting, but there had been no way Sally would have let him proceed alone. He considered bluffing and making up some explanation to play down what they were doing, but realised it would be a waste of time and only limit any cooperation he'd receive in return. "Okay," he began, "we know very little so far, and it's true we're examining what's been happening at RNB. They've been having an awful lot of bad luck recently. We think it's too much of a coincidence. Either someone's doing it to them, or there's someone inside trying to make it self-destruct. We want to see if we can detect any pattern."

"And this takes three of you?"

"Probably not, but both Sally and I pitched for the job and Stephan decided we should work together and we went up to Glasgow. Ahmed doesn't work for Global, but joined us to help with the locals and he's tagged along since. We're happy to have him on board, but so far the story's not justified us all being involved." Tom's words were spoken with honesty and sincerity, albeit with the planned spin to downplay what they were doing.

"And how is the noble Stephan? Still puffing and blaspheming his way into hell?"

"You could say that," Tom agreed. "He's doing fine, never changes."

"Pity, he could do with making some changes for his own health. Mind you, after all these years the shock would kill him. It might let him have a healthier passing though."

"I don't think he'd see it that way," Sally added.

Gilby studied the three of them, his gaze again lingering slightly longer on Ahmed. "Well, if I'm prepared to help – and I'm not saying I will – what will I get back?"

"There's my undying gratitude for a start," Tom said.

Gilby made no reaction whatsoever, not even an eye flicker.

"I'll give Stephan a call and see how far the budget can stretch." Tom added.

"Don't be obtuse. I don't want your money. I couldn't take your money even if I wanted to. I'd have to declare it if I did, and rightfully, it would belong to the company. I want recognition."

"You mean you'd like a credit on the story, if and when it goes live?" Sally asked.

"If it goes as big as it must do with three of you on it and Stephan backing it, then I want a special mention of thanks. Obviously, I'd also expect reciprocal cooperation from you and your company if ever we're in the same position. There's one other thing; your company has six press passes at next week's test match at Old Trafford, and for some strange reason we've only been given four. I'd like to even the balance."

Tom was stunned, but blurted, "I don't have the authority to do that, but I can ask."

"Ask away."

Tom called Stephan and was given the go ahead. "Affirmative," he announced to Gilby, "But only provided you have something to give me that I can use."

"Okay, what do you want from me?"

"Last month, your paper broke the story about RNB playing fast and loose with their solvency ratios. It sent ripples through the market, affecting many other banks, but mostly RNB. It led to a Bank of England investigation. In the end, RNB were found to regularly take their figures right to the edge of the regulations, but generally stayed within. There were a couple of occasions where they'd strayed across the line. Because of RNB's size and power, there was no real threat, but they were technically in breach of regulations. Many of the banks have done it, and often with more serious consequences, but RNB were the ones who got caught. They were given a severe ticking off and fined, but the amount was only a token for an institution of their size. The real penalty was how it affected their share price when the story broke and the cost of the investigation that ensued in the States as a result."

"So, you're telling me what we all know?" Gilby replied.

"How did you come up with the story? It's not something you happen across. You must have had a tip off."

Gilby steepled his fingers in front of his chin. "Yes, we did."

"We want to know your source."

"You expect me to name names?"

"Not necessarily, we need to know the way you came upon the information, and then see where we can take it," Tom said.

Gilby shook his head. "We don't have a name. It was an anonymous tip off."

"How did you receive it and who was it sent to?"

"One of our news reporters received it. The story went out under his by-line. The information came by post."

"Do you have it? Can we see it?" Sally chipped in.

"I suppose so. I have the file on my desk. I extracted it when I knew you were coming."

Gilby stood and lifted a cardboard folder from his desk. He flipped open the cover and extracted a lightweight, A5 size manila envelope which was stapled to two, A4 size sheets of copy paper. He placed the package on the table.

The paper was a print of an email between two RNB executives, both based in Manchester. The only narrative was at the top, a heading stating, 'Last Month's Stats'. This was followed by a table of figures which ran onto the second page.

In three places numbers shone out, having been illuminated by a bright yellow marker pen.

Tom fingered the pages carefully and looked up at Gilby, confused. "It came in like this? No explanation?"

"Exactly as you see it."

"The highlighting was done before it was sent?" Sally asked.

"Yes, and just as well, I don't think we'd have made head nor tail of it otherwise. Even so, it doesn't mean much to me, or to you, judging by your reactions. However, it was sent to our man Bissett; he has a degree in economics and a background in banking and knew what it was right away. He was able to interpret the letters used as the column headings and knew that what he had was dynamite."

"So you ran the story?" Tom asked.

"Not immediately, we made all the standard enquiries first, but it was out within a day or so."

"Did you check the names on the email? Speak to anyone at RNB?"

"We're not amateurs, what do you think?" Gilby snapped, showing a little irritation.

Risking further annoyance, Tom continued. "Did you take any steps to research who sent the letter?"

"No, how could we? You can see how it came, plain paper in a plain envelope."

As he had in Glasgow, Tom extracted his magnifying glass and studied the papers intently, making notes on a pad as he went.

"Did you see something that we've missed?" Gilby asked.

"Probably not," Tom replied, guardedly. "I want to see if there are any clues about where it came from and who sent it so I can compare it with what we saw in Glasgow. Can I ask you another big favour? Will you unstaple it and give me a photocopy of all of this? The envelope as well as the email."

"Yes, no problem, give me a moment." Gilby lifted the papers and stepped out to use the machine in the general office, leaving the door slightly ajar.

Taking the opportunity for a semi-private conversation, the three exchanged some comments in hushed tones.

"It seems to be the exact same formula as in Glasgow," Sally said excitedly.

"Never mind the story, for a moment back there, when you were bartering, I was scared that I was being requested as the peace offering," Ahmed blurted.

Sally grinned. "Don't worry, although Tom may have agreed, there was no chance I'd have allowed that as I'd have been the one left to explain to Morag."

Gilby returned with the copies, eyeing the three chuckling reporters. "Have I missed something?"

"No, it was nothing," Tom answered. "We were winding up the young lad." This was followed by even more guffaws.

Gilby handed over the copies and Tom checked them before he placed them carefully in his inside jacket pocket. They expressed their gratitude as they stood to leave.

"Are you staying in Manchester tonight?" Gilby asked. "I thought you might like to join me for a meal or a drink."

"Thanks for the offer, but we need to be away. I'm going back down south, Sally's visiting family locally and Ahmed's going north."

"Ah, the parting of the waves. Well, if you're sure." Gilby extended his arm for a final round of handshakes.

* * *

Travelling down in the lift, they were euphoric.

"Before Gilby came back in, I was starting to ask about the similarities to what we saw in Glasgow. You checked the envelope, Tom, but you didn't say anything. What did you find?" Sally demanded.

"Was it the same postmark?" Ahmed added.

"The letter was sent using a postal frank, the same sort as in Glasgow, but I haven't had time to check yet. From recollection the number was different, but I can't be sure until we've done a proper comparison."

"Yeah, but if they both used the same sort of postage machine...?" Ahmed said.

"You can't read too much into that, not yet. Nearly every business in the country uses franking machines to send their post. There must be a variety of machines giving different stamps, but not that many. We'll need to check if it's the same licence number and if not, see if we can trace where this one's from." Tom patted his pocket. "But I can't deny it's encouraging. I always thought it was promising, but now I'm even more certain we're really onto something."

"What about RNB? Do we need to see them or tell them anything?" Ahmed asked.

"I don't think so," Tom replied. "There's nothing further we can get from them yet and it won't make any difference telling them any sooner. No, it can wait until Monday when we see Matthews. It means we'll have something to give him and hopefully, his people will have discovered more information for us. So there's the potential of a trade of information."

"In the meantime, we can finish up for the weekend and you two can catch an earlier train which would let you be back at a reasonable hour," Sally added.

"Sounds good," Tom agreed.

As they exited the building and crossed the courtyard in front, they caught sight of a gleaming motorbike parked at the roadside.

Ahmed stopped to admire the bike. "It's a Honda Goldwing, a GL1800. It's beautiful, the graphite black is so stylish. A good twenty-five grand's worth there. It must go like the wind."

Tom turned at the sound of approaching footsteps. The figure coming towards them was large and broad, towering above Tom. As if his sheer size wasn't imposing enough, he was wearing bikers' leathers in bright red and his head was covered by a helmet with the visor down, obscuring his face. Both the jacket and helmet sported a logo of a white horse rearing up on its hind legs. He was wearing thick leather bikers' gauntlets, but in his right hand he was carrying a parcel about fifteen inches' square and an inch deep, wrapped in black and white chequered paper. In his left hand was what appeared to be an electronic scanning device.

"Are you Bishop?" A muffled voice escaped from behind the visor.

"Yes, that's me," Tom replied, eyeing the man warily.

"You'll need to sign for this delivery," the stranger continued.

Tom was aware that a few people knew where they were and whom they'd been seeing, but thought it strange to have been specifically located at this place and time by a courier. He leaned forward reflexively, to examine the screen. He had a fraction of a second to make out the words, **'You've been warned'**, before he became aware of swift movement in his peripheral vision. The biker swung the parcel, walloping him on the side of the head and Tom went down like a stone, his crown impacting with a raised paving stone bordering the pathway. The biker dropped the parcel, picked up Tom's laptop bag and made off.

Tom vaguely heard the Honda's engine roar into life, just before everything went blank.

* * *

Tom was lying prostrate with blood gushing from a gash on the side of his head. For several seconds, Sally and Ahmed stood transfixed gazing after the dot, rapidly vanishing into the distance, trying to make sense of what had happened.

"Oh my God! Is he dead?" Ahmed's voice when it reached Sally's ears was a high pitched squeal.

The yell brought Sally back to her senses and she collapsed onto her knees beside Tom, first searching for vital signs and then trying to stem the bleeding with tissues from her bag. "Quick, call 999, ask for an ambulance! Don't just stand there!"

Tears of fear, anger and frustration streamed down Sally's cheeks as the minutes ticked by before she heard an approaching siren. Tom was already regaining consciousness by the time the paramedics arrived. They dressed the wound, but made Tom stay on the ground for a few minutes longer, asking him questions to confirm he was lucid before moving him onto a stretcher and into the ambulance.

Sally and Ahmed made to follow Tom into the vehicle, but they were stopped. "Are you with him?"

"We work with him," Sally replied. "He has no family in Manchester."

The paramedic nodded, making a decision. "Okay, one of you can accompany him in the ambulance. The other one will have to make their own way to the hospital."

"I'm staying with him," Sally insisted. "Where are you taking him? The Royal, I suppose?"

Seeing the paramedic's nod of confirmation, Ahmed pulled out his mobile phone. "I'll grab a taxi and meet you there."

"There's really nothing you can do and it may take hours before we'll know what's happening or when he'll be released. Perhaps you should go ahead and take a cab to the station, and catch your train home," Sally suggested.

"I'm not leaving him – or you for that matter – until I know he's okay. I don't care if I miss the train and have to stay here all night. Besides, I want to make sure the police get a full report so they can catch the bastard."

Sally gave Ahmed a gentle hug. "Thank you," she whispered.

Tom was already sitting up and protesting when the trolley carrying him was wheeled to a booth at the Royal Hospital. Sally was asked to take a seat in the waiting area and she was joined by Ahmed.

How's Tom?" Ahmed questioned.

"He seems to be okay. He's recovered consciousness and is aware of what happened. He wanted to get up and leave, but the medics want to run some tests and ensure there's no internal damage. I think they suspect a concussion, so they'll keep him under observation for a while."

"Is there anything I can do?" Ahmed asked.

"Not really, we just have to sit and wait. Once they've finished checking him over, they'll probably move him to a ward and keep him overnight. I'm hoping he might get released in the morning." Sally chewed at one of her nails for a moment. "There is one thing I'm worried about, before Tom was fully 'compos mentis', the ambulance crew asked me about next of kin. They saw he was wearing a wedding ring, so I told them his wife's name was Anne and I fished out his home number from my mobile phone from when he gave me it yesterday. I don't know if I did the right thing, because they've been going through a rough patch and I don't know if Tom would want the staff to know her details and contact her."

"You did the right thing," Ahmed reassured her.

"I hope he thinks so. Do you think we should call Anne ourselves and let her know what's happened?"

"Better wait and see what Tom says. If he confirms he wants us to, then we can call."

"Yes, you're probably right," Sally replied doubtfully.

"I still can't get my head around what happened back there," Ahmed said. "It obviously wasn't a straightforward mugging, because the biker asked Tom his name first."

"Yes, I think it must be connected to the warning letter he got. When he regained consciousness, Tom told me he saw a message on the scanner device, saying 'You've been warned', a second before he was assaulted."

"What warning letter?" Ahmed demanded.

Sally explained the strange letter Tom had received and the useless reaction she'd received when she tried to report it to the police.

"Where's the letter now?" Ahmed asked.

"I don't know," Sally replied. "Tom might have had it in his jacket, but it could have been in his laptop case, and that's been stolen."

"This analogy to chess may be relevant. The weapon used to hit Tom fits in. It was about the size of a chess board and it was wrapped in chequered paper. What happened to it?"

"I've got it here, with Tom's other stuff. I haven't taken the paper off it, because I thought the police might want to check it for evidence."

"Assuming they're more interested than they were last time," Ahmed stated cynically.

"They should be. The useless detective I spoke to, McAvoy, said he couldn't do anything because no crime had been carried out. He doesn't have that excuse now."

"Can you remember exactly what was in the letter?" Ahmed asked.

"Not exactly, but I did read it a few times. It played on Tom's name being Bishop. The gist was that he was attacking the King and he was being threatened by Knight."

"More than threatened, he was bloody assaulted?" Ahmed retorted.

Sally was puzzled. "What do you mean?"

"Didn't you realise? The symbol for the knight in a game of chess is a horse. That biker had a logo of a horse on his jacket and his helmet."

Sally's mouth dropped open. "You're right, I should have realised. I thought it was something like a Ferrari logo."

"No, the Ferrari symbol is a black horse on a yellow background, and it's often surrounded in red. This was different. He was wearing a red suit with a white horse," Ahmed informed.

"Yes, I remember now. It might only a co-incidence, but it's a different logo. The white horse on a red background is the symbol of Kent county," Sally said

"Surely that ought to make it easier to find the guy who attacked Tom. There can't be many courier companies using Goldwing motorcycles. There can't be all that many Goldwing's in the country. If we then narrow it down to Kent, how difficult can it be?"

"You're jumping to a lot of conclusions. Firstly, we don't know it's a genuine courier company; he could have just been behaving like a courier to get close to Tom. Secondly, we can't assume the biker has any relationship with Kent, solely based on the white horse symbol. He might have used the logo to match in with the 'Knight' story. I didn't get a chance to study it closely enough. It might not have been a permanent logo; he might have just stuck it on the jacket and the helmet temporarily." Sally paused for breath before continuing. "And even though the Goldwing is very expensive and unusual, who's to say how many there are in the country, particularly if you include specialist hire companies and dealerships? It won't be easy to track down the owner of this one without the registration number and I didn't see it. I presume you didn't either, or you'd have mentioned it before now. Finally, even if we did track down the exact bike, that won't automatically lead us to the driver."

Ahmed looked crestfallen, "I just thought—"

Sally offered him a reassuring smile. "Don't be too despondent. It's a good lead, but that's far short of having the answer."

"What do you think the chances are of the police tracking him down?" Ahmed asked.

"I really couldn't say. But what I can tell you is even if they do get a result, they're not going to tell us too much about it. They might advise us what progress they're making, but they won't give us any details and the first we're likely to find out about who's responsible, is if a prosecution gets raised."

"Why don't we try to find out for ourselves? We must have our own information sources."

"Exactly what I was thinking," Sally replied. "You wait here, and I'll go outside to call Stephan and see if we can get the ball rolling." She slipped from her chair and Ahmed watched her hurry out of the building.

When Sally returned, she was about to brief Ahmed about her phone call, when two police officers appeared in the doorway, ambling toward the reception desk.

"Do you reckon they're here for Tom?" Sally suggested to Ahmed, before she marched towards the two police officer. "Are you here to take a report regarding the assault on Tom Bishop?"

The taller of the two young constables stopped in his tracks and looked down at Sally, a quizzical expression on his face. "No, what are you talking about?"

Sally rolled her eyes. "Christ, the incident happened hours ago! I thought the police were meant to attend all '999' incidents straight away. Isn't that why it's called an emergency service?"

The two officers seemed dumbfounded. "I'm sorry, Madam," the smaller of the two responded. "It's Friday night, we're in the centre of Manchester. It's been a busy night for us between petty crime, drunkenness and assaults. I don't have a clue what you're talking about, but if you have a complaint then you can pick up a form at any police station or you can fill it in online." With that he made to turn away.

"Where do you think you're going?" Sally challenged. "I want you to file a report! No, more than that, I want you to find the bastard who assaulted my friend and I want you to charge him!"

The taller officer spoke again, indicating some empty seats. "Please calm down, take a seat over there. First of all, we'll need to take your details."

Once again, tears of anger and frustration streamed over Sally's cheeks as she made an attempt at giving a coherent account of what had happened. Although it was her profession to assimilate facts and report them in a clear and concise manner, Tom's assault had shaken her confidence and Sally's skills abandoned her, so her report came out as a confused montage of facts, observations and accusations.

"We've noted everything you've told us, but unfortunately, there's not really anything to go on. Your friend's been assaulted and his laptop's been stolen. I'm sorry to say this, but it happens all the time. It sounds like a random mugging to me. We'll need to talk to Mr. Bishop as well, but I doubt we'll get very far. It's unlikely he'll see his laptop again."

"How can you say that? There's no way this is random." Ahmed intervened. "The assailant said Tom's name before he clobbered him! We have the weapon which was used to hit him. You can surely check it for prints or other forensic evidence, for a start. And then there's the assailant, we've given you his description and what he was wearing and we've told you the type of bike he was riding. So what are you going to do about it?"

"And who might you be?" The shorter officer questioned.

Ahmed explained who he was and gave his details before the officer spoke again.

"Your friend's already told us the biker was wearing gauntlets, so there aren't going to be any prints, are there? I'm afraid the best we can do is file a report with the statements you've given and then it's up to C.I.D. whether it will be investigated further."

"That's bloody ridiculous, it's incompetent. First no-one was sent in response to an emergency call and now that we've pinned you down, you're not interested. Is this some sort of conspiracy?" Sally barked.

The taller of the officers spoke up again. "Now, now, if you're going to make a nuisance of yourself, we're going to have to issue you with a caution. If you're not happy with our service, you already know how to file a complaint."

"And no doubt it will receive as much attention as the report we've already given, filed under B, one, N, into the trash," Sally's tone was caustic.

The taller officer shrugged and turned to go.

"Before you leave, I want your badge number," Ahmed demanded. "We're both journalists and we'll be placing our own report to the Police Complaints Commission."

The policeman pointed to his badge, only giving Ahmed a second to focus on the detail and then turned and brusquely walked away with his partner towards the reception desk.

Chapter 11

Hours passed after Tom's admission and Sally repeatedly tried to encourage Ahmed to go, so he could catch the last train north, assuring him there was nothing he could do. Ahmed refused each time, adamant he wouldn't leave her until they'd seen Tom and could confirm he was okay.

Sally made arrangements for a private room to be allocated on the ward in anticipation of Tom being released from A&E.

It was well after eleven o'clock when Tom was wheeled out of the emergency department on a trolley. Sally and Ahmed jumped to their feet and ran after the porter.

"Tom, are you okay? Is he okay? Where are you taking him?" Sally asked.

Tom was lying flat on the stretcher with a sheet pulled up over his chest and tucked under his arms. His complexion was pale, except for the area around his left eye, where the skin was puffy and discoloured to a deep blue-black colour. Butterfly stitches ran down the side of his forehead, and a transparent plaster covered them. There was still a blood mark running down his neck and his shirt was badly stained.

"I'm okay," Tom replied. "I've got a bit of a headache and I'm bored to death having lain there alone in a cubicle for God knows how many hours." He studied Sally for a moment. "What happened to you? You look as though you've been dragged through a hedge backwards. Still attractive, but different," Tom added with a chortle, before he winced from the pain caused by his head's movement.

"What?" Sally asked, raising a hand and touching her face. She glanced at Ahmed. "What does he mean? What's wrong with me?"

"You've been crying, your make up's run and you have some blood stains on your clothes," Ahmed replied matter of factly.

"For pity sake, why didn't you tell me before now? No wonder the police thought I was a mad woman." Sally rolled her eyes, and made a brief attempt at wiping down her shirt, before she gave up and turned back to the porter. "Where are you taking him?"

"He's going to a side room off the male surgical ward. Follow me up, but you'll need to wait outside for a few minutes while we get him registered in and changed into a gown."

Ahmed rushed back to the seating area to collect their belongings and caught up with them at the elevators.

As soon as they reached the ward, Sally lifted her handbag from the rest of her belongings, excused herself, and found a ladies' toilet to check her appearance. She'd thought, or at least hoped, Ahmed had been winding her up and exaggerating, but she was truly appalled by what she saw in the mirror. Her normally immaculate, curly, blonde mane was straggly and unkempt. Her mascara had run and she must have wiped or dabbed at her face on a few occasions because it had left her with a dappled look, giving her markings like a Dalmatian. Her lipstick was smudged, leaving a blotchy mark between her lower lip and chin. Her jacket and blouse were speckled with Tom's blood, and because of her diminutive stature, the overall impression was clown-like, only lacking the enormous shoes to complete the image. If it wouldn't have made matters worse, Sally would have wept. But she composed herself, had a laugh at her own expense, and took some paper towels from a dispenser to wipe off what was left of her make-up. She scrubbed her face clean and then carefully reapplied the lightest touches of cosmetics. Finding her hair brush, she restored her hair to something resembling tidy. There was nothing she could do about the blood staining. Returning to the ward, she looked natural, fresh and pretty.

"Why couldn't you have told me what I looked like before?" she chided Ahmed.

He shrugged. "Under the circumstances, I didn't think about it."

"You're such a... a... man," Sally spat the words in annoyance.

Ahmed smiled, his expression smug. "I guess I should take that as a compliment."

A few moments later, a nurse opened the ward door, held her finger to her mouth to indicate silence and beckoned them into a side room. The main ward had only subdued lighting.

"How is he, nurse? What can you tell me?" Sally whispered.

"We think he should be okay. He had two head wounds, the one where he was hit and the second from when the back of his head hit the pavement. The first looks nastier, but it was the second which caused more damage, knocking him out and causing the concussion. He seems to be fine, but we'll monitor him for a while longer. The doctor does his rounds mid-morning and hopefully, he can be released then. You can stay with him, but I must emphasise that he needs rest."

When Sally arrived at Tom's bedside, she saw the plaster at the back of Tom's head, which she'd missed on her earlier inspection.

"You look better now, how am I?" Tom asked, amusement in his eyes.

Tears welled again in Sally's eyes, but she managed to hold them back. "Tom, I was so worried. How are you? Are you in pain?"

"No real pain, but I'm still a little dazed. I've been trying to work out what happened and make some sense of it. I really walked into it, I suppose. I should have been more guarded about a stranger approaching me, knowing where I'd be. I guess I was tired and thinking about what we'd achieved and my defences were down."

"Tom, it wasn't your fault. How were you to know? Neither of us saw it coming, either. Now you need to relax and get some rest. Nurse's instructions, so you can't argue."

"Yes, yes, but first we need to talk through a few things. This is obviously no ordinary investigation. We're up against someone or something very powerful and it's getting really dangerous. I'm more determined than ever to follow this through, but I can't take responsibility for you and Ahmed. I don't want any harm to come to you."

Sally patted his hand. "Now you stop right there. It's not your responsibility. We have minds of our own and there's no way you'll take me off this enquiry. I'm not scared. I spent a week in Afghanistan, for God's sake, with buildings blowing up around me. I don't scare easily, so I'm definitely in."

"Yes, but in Afghanistan you would have been an observer; here, you might be the target."

She shook her head firmly. "I've said my piece; I'm not giving up."

"You're not getting rid of me, either," Ahmed said. "These last two days have been the best and most exciting of my life." He looked at Tom's damaged face, then added, "Sorry, I didn't mean—"

"I doubt Morag would be happy to hear you say that." Sally said.

"And you're not going to tell her either, or your life might really be at risk," Ahmed replied.

"I'm really happy you're both in, but if things get any messier, don't be afraid to back out at any time. Nobody will think any the less of you, and that applies to me too."

"Okay, it's a pact," Sally said, and they each put one hand forward theatrically, one on top of the other. "Now get some rest," she added.

"No, first, I need to talk this through. I've spent so much time lying around with nothing to do and I've been thinking. The timescales on this are really strange."

"What are you talking about?" Ahmed asked.

"This whole thing kicked off on Wednesday, when Sally and I met with Stephan. At that time, no-one, other than the three of us, knew about what we were trying to do. Stephan called your paper, Ahmed, and someone assigned you to help us. So far, everything is bland and there's nothing out of the ordinary. Still, nobody else knows what we're doing. Yesterday, we met with each other to begin our investigation. We talk to Charlie McMillan and then to Oliver Matthews and some of his people – then within a couple of hours, I received the first threat."

"You're not suggesting Charlie had anything to do with it?" Ahmed asked.

"I very much doubt it, but what I'm saying is there was limited knowledge of what we were doing, but it got back really quick to whoever is behind this. The implication of me threatening the king is that their top man knows about it. That means someone we've talked to, or dealt with, has a hot link through to him – or else has said something to someone with such a link."

"I see what you mean," Ahmed replied thoughtfully.

"It doesn't give us any clues as to who it might be, but it gives us an indication of the strength and effectiveness of his communication lines," Tom added.

"There's another possibility," Sally said. "When we were talking to Matthews, we debated that whoever's behind this might have the technical resources to hack the bank's communication system and possibly their telephone lines. If they can do that, surely they could be hacking our communications, too."

"Yeah, we can't rule it out," Tom replied. "But if that's the case, they'd still need some lead, to make them think we were a potential threat. Taking what you've said on board, I think we should do the same as Matthews and all purchase separate phones which we can use just to contact each other. There's something else too – although it may or not be related – there's the problem I've had with my credit cards."

"If we're really getting into this as a conspiracy theory, perhaps that would explain why the police didn't respond to the '999' call. Maybe their communication system's been hacked too," Ahmed suggested.

"But they did respond," Tom replied. "Two constables came in to see me when I was in the cubicle in A&E. They said you'd spoken to them too."

"They didn't come as a result of the emergency call," Sally corrected. "I saw them coming through the hospital and insisted they made a report about your assault. They didn't seem interested either, but now that I know I looked like a demented clown at the time, it might explain their unwillingness to take me too seriously."

"They seemed pretty professional to me," Tom replied. "They took my statement and said they'd pass on the information to C.I.D. and I'd probably be hearing from them."

"Did you tell them about the threatening letter and the chess analogy, or the knight symbol on the biker?" Sally asked.

"Yes, I think so. They said you'd already given them a story which they weren't too sure about. They asked if I had the letter and I told them it was in the laptop case, so they said that was a dead end, but noted it all down anyway."

"What else was in the bag?" Sally asked.

"My laptop, surprisingly enough," Tom forced a grin. "It's a bloody nuisance, but not too serious a loss. I keep most of my files on a memory stick and not in the same bag. There were no files on the computer which say anything about what we've found so far about RNB. Mind you, a good computer pro would be able to check the websites I've visited recently. There were some other articles I'm working on, but they won't be much use to anyone else and they're encrypted, so they'll have a job getting into them. As well as that, there's some personal files with finances and address books, you know the sort of thing."

"What about the copies you picked up from Gilby?" Ahmed asked.

"I put those in my jacket pocket, but I haven't been able to see if they're still there. Will you check for me please? The porter put my clothes in the locker over there."

"Got your jacket, yes and here's some papers, yes, they're still here," Ahmed confirmed. "What else was in your bag?"

"My bloody mobile battery charger was there too, and the spare battery, the one I bought yesterday. Shit, I'll need to go through all that again."

"We can pick them up at the same time as we get the new phones," Sally suggested. "Have you got any charge left in your battery now?"

"Have a look will you? It should be in my jacket as well."

"I can't find it," Ahmed replied. "Could it be in your trousers or anywhere else?"

"I don't think so, but try all the pockets," Tom replied.

"Sorry, it's nowhere to be found," Ahmed said.

Tom groaned. "Between the laptop and phone, I keep all my contact details and addresses. The last independent backup was weeks ago. I've lost everything in between."

"Maybe it fell out your pocket when you were assaulted," Ahmed suggested.

"No," Sally replied, "I checked the ground to make sure we had everything before we left in the ambulance."

"Could it have been in your laptop case?" Ahmed asked.

"No, I'm certain. I never keep it in there."

"Well in that case, it must either be in the ambulance or the hospital," Ahmed said.

"Unless the biker took it as well," Sally suggested.

"He wouldn't have had time, we'd have seen him surely," Ahmed protested.

"It's possible," Tom concluded. "He was very professional."

Their conversation was interrupted by the door opening and a nurse poked her head in.

"Two things," she said. "First, there was a phone call from a Mrs. Bishop."

"Anne?" Tom whispered.

"She didn't say, but it sounded like an older lady."

Tom frowned. "It must be my mum, but how would she know?"

"We'd have telephoned the number we were given for next of kin. Anyway, she asked how you were and said she'd call back in the morning. The second thing is that you need to get some rest. I'm going to ask your visitors to leave unless you switch off the light and try to get some sleep, now."

"Okay, nurse, thank you," Tom said. He waited until the door closed and spoke again. "Like I was saying—"

"No, no, no," Sally held up a finger, admonishing him. "You heard what the nurse said." She walked to the doorway and turned off the light, before resuming her position at Tom's bedside.

"Aw, Mum," Tom joked in a whiny, child-like voice, but nevertheless he lay back, resting against the pillows.

Sally and Ahmed each stretched out as best they could in their individual armchairs, trying to steal some sleep.

Tom remembered lying there for some time before he drifted off, but when his eyes sprung open again it was already half past six. It took a few moments to familiarise himself with his surroundings and remember where he was and what had happened. He became aware of a weight on his chest and glanced down to see Sally's head resting just below his shoulder. His arm was crooked and his fingers were enmeshed in her hair, gently holding her against him. Tom had no recollection how'd they'd come together in such a way, but he was comforted by her close-ness. He was aware of her rhythmic breathing and there was a slight sense of dampness on his chest, where his hospital gown had been moist-ened by her gentle exhalations. He didn't move, instead letting his eyes scan the rest of the room to discover Ahmed was also asleep, lying back in an armchair.

Tom heard activity in the ward outside and prayed they'd stay quiet and not disturb Sally, so he could enjoy their embrace for a tad longer.

Inevitably, the clattering of trolleys and uninhibited volume of conversation outside had an effect and Sally's eyes fluttered open. She sat up in the armchair and stretched. Her hair slid through his fingers as she moved and it was with great reluctance that Tom relinquished the contact. Ahmed, too, was rousing.

Tom recollected Stephan's witticism about them 'not sleeping on the job, not together,' and he anticipated what Stephan's reaction would be if he told him that not only two, but all three of them, had specifically ignored his instruction.

"Oh, is it morning?" Sally asked.

"In a manner of speaking," Ahmed replied, glancing at his watch. "Technically, it's morning but it's an unearthly hour. Why is it hospital wards start their working day so early?"

"Probably a tradition from the middle ages, so they can remove the bodies of those who haven't made it through the night, before the rest of the world knows what's happened," Tom replied.

"Are you serious?" Ahmed asked, sounding shocked.

"No, not really." Tom smirked. "I just made it up, but it sounds quite credible, doesn't it?"

Sally punched Tom's shoulder lightly and he winced and drew back in mock pain.

Becoming more earnest, Tom addressed Sally and Ahmed. "Thanks for staying with me last night, I really appreciate it. Now if only we can all get out of this place, there's a lot to catch up on"

"I'm going out to get washed and cleaned up. At the same time, I'll check with the staff what the plans are, and when you're likely to be seen."

Chapter 12

Being a Saturday, there was no set time prear-
ranged for the doctor's rounds to take place, if
at all. Tom's greatest fear was being stuck in hospital until Monday. With an expected minimum
of three hours to kill, Tom, Sally and Ahmed sat
together, analysing every aspect of their enquiry
to date.

"I'll need to call Stephan and let him know
what's happened," Tom said.

"No need, I spoke to him last night," Sally
replied. "He told me he's already been in contact
with the Barcelona paper to smooth our way.
He's told them we'll be across on Monday afternoon or Tuesday morning and arranged for the
reporter to speak to us. It seems he has a friend
there, too."

"The old bugger has friends everywhere. He must be one of the best connected people in the industry," Tom suggested.

"Mind you, the arrangements are dependent on you being well enough to travel," Ahmed pointed out.

"Nothing's going to hold me back from this." Tom's assertion left little room for argument.

"You might have to wait and see what the doctor says first," Sally warned. "Anyway, I spoke to Stephan about what happened last night. He didn't have confidence the police would be too active in tracking down your assailant and it looks as though he was right. He agreed for us to try using our own resources and said he'd see what he could find and get back to me today."

"What did he hit me with? Did you see? I remember seeing some sort of package."

"It was, and he dropped it to pick up your laptop. I still have it here. I was planning to give it to the police to investigate, but they didn't show any interest," Sally answered.

"Let's have a look," Tom requested. Sally retrieved the parcel and handed it to him. He held the package and examined it carefully. The paper wrapping was squashed and torn at one corner and there was evidence of blood and skin fragments. Tom carefully parted the sticky-tape binding the cover and removed the contents. As expected, it was a wooden chess board. It had inlaid squares of light and dark coloured boxwood. There was also a single sheet of paper. Tom extracted it and turned it over to see the same chessboard letterhead as the previous one had included. The typed message below read -

'Black has advanced into opposition territory and is behaving erratically.
White Knight has Bishop pinned and facing continued danger.
Is White prepared to sacrifice Bishop?
The danger continues.'

Sally leaned over Tom's shoulder to read. "I really don't like the sound of it," she said.

"We set the rules last night and this doesn't change anything," Tom replied. "I can't walk away. I need to get to the bottom of this."

Before further discussion ensued, the door opened and a doctor walked in, accompanied by two nurses.

"I'm Mr, Chung, your consultant," he began. "Can we have some privacy?" he continued sharply, looking pointedly at Sally and Ahmed until they meekly left the room.

He checked Tom's chart, pulse and blood pressure, asking some standard questions and running some more rudimentary tests. "Well, Mr. Bishop, you've taken a hard knock to the head and you've suffered a concussion. We're satisfied there are no broken bones and the CT scan showed nothing unexpected."

"Can I leave then?"

"Let me run through a few items first. The main things you need after a concussion is to get plenty of rest and to avoid stress, also, don't allow yourself to become dehydrated. You should take some time away from work if you can, avoid alcohol, loud noise and no strenuous exercise. You'll probably continue to experience headaches for a while, but they'll be much worse and last a lot longer if you don't follow my advice. I can prescribe you some pills which might help. You must avoid driving as your judgement will be impaired. You need to advise the DVLC and get their authority before you drive again."

Tom began to protest. "Oh, come on, I need my licence for work!"

"Don't blame me, I don't set the rules. However, it has been scientifically proven that your awareness is diminished after suffering from even a mild concussion."

"I'm meant to be flying on Monday. Is there any problem?"

"There are no set rules to stop you, but you'll be more inclined to suffer from headaches because of the pressure and lower oxygen levels in-flight, also if there's any turbulence. I won't tell you not to, but you should seriously consider the risks and if you do insist on flying, take some analgesics. Ibuprofen would be suitable." The doctor turned to leave.

"So can I go now?" Tom asked.

"Yes, but not until you've settled your account, you've had the use of a private room"

* * *

Tom dressed quickly and made ready to leave. It occurred to him that he didn't have much cash and he'd suspended all but his business credit card. By rights, he ought to ensure he had permission before charging his medical costs to the company, but he didn't have his phone, nor did he have Stephan's number to use a hospital phone. Tom cursed inwardly; there seemed to be no easy answers to anything.

It wasn't long before Ahmed and Sally charged back through the door.

"What did he say? Nobody would tell us anything," Ahmed said. "I'll excuse his rudeness if he's said you're okay."

"I can go, but he's given me some rules. Would you believe I've got to avoid stress? Go figure that one out. I'm not allowed to drive and there are various other things I've got to do – or rather, not do."

"While we were waiting, there was a call to ask how you were. I think it was your mother again. I overheard the nurse saying she couldn't put them through, because the doctor was with you, but she'd pass on the message. You'd better check with her before we leave."

"I'll do that. I hope she left her number, because I can't remember her new one since she moved house. I don't know anyone's number. I'm going to be lost without my phone."

"You'd better call your service provider too and put a block on your account, in case anyone else has the phone, so they can't run up a bill," Ahmed suggested.

"That might be the least of your problems; it's more important to ensure that no-one else can access your incoming calls and messages," Sally added.

"You're right. I'll get straight onto it as soon as we're out of here. But first, I need your help. The only working credit card I have is my Global one and I'll need to use it to pay the hospital bill. I have to call Stephan to get his permission."

Sally shook her head. "Forget it, Tom. When I spoke to him last night, he told me you have private medical insurance as part of your employment contract. He gave me a note of the company and the contract number, so you won't need to charge anything. That's one element of stress you can chalk off."

"Allah be praised," Tom uttered. "I'm relieved about that."

"Don't mock the great prophet. Islam followers won't tolerate it. You don't want to be like Salman Rushdie, do you?" Sally chided.

"Why not? He's written a string of bestsellers and must be a multi-millionaire. He's won the Booker Prize, been knighted by the Queen..." Tom replied.

"I was thinking more of his years in hiding after Ayatollah Khomeini issued the fatwa against him. Do you want to be living in fear of your life?" Sally asked.

"Perhaps you forgot – after what's happened, I already am," Tom answered. "Besides, I wasn't mocking, it was only an expression like *Oh my God* or *thank Christ*," Tom argued in his own defence. "For an atheist like me, what difference does it make?"

"It's not the same. Christians aren't so intolerant of people blaspheming against their Gods and prophets, at least not in this day and age and not in this part of the world."

"Okay, point made, I'll be more restrained in future but just to check – you weren't offended by what I said, were you, Ahmed?"

"I wasn't, but I doubt that's anything to go by," Ahmed replied.

The three made their way to the nurse's station to finalize Tom's discharge, then made their way downstairs.

"I forgot to tell you, Tom," Ahmed began, "I was able to phone the hotel I'd booked for last night and cancelled the booking. Under the circumstances, there was no penalty, so I've saved you some cash. I think you owe me one there."

"I appreciate it, but as for the 'owe you' – you can add it to my tab," Tom replied. "Now, let's get these new phones and exchange numbers, and I'll need Stephan and Matthews phone numbers also. If there's a Carphone Warehouse nearby, I'll be able to download my address book. It won't be up to date, but it's better than nothing."

As soon as this task was completed, they caught a taxi to the station where they purchased tickets for their respective journeys.

Tom phoned his home landline, but unsurprisingly, there was no reply. He didn't have Anne's mobile number yet, so his next call was to his mother, to reassure her that he was okay.

"How did you know what happened?" Tom asked.

"Arthur called to tell me; he'd heard about it from Anne. Have you called her?"

Tom paused for a second, wondering what his mother knew, "No, I've not spoken to her yet. I tried the house and didn't get a reply. I thought I'd best return your call first and see if you had a note of her mobile because she recently changed it and I don't have it on storage."

"I'm sorry, Tom. I only have the old one. I didn't know it was changed."

"Can you give me Arthur's number? I can call him to see if he has it.

"I'm sorry Tom, I never call his mobile. Are you coming back home now? I'm worried about you, Tom"

"Yes, I'm on my way home now and I'll drop by and see you later so you can see for yourself that I'm okay."

"Tom, you work too hard. You need to be at home more. You shouldn't be travelling so much.

It's not right being away from your family," then after a pause she added, "they need you."

Tom inhaled deeply, taking account of what his mother had said, but more to what she didn't say. "Mum, it was business, I had to go away. It wasn't my fault... I've tried to call, over and over. What do you know? What can you tell me?

"You need to sort this yourself"

"Yes, I know I need to sort it myself ... I'll see you later."

Tom hung up, frustrated. He had no means of contacting Anne or Arthur, not that they'd be likely to take his call. If they hadn't phoned to see how he was when he'd been taken into hospital, then they obviously didn't want to speak to him. He was surprised they'd passed on the message to his mother.

Tom turned to where Sally was sitting, concerned to see her face was ashen and strained. She was still holding her phone, but her hand was quivering.

"What's wrong?" Tom asked.

Sally glanced up, and Tom was alarmed to see tears welling in her eyes. "My sister, she said she doesn't want to see me."

"What?" Tom exclaimed. "I thought you were planning to spend the weekend together?"

"I was," Sally replied. "I spoke to her yesterday from the train, you remember? Perhaps it was while you were talking to Stephan. Anyway, I haven't seen her for about two years. I told her I'd be there after I finished work. I didn't know, but she arranged for all the family and many of my old school friends to come over to her house to surprise me. I hadn't expected it. Of course with everything that happened, I didn't turn up. I was waiting in the hospital to find out how you were. By the time I knew anything, it was late and I didn't call her back because I thought it was too late and I didn't want to disturb her. My phone had been switched off in the hospital so I didn't realise she'd been leaving messages. At about eleven or twelve, I switched it back on to send her a text, apologising for the inconvenience and explaining there was an emergency and I was with a friend at the hospital. I didn't think to check my messages at the time or I'd have realised she was trying to contact me."

Tom nodded.

"When I called her a moment ago, she nearly bit my head off. She told me I was a selfish and insensitive bitch; said I'd always been that way. She called me a snob and claimed that since I'd had my education I'd looked down on the rest of the family and didn't want to know. She said now it was their turn and they didn't want to know me anymore. I tried again to explain but she hung up on me." Tears were welling in Sally's eyes.

"Do you think she really meant it or was she just angry that her arrangements had been ruined?" Tom enquired. "Maybe once she's had time to calm down …"

"I don't know," Sally replied. "She's a couple of years older than me and she's the oldest of my siblings. She's always been spoiled and likes to be the centre of attention. She sulks when she doesn't get her own way. She can sulk for Britain if it becomes an Olympic event. She can go on for weeks."

"In that case you need to see her and sort things out," Tom said. "If you don't the anger will fester and if you aren't able to get back it will only be worse."

"I suppose you're right, but I don't want a confrontation and what can I do if she won't speak to me?"

"You need to take it one step at a time. Hopefully she'll see you and resolve any issues. But if she doesn't you need to see the rest of your family and any friends who'd been invited. That way you can apologise to them directly and regain their trust and friendship. If that works, then your sister will be alone with her condemnation and I'm sure she'd then come round as well."

"Thank you, Tom." That's good advice. Sally swabbed at her eyes with the back of her fist to wipe away any tears then thought better of it. She lifted a tissue and gently dabbed instead. She opened her handbag and removed a small vanity mirror, checked her face then re-applied her make-up.

They each moved off in different directions to catch their respective trains.

* * *

Once aboard the train, Tom called Stephan's mobile number.

"I gather you've been through the wars. Are you back in the land of the living and ready to do some work for a change?" Stephan joked when he answered.

"Thanks for your concern. I always know I can rely on you." Tom responded sarcastically.

Stephan's tone changed. "Seriously though, Sally told me what happened and I don't like it. I'm thinking of pulling the rug on your enquiries."

"Don't you bloody dare! I'm sure I'm getting somewhere, and I'm not giving up. If you're not prepared to back me, I'll quit and go freelance. I'm not letting go of this, no matter what you say."

"Calm down, calm down!" Stephan appeased. "I want to go forward as well, but I don't like the idea of you being in danger and I didn't want you thinking I was pushing you into it. It's particularly the case with you having such a young family. Your wife'll probably blame me for what's happened already, and she'd never forgive me if anything more serious occurs."

"You needn't worry on that score. I have doubts my wife cares whether I'm alive or dead.

She might even prefer dead, if she'd get an insurance pay-out. As far as the work goes, I'm in and I'll sign a waiver saying it's my decision if you'd like."

"That won't be necessary, but what's the problem with your wife? No, on second thoughts, don't tell me now. Come into the office as soon as you're back in London"

Tom rang off and tried his home number again. There was no answer –and he didn't leave a message.

Chapter 13

The normally buzzing office was ghost-like and silent when Tom walked through to discover Stephan's door already slightly ajar. He rapped briefly and poked his head around to discover Stephan battering fiercely away at his keyboard. "I don't think they're designed to withstand that sort of pressure," he said.

"You're probably right. I go through two or three keyboards a year. I learned to type on an old Adler manual machine and they didn't work well with a light touch. I've never managed to train myself out of it." Stephan stood and walked around his desk to greet Tom. "How are you, my boy? And what's all this about family problems?"

The pressures and trauma of the last few days caught up with Tom. It was completely out of character for Tom, but he was overcome by emotion. He stepped back into the general office and slumped into a chair, tears ran down his cheeks.

Stephan patted his back and gripped his shoulder, in a gesture of fatherly support. "It's okay, it will all be okay," he comforted. The gesture was stiff and he stared at the floor, embarrassment making his movements seem awkward.

Tom pulled away. "I'm sorry, I don't know what came over me. Must be a result of the concussion." He swivelled the chair back round to face Stephan. He explained in detail about the progress of the enquiry and then hesitantly confided his worries about his relationship with Anne.

"Do you think it's repairable?"

"I really don't have a clue. So far, neither she nor Arthur have said a word to me and they're both avoiding my calls. There's no way anything can be fixed if we don't talk. I'm planning to head over to the house now, but I've got no idea if anyone's home or what's likely to happen if they are. If I'm honest with myself, I don't think I'd want to go back to the relationship we've had for the past couple of years. A split from Anne might not

be a bad thing, but as for the kids –that's another matter. I'm not giving up on them. I won't
do that without a fight. Then there's Arthur. If
my suspicions are correct, I can't stand by and
let him take away everything that's mine; I'd kill
him first."

Stephan fished in his pocket and pulled out a
packet of cigarettes. He placed one in his mouth,
took out his lighter but then thought better. He
drew deeply on the unlit cigarette, "Keep calm,
Tom. You need to deal with this dispassionately. I
know it's difficult, impossible even, but you have
to try."

"So what do you suggest?" Tom asked.

"Go home and try to talk things through with
Anne,. You'd be best to take someone with you
if you can, in case Arthur's there. See if you can
work out what you both want and then take it
from there. If you can come to an agreement then
fine, but if you don't, or you agree to split, I'll
put you in contact with my brother-in-law, he's
a lawyer."

"Your brother-in-law? I didn't think you were
married anymore."

"I'm not. He's my sister's husband. Specialises in family issues, he's one of the best. He represented me at both of my divorces and, as you can see, I'm still alive and I'm not broke. Well, not completely broke. As you're on the road, I can try to get him to see you tomorrow if you need him."

"I'd really appreciate if you would. I won't know until I've seen Anne what the situation is, but it wouldn't do any harm to know where I stand," Tom agreed.

"Fine, I'll check his availability and you can call me when you know your situation. One other thing – I'd suggest you write down everything pertinent. You do remember how to write, don't you?" Stephan added, revealing his nicotine-tainted teeth in a smile. "You want to note everything important about your relationship with Anne. Things like your joint and personal assets and liabilities, what you'd want to achieve out of any settlement and what you're not prepared to give up under any circumstances. Not only assets, but rights over children, pets, memberships, etc. Also make notes on any strengths and weaknesses that you each have. You don't want something dragged out of the woodwork at the eleventh hour, stuff that your lawyer's not prepared for. On the other hand, you want him equipped to be able to apply leverage or use dirty tricks if he needs to. You told me Anne had suffered from depression in the past. Write down the details. Was she medicated? Was she hospitalised? That sort of thing. You want to be able to give your lawyer a sensible and cohesive account, so he can work efficiently for you. You don't want to waste time with your story coming out more as a rant."

"That's sound advice. I'll see what I can do."

"Now back to work issues. I've ordered you a new laptop, but for the time being take this one I've filched from advertising. It'll tide you over."

"Thanks Stephan, I felt naked without my computer and when I didn't have my phone either—"

"Enough said. Now listen, I've been trying to do some research on this biker. Sally said Ahmed recognised the bike and it was a rare one, a Honda Goldwing. It might be rare, but there's been more than one million produced worldwide since they first came out in 1974. The version he thought it was *is* special though. The first generation of the model was manufactured in the USA up until 2010, but the '1800' is second generation and built in Japan and that only started in 2012, so it is special. Nevertheless, there are still a few about. There's been about one hundred registered in the last three years. Sally told me about the 'White Knight' emblem, the symbol for Kent, so I concentrated my efforts there. I couldn't find any courier services using the 'Knight' symbol, in Kent or anywhere else. Next I used one of my contacts to get information from the DVLA to see what Goldwing's had been registered. I didn't find any 1800's registered to any courier services. I tried searching for recent Goldwing's registered in Kent. There weren't many and none that jumped out as likely suspects. The owners are all wealthy, as you'd expect and weren't always likely to be the drivers. For example, we have a Fred Williams, who's eighty years of age, and a Francis Leroy, who owns a massive fleet of cars and bikes, and then there are two brothers who each own one; Safdar and Taraq Ali. I'm having each of them checked out."

"Let me know what you find."

"I will do, but I'm not optimistic. There isn't a high probability of finding the bike. Even if we did, we'd also need to pin down the rider. It might open a whole new set of doors on the enquiry, but it wouldn't give us any automatic solutions. We have strong reason to suspect someone has mounted a campaign to damage RNB, but we don't know who or why, or how far they're prepared to take it. They're obviously powerful and well connected, so they're not a good enemy to have. You've obviously done something to upset them, or else they're worried because you're getting too close. You've become their enemy, so you need to be really careful."

"I'll try, but it would be easier if I didn't have so much other crap to deal with. I'm not going to get anywhere with anything unless I make a start, so I'd better be going."

Tom stood and they shook hands. "Do you have someone to go with you? Would you like me to arrange for one of the juniors?" Stephan offered.

"Thanks, but I don't think so. I don't want everyone knowing my private business," Tom replied.

"Don't you have some double standards there, Tom? Isn't it every good reporter's duty to expose the private life of anyone who Joe Public wants to read about?"

"Yeah, yeah. I'll keep you informed if anything comes up and I'll get back to you about a meeting with your brother-in-law."

A cool fresh wind assaulted Tom on his way from the building. The breeze was cold on his face and particularly against the wound. He found it invigorating and decided to take full advantage by walking to the station, knowing he'd need to grab a cab at the other end. On the way, he considered the implications of the driving restriction the doctor had told him about. He wasn't normally an enthusiastic driver and more often chose to use public transport or taxis. However, the idea of the choice being taken away from him seemed oppressive and restricting.

Arriving at home, Tom exited the taxi, opened the gate and cautiously walked up to his front door. As he moved, he chanted Stephan's words to himself like a mantra. "Keep calm. Whatever you do, don't lose your temper." With a mixture of fear and apprehension, he reached into his pocket to check his keys were there, but changed his mind and pressed the doorbell instead. Each second seemed like hours had passed as he waited with no response. He pressed the doorbell again, then gave up and took his key from his pocket. The tip had barely made contact when the door was pulled open and Arthur stood in front of him.

"Hello Tom. Mum told me she'd spoken to you and you were being released from hospital. How are you? Are you in pain?"

"Why the sudden interest?"

"Please come in, we can talk better in the lounge," Arthur suggested.

"Where do you get off, inviting me into my own house?" Tom barged into the hallway. "I want to speak to Anne, and I want to do it privately." Tom spoke slowly and quietly, remembering Stephan's instructions about remaining calm.

"Anne's next door with the children. She's left me to talk to you. I— no, we, thought it would be better and simpler that way. She's packed all your bags to make it easier and I can give you a hand out with them."

Despite all the preparation and good advice, Tom saw red. "Who the fuck do you think you are, telling me what to do in my own house, and with my own wife? Get out of my way, or I won't be responsible for what I do to you."

"Daddy said a bad word."

Tom looked around, shocked to discover Jenny standing in the doorway. Anne was immediately behind her with one hand protectively holding her shoulder, the other supporting Colin, who she was carrying with his arms around her neck.

"Jenny, I'm sorry, sweetheart, I shouldn't have said that. Now come and give Daddy a big hug." Tom forced a broad smile. "You too, Colin."

Anne released her grasp and the girl stepped forward cautiously. "Daddy, what happened to you? What's that on your face? Did you fall down?"

Anne placed Colin on the floor and he followed his sister to investigate.

Tom swept his daughter off the floor and held her close, then scooped up Colin to join the embrace. He hadn't planned for this and didn't know what to say. "I was away working and a bad man hit me," he said lamely. "But don't you worry," he added, suddenly fearful of upsetting the children, "I'm fine now and the police will lock the bad man away."

"Mummy said you were away working and we might not see you for a long time, but you came back," Jenny announced seriously

"Yes, darling, I'm back and I'll be here for you whenever you need me." Tom kept his voice gentle but he stared at Anne, his expression fierce.

Her reaction was to look back just as sternly. "Arthur's already told you what needs to happen. You don't want to upset the children, do you?"

It wasn't like Anne to be so prepared, calm and manipulative. He guessed she'd had help in planning this ambush and he suspected it was Arthur's work.

Fighting to keep his emotions in check, he replied. "You're wrong Anne, we need to talk and we need to talk alone. We've got ourselves into this and we need to agree on the way out of it. No-one else, just you and me."

Anne seemed uncertain and glanced at Arthur for support.

"He's got no part in this." Tom found him-self wishing he'd taken Stephan's advice to bring someone with him.

"I don't want to be alone with you. I'm afraid of your temper," Anne said quietly.

Tom stared at her in disbelief. "What? What temper are you talking about? I've never, ever raised my hand, which is more than I can say for you," Tom said remembering Anne's assault with the spoon a few days earlier.

"But you'll shout at me and bully me," Anne continued, as if she was genuinely afraid.

"I've never bullied you either. But if it will make you any happier or feel any safer, we can sit in the dining room with the door slightly open. Arthur can sit in here, and he'll be only a few yards away so you needn't feel threatened."

Anne picked up Colin and placed him safely in the playpen, then selected a Shrek DVD, one of Jenny's favourites and set it up on the player.

"You don't need to do this," Arthur said. "We've already talked through the best way to handle this." But despite his protestations, Tom and Anne went through to the dining room and took up positions at opposite sides of the table.

247

"So, what do you want to talk about?" Anne asked quietly.

"Don't you think I'm entitled to an explanation?" Tom replied. He watched Anne sitting nervously in front of him, her gaunt complexion and almost skeletal frame. He couldn't help drawing a comparison to Sally's appearance, healthy and wholesome, with her sharp wit and challenging conversation. Given a choice, right there and then, it was a no-brainer who he'd prefer to partner. But it wasn't a choice, Anne didn't want him and Sally wasn't on offer. Nevertheless, Tom thought his marriage's days were numbered.

"I don't think you're entitled to anything. Arthur says—"

"Let's forget everything Arthur says," Tom interrupted. "He doesn't make the rules here. We've been man and wife for nearly ten years now, and most of that time was bloody good. I'll be first to admit the last two years have been hell, but a lot of that wasn't my fault and I can give a good case proving that."

Anne's eyes softened and welled with tears. "You're right, you don't deserve this. You don't deserve any of it."

Tom drew in a sharp breath, suddenly uncertain. He was apprehensive, not sure what direction the conversation was taking. He looked at Anne questioningly.

She chewed at the inside of her cheek for a moment, tapping her fingers nervously on the table. "Maybe it's time you knew the truth. I should have told you a long time ago, but there was never a right time. I thought about telling you on a couple of different occasions, but I never had the courage to go through with it."

Tom couldn't stay silent. "So this has been going on for some time. You and Arthur have been getting together behind my back?" He threw out the accusation bitterly. "And then you've got the audacity to accuse *me* of being a bad husband and father?"

"No, no," Anne cried, tears in full flow.

The door flew open, the void instantly filled by Arthur's advancing form. "Get away from her, you bastard. I should never have let you see her alone!"

"No, Arthur! It's okay!" Anne yelled. She took a deep breath, visibly settled herself. "There's nothing wrong. Please, leave us alone for a while. I need to do this. It's okay to shut the door."

Arthur's eyes flashed between them, unhappy at the suggestion, but nevertheless he followed the instruction.

Anne turned back to Tom. "You've never been a bad father, a little less attentive than ideal at times, but never bad. You've been a good husband as well, better than I deserved."

Tom shook his head in disbelief, but was instantly sorry, when it began to throb. He raised his fingers to his brow, rubbing at his temples. "What are you trying—" he began.

Anne held up a hand in a stop motion. "Please, no, don't speak. This is difficult enough without you interrupting. Do you remember about three years ago; the time you went away for that training course in Bristol?" The words were spoken quietly, punctuated by sobs. "Jenny was nearly five, looking forward to her first day at school."

Tom nodded, not trusting himself to speak.

"I did something stupid; something very stupid."

"What?" Tom mouthed the word, but no sound escaped.

Anne lowered her gaze to the floor, unable to meet Tom's penetrating glare. "I went for a night out with some of the girls from the play-group. It was someone's birthday; I can't remember whose. Arthur came to babysit, to let me go out. It turned out to be quite a wild evening; we had loads of wine with dinner then went on to a club for some more drinks. I got quite tipsy."

Tom nodded, but his gesture went unseen, Anne's eyes were focussed on her shoes.

"The evening was drawing to an end and I was about to call for a taxi when I met an old school friend. I hadn't seen him for years, so we sat down again to reminisce and talk about what had happened with the old crowd. It was a mistake, because we shared another bottle of wine as we chatted. Danny told me he had a stack of photos from the old days and invited me to go with him to see them. He had a flat, only a few minutes' walk from the club. I accepted the invitation and we staggered around to his place. He'd no sooner closed the door when he told me how much he'd always fancied me. I laughed, thinking he was joking, but then he kissed me and started fondling me. For a moment I responded,

251

it felt good and dangerous at the same time. I felt like a schoolgirl on a first date. Then I remembered who I was and how much I loved you. I told him no, and tried to push him away, but he wouldn't take no for an answer. I struggled and pushed and tried to punch him. He said he liked a fighter and kept going until he, he—" With a strangled sob, she stopped.

"He raped you?" Tom asked, unable to keep the tremor from his voice.

"Yes, he did," she said quietly. "I should have yelled. I should have screamed, but I didn't. I was so drunk, I hardly knew what was happening at first and when I did understand, it was too late. I just wept. Afterwards, he said he'd call me a cab but I grabbed my bag and ran away. I was still dazed by what had happened, but I'd sobered up instantly. I hated myself. I wanted to be home and safe, but at the same time I was too ashamed to come home. So I walked all through the town for ages, before I stopped a taxi. I let myself in the front door and heard Arthur call out, joking that it must have been some night. Then he saw me and he was shocked. He hugged me and asked what had happened. When I told him, he said he'd take care of me, that it would all be okay."

"Why didn't you phone the police?" Tom demanded. "Why didn't you tell *me* what had happened?"

Anne shook her head hopelessly. "Arthur and I talked about it for ages. We debated what I should do. If I'd gone to the police, they would probably have thought I'd asked for it. Even if they did prosecute, the chances of a conviction would have been slight and the whole world would have known how stupid I'd been. Everyone would have thought I was a slut."

"Why didn't you tell me?" Tom's voice was unsteady when he repeated the question.

"I wanted to, but I was scared. I thought you'd blame me. Arthur thought so too. He said you were so prim and proper, you'd never understand and that you would only chase me away if you knew. He said he'd protect me. He knew my secret and nobody else need ever find out.

"It didn't work though. I felt so stupid and ashamed. When we made love after that, it never felt right. I kept thinking you'd know. I couldn't relax and that made it even worse. I went through the motions, but I found it difficult to even be in your company. I kept thinking you would see through me, discover my secret.

"Then I discovered I was pregnant and I was terrified the baby wasn't yours. The pregnancy gave me the excuse for not making love. I made up the story, you'll remember, that I was risking a miscarriage and it also covered for my mood swings."

Tom nodded soberly. "Colin?"

"Yes."

"He's not mine?"

"I don't know." Anne pressed her hands to her eyes for a moment, before she looked up again. "I wanted him to be yours. He looks like you, everyone says so, but I was always too scared to find out for sure."

"That's not good enough! For over two years I've been raising that boy as my son and he might not be!" Tom had a deep stabbing pain in his gut. He felt betrayed and wanted to hurt her back. He spoke coldly, "And how many other potential fathers might he have?"

Racking sobs escaped from Anne as she fought to reply. "That's exactly how Arthur thought you'd react. He is yours, I'm positive of it. There was only that one time, and I didn't want it to happen."

Tom's venomous jibe had given him no satisfaction. He regretted saying it and experienced a desire to reach out and offer Anne a reassuring hand, but he didn't. He was hurting too much himself to offer her comfort. "Only one time, okay. And what about now? What's going on with you and Arthur?"

"That's different. Let me go on. When Colin was born, I was really low. For a while, I couldn't bear to look at him. I didn't want to be near him, I was so scared that he wasn't yours. I didn't want to be near you either, because I was so ashamed."

"It was diagnosed as post-natal depression at the time."

"Yes, it was and you were so wonderful. You did everything for me and Jenny and Colin. Somehow, , that only made matters worse. I felt as if I didn't deserve you. I pushed you away, I guess. Afterwards, you went back to work and it seemed easier – the more you worked the easier it became. It gave me the chance to blame you, but truly you'd done nothing wrong. I fell out of love with you, but it wasn't your fault. It was my defence mechanism."

"And Arthur?" Tom questioned.

"He was there for me all the time. He was my confidant, my rock. I could tell him anything and he'd reassure me and tell me it was okay. Over time, we grew closer and closer and in the end, we became lovers. It's all my fault. I pushed you away."

Tom could feel a modicum of sympathy for Anne. He fought it down though, because he wanted to stay angry with her. He needed no such effort to focus his loathing on Arthur. All of this was his fault, at least a good part of it. He'd manipulated the situation to his advantage. He'd convinced Anne to keep the secret, stopped her from being honest. By doing that, he'd inflicted the guilt and consequent depression onto her. He'd poisoned their relationship and killed their marriage and now he'd picked up Anne on the rebound. Tom conceded there was some truth in how Arthur had predicted his reaction might have been, but he'd grossly exaggerated. If Anne had only been honest with him, there would have been some difficult times, but Tom was sure they'd have survived it. He'd have reconciled what had gone before and they'd have come through it. But not now. Now it was too late.

"For how long, with Arthur?" he demanded.

"Not long; does it really matter?"

"Yes, it matters to me! And where? Has he been fucking you in my bed? In our bed?" Tom's tone was harsh. "And where were the children?"

Anne couldn't meet his stare. At first, she couldn't speak and when she did, she whispered. "The children were never at home. Not until the last few days, at least."

"While you're in the mood for confessions, do you want to tell me who else you've dropped your knickers for? This Danny, then Arthur – were there many more?" He knew he was being deliberately cruel and didn't wait for an answer; his head was buzzing. The doctor had warned him about headaches and avoiding stress. If he'd been consciously trying to oppose the advice, he could hardly have been more successful. He lifted a drum of tablets from his pocket and popped two of the painkillers into his mouth then walked through to the kitchen for some water to help him swallow them down.

When he returned to the dining room, Anne looked up at him, tears streaking her cheeks. "What now?" Anne asked.

"I don't know; I truly don't know. I need time to think, to come to terms with all this."

"I've packed all your things," Anne said.

"So Arthur said, but I don't want them now. I've got to go away for a few days; I'll take the stuff I packed and left in the car. But just so you know – this is my house too. You can choose to pack up and go, but I haven't done anything wrong and I'm not leaving. I've got as much rights as you, probably more under the circumstances."

"You can't want to disturb the children?" Anne admonished.

"It's not me who's wrenching the family apart. Perhaps you should have thought of that before." He stood to leave.

"Tom, I've had a problem with the bank and the credit cards. What have you done? I haven't been able to buy any shopping."

Tom stared down at her. "You tell me, I put a stop on any withdrawals after you lifted the two grand." Tom didn't know who had withdrawn the money, but with Anne having brought the subject up, it was a good opportunity to test her reaction.

"What are you talking about? What two grand? I tried to take fifty quid from the hole in the wall and it ate my card. I tried using the Visa at Waitrose and it got rejected. It was really embarrassing. I only had enough cash for half the items and I had to put the rest back. They looked at me like I was a criminal. What have you done?"

Tom shrugged. Anne's reaction seemed authentic, but how could he be sure about anything? If she hadn't withdrawn the money, he had another mystery to solve. If it caused her some inconvenience in the meantime, then so what?

Tom walked back through to the lounge to say goodbye to his children, confirming in his own mind that he still thought of both of them as 'his'. It didn't matter how Colin had been conceived, Tom thought of him as his son.

"I guess you're not man enough." Arthur sounded self-satisfied, enjoying the opportunity to goad Tom.

Tom had never been violent in his life, but with a combination of pent-up fury and frustration, he summoned up a strength he never knew he had and landed a punch deep into Arthur's midriff. It was an unexpected blow and Arthur collapsed to the floor, wheezing and coughing.

The children hadn't seen it happen, but turned around upon hearing Arthur's gasping response. Tom gently kissed each of them, told them he loved them and would see them soon. He rushed through the front door before tears overcame him.

He heard Arthur's spluttered voice in the distance. "I'll give you that one, but I'll squash you if you dare come near me again!"

Tom resisted the temptation to return and confront Arthur. He so wanted to do it, but not in front of his children. They must be confused enough already, without having to witness a blazing argument or worse still, a fist fight. He lifted his case from the car's boot then shuffled

slowly along to the end of the street before calling a taxi.

Chapter 14

The ride to Tom's parents' house took a little over fifteen minutes. All the while, as the vehicle sped on its way, Tom felt distant and detached. He mulled over the circumstances of his relationship and the possible consequences as if he was analysing someone else's life, preparing to write their story. Tom's parents lived in a suburban villa in a tree-lined avenue on the far side of town. He settled the cab fare –his driving restriction was going to prove expensive. He lifted his case, bag and laptop and struggled to keep them in balance as he staggered up the driveway.

He hardly had time to press the bell before the solid timber door sprung open and his mother stepped forward, enveloping him in a hug.

She stood back, examining him for damage and raised her hand to touch his face. "Oh Tom, are you okay? Tell me what happened." Then she caught sight of his case and her face dropped in dismay.

"Physically, I'm fine. I was in Manchester on business and I was mugged. I was walking out of an office in the centre of town. It was early evening, in broad daylight, when I was hit, knocked over, and my computer and phone were stolen." Tom had made up his mind not to tell his mother the whole story for fear of upsetting her further.

"Tommy, son, it's good to see you!" His father approached and shook his hand, drawing him forward for a hug.

Tom's father wasn't normally so tactile and Tom knew this sudden show of affection betrayed his fear. The enormity of his situation was only now coming into focus. Tom clung to his father as if needing the support to stop him from collapse.

"It's all gone wrong. My marriage is over and it can't be fixed."

"Come inside," his mother beckoned. "Come in and sit down. I'll make you a nice cup of tea. Are you hungry? Can I get you a sandwich? Then we can talk." She was busying herself to avoid hearing bad news, thinking if she didn't hear the words then it wouldn't be real.

"Come sit down," his father added. "I reckon you're ready for a whisky. Can I get you one?"

"I'd love one, Dad, but I'm meant to stay off alcohol for a while. It's because I've had a concussion, it can cause headaches."

"Whisky can give you headaches at any time. It depends how much you have though."

Tom grinned. "Thanks Dad."

They sat down in silence and a few minutes later, Tom's mother joined them carrying a tray with three mugs and a plate piled high with biscuits.

Tom nibbled on a digestive then asked, "How much do you already know?"

"We've known you've had problems for a long time. Way back from when you took a sabbatical from work. Things seemed to improve, but they were never right after that," his mother began. "You'll remember, we wanted to help. We offered to babysit and everything, so you'd have time together. Arthur wanted to help too. Much as we were upset, we were so proud at the time – all the family pulling together. It was the first time we'd seen Arthur act in a really positive way since his accident." Tears were flowing down his mother's cheeks. "He'd had so much potential."

"This isn't about Arthur and his problems," Tom spat. He felt hurt that even at this critical time in his life, his mother's thoughts and sympathy were focused on Arthur.

Arthur had been the golden child, strong, attractive and smart. He was skilled at all sports and had shown the potential of having a professional career in rugby. He was a brilliant scholar, in his second year studying for a law degree when he'd broken his leg in a stupid accident while playing a bounce game of football in a local park. He was in plaster for weeks and warned off sports for months. He descended into a deep depression and dropped out of university, never to regain his former potential. He'd had jobs, but they seldom lasted more than a few weeks and he survived, living in his own flat, paid for out of the benefit system, supplemented by hand-outs from Tom and his parents. Physically, he'd fully recovered and now attended a gym almost daily. He was super fit but unequipped to return to competitive games or life's challenges. Their

parents had cosseted and spoiled Arthur to protect him from outside influences, but the effect
had been negative; rather than helping him, it
had left him unable to cope or function indepen-
dently.

"Arthur was there and you weren't," his
mother said simply, as though that explained everything.

"What?" Tom yelled. "Don't tell me you think
what he's done has been alright?"

"No, I didn't say that. At first he was just being supportive. It was only after some time had
passed when we realised he'd fallen in love with
Anne."

"Fallen in lust, more like," Tom cut in angrily.

"We tried to talk to him, to tell him to stay
away, but you know Arthur when he gets something into his mind. He won't listen to anyone."

"So you've known this has been going on for
some time? Who else knows? Am I the only
schmuck who's been kept in the dark?"

His mother leaned forward in her chair, her
voice soothing. "It's not like that. It's not been
long. We tried to make him stop."

Tom was incensed. "And what did you do to stop him? Tell him he was being a naughty boy?"

"We tried talking to him."

"That's it; you tried talking to him? He does nothing for himself. He's virtually dependent on you to allow him to maintain his lifestyle. He behaves like this and all you do is 'TRY' talking to him? That's the equivalent of an endorsement. You've practically encouraged him."

"That isn't fair, you two boys have always argued and fought, ever since you were little," his mother protested.

"Don't you see? This isn't a playground squabble! It's not a matter of him taking away and hiding my toys. This isn't a question of a few Lego bricks. Arthur has always been jealous of anything I've had. Anything he could have had too, but he was too lazy to work for! Now he's stolen my wife and he's trying to steal my kids and my house too. He'd totally fucked up his own life and you're happy for him to fuck up mine as well, not to mention the kids!"

"You mind your language. I'll not have you using that gutter talk in this house," his mother warned.

Tom stared at her in disbelief. "Am I hearing you right? You don't want me saying the word 'fuck' but it's okay to let Arthur destroy everything I have, everything I've worked for and everything I live for! That's typical. Well, my answer is fuck, fuck, fuck! That's what I think of your rules. You've obviously made your choice and you've chosen Arthur over me. If that's how you feel, then I'm out of here." Tom got to his feet.

"Stop, Tom, sit back down and let me speak." His father piped up for the first time. "We aren't choosing Arthur over you. We couldn't. We would never show preference for one of you over the other. It's true, over the years we have given more to Arthur than to you, but that wasn't because of favouritism, it's because he needed help where you were always the strong one, strong and independent. We've always been there for you as well, but you didn't need us in the same way. What Arthur's done is wrong, very wrong and we've told him so. But as your mum has said, he doesn't listen, he does his own thing."

"But you're still supporting him?"

"We're not supporting him. He gets benefits and sometimes he makes some money. Occasionally, we'll give him some cash to help him out of a tight spot or to pay for the odd luxury, but not enough to influence his behaviour or regulate what he does. Besides, we're afraid, we don't want to lose our contact with our grandchildren."

"I think I need that whisky now. The headache can hardly get any worse." Tom walked across to the sideboard, lifted a bottle of Glengoyne and poured himself a large measure, then sipped a mouthful of the golden liquid.

"I don't know if you should—" his mother began, before being shushed to silence by his father.

"I think you'll need to explain that one," Tom replied, staring directly at his father.

"You and Arthur are our only family, we have nobody else. You are our whole life." He stopped to look at his wife for encouragement to continue. "We dearly love our grandchildren; Jenny and Colin mean everything to us. We see them several times a week. We babysit, we take them out. We go to events. We couldn't stand to lose that."

"So?" Tom demanded.

"If you and Anne were to separate and Anne had custody, we might never get to see them."

"And you thought if it was Arthur who took over my role, then your position as grandparents would be maintained?"

"No, it's not like that," his mother protested.

"And what if they're not really your grandchildren?" Tom snapped.

"What do you mean?" his father demanded.

Tom shook his head. "No, forget I said that, forget I said anything. You've made your position clear and it seems I don't have a place in your lives any more, in any of your lives." Tom swallowed down the remainder of the whisky in one gulp, coughing a couple of times when the spirit burned its way down his throat. "I'll get my things and be out of here, but there's one other thing you should know. I'm not going to make this easy for Arthur or for Anne. I'm going to fight for what's mine."

"I'm pleased to hear it," Tom's father said. "It would be best for the children if you could work things out and get back on an even plane. In the meantime, please don't go. You're welcome to stay here. We can make up the spare room. It would be no trouble."

"If you give me your dirty washing, I'll get it done for you," his mother added.

"Always practical," Tom said bitterly. He didn't want to stay at his parents' house, but he didn't have many choices. He was already exhausted and his head felt cloudy and sore. Would it be so bad to move back in with his parents for two nights? Besides, he had little cash, and no credit cards. His options were limited.

"Fine, but I need to do some work. The pub at the end of the street offers free Wi-Fi. I'll be able to use my computer there. I want to get washed and changed then I'll take a walk down there and do what I need to."

"Can I make some dinner for you? You must be starving," his mother offered.

"No. Thanks for the offer, but I need to get this work done before I'm too exhausted to think. I'll grab a bite to eat at the pub."

"You look exhausted," his mother said. "You can't possibly work now. You need to lie down and rest, but I can make you something first, even a sandwich if you don't want anything substantial."

Tom hesitated for a second. "You're right, I'm tired, but this needs to be done now. I'll go straight out, do what I have to, and I'll be back in an hour or so and go straight to bed then."

With their protests ringing in his ears, Tom collected his computer and phone and fled out of the door. Once through the gate, his exhaustion truly caught up and his footsteps became slow and laboured. Staggering more than walking, he reached the bar five minutes later.

Tom checked the pub grub menu and ordered and paid for a serving of steak and ale pie, accompanied by mashed potatoes and peas. He requested a pint of bitter to wash it down. He knew he would have been better to completely avoid alcohol, but after the day he'd had, he figured he was entitled to break a few rules.

The bar was busy with Saturday evening revellers, but Tom was able to secure a brightly lit booth in a quiet corner where he removed his laptop from its case and powered it up. He took out his phone and called Stephan to set up a meeting with him and his brother-in-law for the following day. Stephan offered to book them a table for lunch at a tapas bar close to where he lived. Tom thanked him, hung up and tried to call Sally. There was no answer and he left a bland voicemail in response to the standard outgoing message.

Waiting for his food to arrive, Tom supped at his ale and used the laptop's search engine to locate the franking machine licence number he'd identified on the letter at the Manchester Sentinel. He was delighted, if not totally surprised, to find it was an RNB machine, but this time from an office in Manchester.

He plugged in his portable memory card and made some notes, then proceeded to draft some Diary column items for inclusion in his magazine's next edition. He knew it wasn't critical for him to do this work now, but he wanted a justification for staying out of the house.

His food came while he was working and although not a small portion, he devoured it with enthusiasm. He was tempted to order a second helping, but instead opted for a second beer and a slice of treacle tart with custard.

After a while, the laptop screen became indistinct and the letters grew fuzzy. Tom slumped back in the chair, totally exhausted. He was physically weak and emotionally wrecked.

He wasn't aware of dozing – the first he realised was when a hand gently squeezed his shoulder and he blinked a few times, trying to focus.

"Tom, are you okay son? You'd been gone for ages so I came to bring you home. I think I might be better to take you to a hospital?"

Tom tried to speak, but his mouth was dry and his tongue felt like sandpaper against the roof of his mouth. He saw his father reach for his phone and lifted a hand to stop him. "No, Dad, I'm fine, I'm just dog tired."

"Let's get you home to rest. You can't sleep here."

Tom packed up his laptop, struggled to his feet and began to stagger out of the pub, with his father providing support.

"You're not well, I'm going to phone for help," his father suggested again.

"No, Dad, definitely not, I'm fine, I need a few seconds to wake myself up. I'm tired and more than a little sozzled, but I'll be okay in a minute. I can't go to the hospital, they're bound to admit me and, being the weekend, I might not get released for a couple of days. I can't afford to lose that time. It would be catastrophic both personally and for work."

"Nothing's more important than your health."

"Dad, please, trust me on this, I'm okay."

With a burst of intense concentration, Tom summoned up his strength and his composure and managed to stand straight and walk unaided. His father strode alongside, cautiously watching every step.

Approaching the house, Tom saw his mother at the bay window of the front room. All the lights were on and the curtains were open. She was standing, wringing her hands and staring out apprehensively. Seeing his approach, her face lit up and she ran to the front door.

"What happened to you? You were gone for so long! Did you meet someone?"

"I'm sorry, Mum. I guess I was more tired than I thought. I started doing some work and then I guess I fell asleep."

"What? In the middle of the pub?"

"I'm afraid so,"

"You're lucky no-one made off with your com-puter."

"Yes, you're right, particularly with the way my luck's been going recently. I'm still really tired. I think I should go to bed. I'm sure I'll feel better in the morning."

"Yes, I think you should. Your bed's all made up and ready for you. I've sorted out your laun-dry too. It's in the machine now and I can tumble it in the morning so you'll have it all back before you leave."

Here he was, a grown man with a family of his own, but he couldn't help feeling he was being treated like a small child. In a remote way it was slightly comforting, but still, it was an imposition and Tom couldn't wait to have his own space.

"Thanks Mum." He washed and changed and went to bed, firmly closing the bedroom door be-hind him.

* * *

Isn't life weird? Tom thought. *I fell sound asleep in the pub, in the middle of everything and every-*

one and all the noise. The best sleep I've had in ages. I'd have still been out for the count if Dad hadn't woken me. And now, here I am, lying on a comfortable bed, totally exhausted and unable to drop off. Tom re-fluffed the pillows and tossed and turned, but it was to no avail. Every time he closed his eyes, he pictured one of the various demons haunting him and his eyelids would spring open again. He tried putting the light on to read, thinking it would make him drowsy, but it had little effect. His situation wasn't helped when he overheard his parents readying themselves for bed and chattering away, talking about his circumstances. Tom lay silently, trying to decipher their comments through the wall. He could tell they were uncomfortable and sympathetic about what he was going through, but not enough to risk their access to the children, or to seriously confront Arthur over his behaviour. Tom tried to fathom his own emotions. He could accept an end to his marriage, but knowing the root cause and how it had been exacerbated by Arthur, he couldn't countenance walking away. He made up his mind he wouldn't let Arthur steal his children or his house. He was less concerned about losing Anne and thought, in some perverse way, that she and Arthur deserved each other. Even so, he'd do anything he could to drive a wedge between them. He grabbed a pad and pen from his bag to make some notes, Stephan had recommended he prepare some information before the meeting with the lawyer, and unexpectedly, he found the thought of doing so liberating. Making a good start, he was considering what to write next, when he remembered resting the biro against the pad, then nothing more.

Chapter 15

The clattering of pots and pans roused Tom and he woke slowly. Seeing the bedside clock, he was amazed to discover it was already half past ten. He realized he'd left the overhead lamp on, but the light streaming through the window counteracted its glow. The strong and pleasant aroma of frying bacon assaulted his nostrils. He looked around, taking a few moments to remember where he was. He saw the pad, checked his notes, and was surprised to see how accurate and complete his summary was. He'd tabulated all their assets and liabilities and given a concise account of the history and nature of his marital difficulties, culminating in Anne's relationship with his brother. He made no mention of her revelation about the rape being the source of their problems. He hadn't yet come to terms with the implications. He knew he'd have to tell the lawyer what she'd said, but had found he was unable to commit it to paper. The list was intended to ensure he didn't forget to talk about anything important and he knew there was little risk of him overlooking that issue. After adding a couple of further details, Tom snuck into the bathroom, quickly showered, shaved and dressed, then descended the stairs.

"Perfect timing," his mother greeted, serving him a stacked plate filled with bacon, sausage, eggs, mushrooms, tomatoes and toast, along with a large mug of tea.

Tom tucked into the feast greedily. It had been a long time since he'd enjoyed a home cooked breakfast. He couldn't remember the last time. Ignoring the high fat and cholesterol consequences, he finished every scrap of the fry up, then mopped up any residues of grease, yolk and juices using the toast.

"Do you feel better now?" his mother asked.

"Mmmmm."

"That'll put some meat on your bones; no better start to the day," his father added.

"Just what I needed," Tom replied, eventually finding his voice.

"What are your plans for today? I thought we could take a walk in the park," his mother suggested.

It hadn't occurred to him that an entertainment programme was being prepared and he wanted no part of it. "I'm sorry, Mum, that won't be possible. I have a meeting planned with my boss. We're having lunch and he's introducing me to a lawyer, so I know how to handle everything."

"But it's Sunday! You shouldn't be doing that today. Besides, you still need rest so you can get well. As for you meeting a lawyer, isn't it too soon for that?" his father said.

"I need to be away early tomorrow. I have a flight booked and I don't know when I'll be back. It's something I have to do. As for the lawyer, I'm only meeting him to see what he has to say and to make sure I don't make any stupid mistakes. I know Anne's already spoken to one herself."

Tom saw his mother's all too familiar pursed lips and knew better than to continue the conversation. Least said soonest mended, was often his principle when speaking to his parents.

Having finished his breakfast, Tom settled into a comfortable armchair in the lounge and picked up the Sunday papers and magazines. After about an hour, he stood up and collected his laptop, hugged his mother, shook his father's hand and made to exit the front door. "I'll leave all my stuff here and I'll see you later. I should be back late afternoon or early evening. I'll need to see how it goes."

"No, wait," his father called. "I'll drive you. Where is it you're going?" His father lifted his jacket and keys and ushered him out the door.

"Are you sure you want to do this? I'm going up to Knightsbridge. I can catch a train. Why not drop me at the station and I can make my own way from there?" Tom suggested.

"It's only Sunday traffic. I'll have you there in no time. I won't risk you falling asleep on the train. God knows where you might end up."

Tom hopped in the car, "Thanks, Dad. I appreciate it."

"I want you to know that we're always here for you. We'll do anything we can to help," his father reassured

Just so long as it doesn't step on Arthur's toes, Tom thought, but chose not to vocalise. Tom detected from his father's attitude that he wanted to be more supportive, but his mother was inhibiting him from taking sides.

When Tom alighted from the car, he saw Stephan standing on a terrace outside the tapas bar, puffing on a cigarette. The sky was grey and rain was falling steadily, so Stephan was huddled under a canopy close to the doorway, reluctantly complying with the smoking policy. Seeing Tom approach, he stamped out his fag and cheerfully met Tom in the entranceway.

"You seem bit more human today, ugly as sin, but human. Come on in and I'll introduce you to Bernard. He's at the bar and was too soft to join me out here. No, I'm being unfair, Bernard is anything but soft. He disapproves of smoking in the rain though. He doesn't like his cigars to get wet. If you like, I can carry out the introductions for the two of you then bugger off, so you can talk in private?"

"No, I'd rather you stayed, if you don't mind. I've nothing to hide from you and I could do with the moral support."

"Of course." He approached the table and waved a hand towards the man already sitting there. "Tom, Bernard: Bernard, Tom, I've already told you both what to expect," Stephan said as he took his seat.

Bernard Carter was not how Tom had imagined. Stephan had made no visual description, but from what he'd told him about Bernard's abilities, Tom had expected someone small powerful and aggressive, a pit-bull of a man. Instead, Bernard seemed benign and fairly average, a man aged in his fifties. Slim and wiry, with a full head of sandy coloured hair, he was clean-shaven and had lazy, grey-blue eyes. His nose was fairly flat, with a kink midway up, and there was the faint line of a scar across his chin, giving an indication of battles lost. He was dressed in Levi jeans and a short-sleeved shirt, and a leather jacket hung on the back of his chair.

Tom glanced around. The tapas bar was one of hundreds of similar eateries. Clean and fresh, it was stylishly furnished and decorated to give the impression of a traditional Spanish restaurant. Menu cards sat on each table, written in Spanish with an English translation.

The three pored over the options and selected a varied buffet to be washed down by a good quality Tempranillo. Tom opted for mineral water, wanting to keep his wits about him and belatedly decided to comply with the doctor's advice.

A pale skinned young waiter, dressed all in black, came to take their order. Once he'd disappeared towards the kitchen, Bernard sat back in his chair and studied Tom for a moment.

"Before we talk about anything personal, remember this is a quiet corner, but it's hardly private," Bernard said. "We can go somewhere else to discuss your situation, if you'd prefer. Stephan set this up and I'm happy to give you a free consultation, but if you want my services afterwards, I'll need you to approve a service agreement. I'll warn you, I'm not cheap. I like to consider myself reassuringly expensive."

"I had a family discount and I can vouch for that, twice over," Stephan added. "But I considered it money well spent."

Bernard grinned. "Thanks for the endorsement. I give the best advice I can, but I can't stop my clients from repeating their mistakes, that's not my field."

"I'm happy to talk here," Tom said. "I'd like to get on with it."

Waiting for the food to be served, Tom provided Bernard with his notes and gave him a more detailed account of his circumstances and what he was hoping to achieve. They continued chatting while they ate and then over coffee, with Bernard quizzing Tom's situation closely.

Albeit the surroundings were pleasant and the company convivial, Tom began to feel as if he'd been dragged through a wringer, having bared his entire life in front of a total stranger.

"You've done well," Bernard said, making a constructive comment for the first time in their long discussion. "That mustn't have been easy. Now I can run through some advice and options. It's down to how hard you want to fight this. The ideal situation would be if you were both able to come to a mutual agreement on what you want, but based on what you've told me, I see that as highly unlikely. In my experience, it's rare. Even when there's a friendly separation, there will always be issues of disagreement. If there wasn't, why would there need to be a separation in the first place?

"You say you'd ideally want full custody of the children, but as I'm sure you'd expect, that's practically a non-starter. The courts will not take children away from their mother unless they consider them to be at serious risk. You've told me about Anne's depression problems, but that wouldn't be enough to deprive her of custody. There's also your availability and the family's history. Unless you give up work, you're not available to raise them, and to date, Anne has been the one taking care of their day-to-day needs, with no adverse circumstances to suggest why she shouldn't continue. On the plus side, I see no reason why you shouldn't be entitled to a share of custody and fairly unrestricted visitation rights."

Tom nodded.

"That takes us onto property and financial matters. Anne has asked you to leave the house, but it's your house as well and there's no reason why you should go. If anything, it weakens your position if you do. You're the injured party here. The house is in joint names, but that's fairly academic under marital homes legislation as you both have rights. You're the one who's working and earning and the one who's been paying the mortgage, so why should you give it up?"

Tom nodded again and gave Bernard a mirthless half smile.

"Whether or not you leave, you can't stop paying the mortgage because if you did, she most likely wouldn't have the resources and sooner or later the house would be repossessed. There's plenty of equity in the house, so that's not a good way to go. Instead, your best route is to stay put and tell her it's up to her if she wants to go."

"I don't want this to hurt the children."

"I understand, but that's not a legal issue. Whatever happens, they are going to be affected and you want to protect them and yourself as best you can. You're entitled to live in the property, as are Anne and the children, but Arthur has no such right."

Tom's face showed a flicker of a genuine smile. "So you think I should insist on my right to continue living there and throw Arthur out?"

"It might not be as simple as that. You're entitled to stay and so is Anne. She's entitled to have her guests visit, but if there was any bother, you could ask him to leave and even ask the police to enforce it."

"Yes, but I have to travel and stay away because of my work."

"Hasn't that always been the case?"

"Yes."

"So move back in and assert your occupation rights. It won't be a comfortable situation, but it may be best in the long term. If Anne chooses to go, then you're in an even stronger position and if she doesn't, you need to sort out a working relationship, at least until the property can be sold. If you continue to pay the mortgage and the utility bills, but supply Anne with no money, that should force her to the negotiating table."

Tom frowned. "I wouldn't want to go back to sleeping in our bed, not after they've, they've—"

Bernard shook his head. "No, I understand, but you told me you have a spare room. Surely you could use that? As for other financial matters, you've said you've already put a stop on bank and credit cards, albeit for a different reason. Make sure they can't be reactivated. Open a new bank account and have your salary paid into there. Then, when the dust settles, try to come to a mutual agreement on how to divide up assets and who'll take responsibility for different liabilities. If Anne has formal custody, you'll be responsible for maintenance payments for the children."

"I wouldn't want or expect any different. I don't want the children to suffer, no more than absolutely necessary."

"Everything will need to be properly valued, including your pension rights. But all that comes later and there can often be trade-offs."

Tom nodded thoughtfully. "Okay. You've been very helpful and I think I know what I need to do now. If you can prepare your contract and send it to me via Stephan, I'll go ahead and sign it."

"One more question, I have to ask. Are you definitely the father of the children?"

Tom's face paled. and he took a deep breath before continuing, "I'm listed as the father on their birth certificates and I've brought them both up as my children, but... but..." Tom started blabbering, almost incoherently, before he calmed himself and repeated what Anne had confessed the previous day.

There was a long pause before Bernard spoke. "That will complicate matters. Would you like a paternity test? If Colin's not yours, it could limit your obligations."

"Colin is mine," Tom asserted loudly, then continued in a hushed voice. "I'm certain he's mine and even if I'm not biologically his father, I'm not giving up on him. If Anne was raped—".

Bernard interrupted. "I'm sorry to say this, but the operative word there was 'if'. When you told me a moment ago what Anne said, she couldn't even speak the word. It may be because she's still traumatised and can't accept it, or, if you'll excuse me being harsh, it might be because it wasn't a rape and she was either compliant or didn't resist and she can't bring herself to accuse an innocent man."

Tom instinctively started to jump to Anne's defence, but stopped himself. He was no longer convinced she deserved to be given the benefit of any doubt.

Tom sat back in his seat and relaxed for the first time since they'd met. He was thoroughly drained. He thought it strange but he felt liberated, unburdening his problems to a total stranger, but it was also exhausting. The serious-ness of the moment was broken when out of the corner of his eye, he saw Stephan sitting squirm-ing in his chair. He'd been so absorbed in his dis-cussion with Bernard, it only now occurred to him how uncommonly silent Stephan had been. Tom had forgotten he was even there. Tom won-dered if Stephan had felt out of place hearing Tom discussing his personal details or maybe he was showing respect to Bernard. In either event it was out of character. Tom looked at him ques-tioningly, "Are you alright?"

"Yes, what's wrong with you?" Bernard added. "You've been squirming around and scratching your posterior ever since we arrived. Have you got ants in your pants?"

"In a manner of speaking," Stephan replied, his eyes downcast. "It's rather embarrassing and bloody stupid really."

"Well?" Bernard pursued.

"You'll make fun of me," Stephan said, stalling.

"Of course we will, but at least let us know what we're laughing at," Bernard said. "You've started so may as well let us know."

"I did something bloody stupid this morning," Stephan began sheepishly. "I had a bath instead of my usual shower and beforehand I laid out my medicinal stuff. After I dried myself I reached out for my haemorrhoid ointment but instead accidentally picked up my athletes' foot cream. I'd already applied it before I realised and it stung like buggery."

"Interesting choice of phrase," Bernard said, but seemed to squirm himself, involuntarily, at the mere thought of what his brother-in-law had described. All three burst out laughing.

"I tried my best to wash it off, but it was too late and it still itches like hell," Stephan managed to blurt in between snorts.

"Well you always have been a pain in the ass. Anyway, I propose a toast," Bernard added. "Bottoms up!"

"Fuck off," was Stephan's only reply.

In contrast to the emotions he felt the previous evening of being bereft at the breakdown of his relationship and the potential loss of his wife, children, brother and even his parents, in a way, Tom was now in really good spirits. He felt he had a plan where he had some measure of control and a means of fighting back. He had also enjoyed the company and camaraderie of Stephan and Bernard and he had laughed, honestly and unreservedly. Tom couldn't remember the last time he had truly laughed. He had a spring in his step as he walked to the station to catch the train back to Reading.

* * *

"I have dinner ready," his mother welcomed when he got back to his parents' house.

"Thanks, very kind, but I don't think I could eat much. Breakfast was amazing and I had lunch while I was out."

"I'll put you out a small plate anyway, and you can eat as much or as little as you like."

"Thank you, but I'm going to head home."

"What? Are you going to collect the rest of your things? Your Dad will give you a lift so you don't have to worry about carrying stuff. Won't you Eric?"

Before his father had a chance to agree or refuse, Tom responded. "No, it's not to get my things. I'm going home to stay. It's my house and I'm not going to be pushed out of it. Anne can make up her own mind whether she wants to stay or go."

"And what about Arthur?" his mother asked.

Tom almost growled his response. "Maybe he'll want to come and stay here and you'll get to console him instead of me. Frankly, I don't give a shit what happens to him."

This time his mother made no attempt to correct his bad language.

Chapter 16

Accompanied by his father, Tom let himself back into the house. He searched around downstairs, but no-one was home. He offered to make tea but his father declined. Tom took his case upstairs to the spare room and unpacked, carefully placing his freshly laundered clothes into the wardrobe and onto shelves. He unpacked the other bags Anne had filled and checked to ensure his small case had everything he needed for his work trip. He set the radio-alarm ready to go for his morning flight and phoned a local minicab company to take him to the airport.

When Tom returned downstairs to join his father, he heard a car drawing up outside and Anne, Arthur, Jenny and Colin walked up the driveway towards the door.

Seeing the light on inside the house, the front door was opened cautiously. "What are you doing here?" Anne exclaimed, on seeing him. Arthur marched forward menacingly, until he caught sight of his father sitting in an armchair.

"Why shouldn't I be here? This is my house," Tom replied.

"And what are *you* doing here, Dad?" Arthur demanded.

"I'm only here as a peacekeeper, not to get involved. If necessary, I can take the children back to our house so they don't have to be stuck in the middle of anything."

"What's Papa talking about?" Jenny asked.

"It's nothing, sweetheart. You take Colin through to the kitchen for some milk and a biscuit and I'll be with you in a moment. It's late and you need to get ready for bed." Anne turned to Tom. "But you said you were going. This is my house and the children's house, so we can't all be here." Anne continued nervously, "Tell him, Arthur."

Arthur made to answer, but his father raised a hand, shaking an admonishing finger. Arthur stayed silent.

"You wanted me to go, but I never said I would," Tom replied. "As I said, this is my house and I'm not going. I've talked it through with my lawyer and I have every right to stay here. We'll have to sell the house, but until it is sold, I'll continue living here. It's yours and the children's house too. You can stay, but if you don't want to live in the same house as me then you'll need to leave. It's entirely your decision what you do."

Anne looked horrified. "But you can't! You need to travel away for work."

"That's always been the case and it hasn't changed, but this will remain my home."

"You can't want to be here. Surely this is a trick? You don't want to be here. Not with—"

Tom shrugged. "I've nowhere else to go."

Anne struggled to come up with an argument. "You can stay with your parents. I heard your mum say she'd be happy for you to stay there."

"But *I* wouldn't be happy. I'm not interested."

"You can move into my flat. Here, take my keys," Arthur suggested.

"You know where you can stick your keys," Tom replied aggressively.

"But what can *I* do?" Anne beseeched him.

Tom raised his eyebrows indicating a lack of interest, then followed up by saying, "Well, I've got an early start in the morning so I'm going to have an early night." He went through to the kitchen and kissed and hugged Jenny and Colin. "Night, night, darlings, I'll see you soon." He turned and walked up the stairs to his new bedroom, leaving everyone else in a stunned silence.

* * *

Anne helped the children get changed and ready for bed.

"Can't you stop him?" Arthur implored his father. "He's spoiling everything!"

"No, I think you've got that wrong," Eric replied coldly. "Isn't it you who's spoiled everything?"

"What can we do?" Anne's eyes were pleading, and she looked to Arthur to perform a miracle.

Arthur's mouth twisted in a wicked contortion. "I've got the answer. I think we should go to bed too. If he hears us banging away passionately in the room next to his, I don't think he'll want to stay for too long."

"Don't be disgusting," his father said.

"You can forget about any of those thoughts," Anne added. "I won't be sharing a bed with you in the same house where Tom's sleeping."

"I wasn't envisioning him getting much sleep, or us for that matter," Arthur replied, giving her a suggestive wink.

Anne's looked at him scornfully. "Your father's right, you are disgusting. I'm going to bed. You can let yourself out."

"No, wait, Anne! I was only joking. It's my stupid sense of humour. I didn't mean anything. Tom got me riled and I said what I shouldn't have. Please, give me a hug. It will all be okay."

Anne relented and they embraced briefly before she pulled away. "I meant what I said, I won't share a bed."

"What can I do?" Arthur whined. "I can't sleep on the couch or the floor, not with my bad back."

"You could come home with me?" his father offered.

Arthur was aghast at the prospect. "No, I'd rather go back to my own flat."

"Would you like me to give you a lift?" his father offered with barely suppressed amusement.

"I think not, I'll be back tomorrow," Arthur replied moodily and left, slamming the front door on his way out.

Eric stood to leave too.

Anne burst into tears, "What have I done?" she asked, more to herself than to him. Eric extended a reassuring arm and she clutched onto him, weeping bitterly on his shoulder.

* * *

Upstairs, Tom was lying on the single bed, wide awake and trying to catch snatches of the conversation downstairs. Although unable to decipher every word, he heard enough to know his plan had worked exactly as he'd hoped. He felt little satisfaction though; his main sentiment was sadness. He wanted to go and thank his father for the support he'd given, but knew it would have to wait.

He decided to try phoning Sally again. After everything he'd been through, he craved hearing her voice, caring little about what they might talk about.

He was about to hang up when the call was finally answered. Sally sounded a little breathless. "Tom? Are you okay? Has anything happened?"

"I'm fine... as fine as can be expected under the circumstances. What about you? Did things work out with your sister?"

"Not exactly. I'll tell you all about it tomorrow. I can't say too much at the moment. I'm at my mother's house. How did you get on? Did you see your children? Have you spoken to Anne? Have you made any progress? What happened with Arthur?"

"Yes, yes and yes, but for God's sake, slow down. I can't really say too much either. I'd rather not talk about these things on the phone. I've made some progress on our enquiries. Not a lot, but Stephan's been researching the Honda and the White Knight angle."

"I haven't been totally idle myself, but as you say, it's better not to talk about it on the phone. I spoke to Ahmed and he's doing some internet research. He's really keen and desperate to stay part of the team."

"Ah, the enthusiasm and naivety of youth," Tom said.

"I suppose so, and old men like you need to get their sleep, particularly when they've got to be up in the middle of the night to catch a flight. I'm not much better with my train. I'll go now so we both have a chance of some shut-eye and we can catch up properly tomorrow."

"Okay, pleasant dreams." Tom rang off with a shudder, remembering that his recent dreams had been anything but pleasant.

* * *

The melodious sounds of the Eagles, singing 'New York Minute' brought Tom back to consciousness. He leapt from bed to silence the radio, hoping he'd been quick enough not to disturb the children. Although he'd only heard a few seconds of the song, he was familiar with the lyrics and as he washed, dressed and prepared for his journey, his thoughts lingered on the meaning, and how quickly everything can change. It was a repeating truth of his recent past.

Tom crept down the stairs, entered the kitchen and switched on the kettle to make tea. He was alarmed when he saw an unopened bottle of White Horse whisky sitting on the worktop. It was a blend he'd seen many times, but he couldn't ever remember trying it. Anne never drank whisky and his father and brother, like him, preferred malts. So what was it doing here? The more concerning question was – could that particular label be a total coincidence? An image of a standing white horse was different to the rampant horse used by Kent, or the chess depiction of a knight, but it was too close for comfort and particularly so in his own house. Tom shook off his apprehension, thinking he was overreacting, and prepared breakfast.

Finishing his toast, he opened the lounge curtains to watch for the taxi. Seeing it approach, he slugged back the last of his tea, deposited the cup in the dishwasher and turned towards the door. Before he got there, he heard footsteps and saw Anne descending the stairs. She had a housecoat drawn tightly around her and she looked pale and exhausted, with dark shadows under her eyes. "Tom, we need to talk."

"Yes we do. It's what I've been trying to do for days and what was said over the weekend only scratched the surface. But now isn't the time. I have a flight to catch."

"Where are you going? When will you be back?"

"I truly don't know. I have a meeting in Glasgow this morning and then a flight booked from there to Barcelona. I don't know how long it will take or where I'll be off to then."

"Barcelona? In Spain?"

"It's the only one I know, yes."

"We need to have a proper talk when you get back."

"Yes, we do…" Tom said, but before he was able to say any more, his mobile rang to confirm the taxi was waiting, " but it will have to wait."

Albeit short, it had been one of the longest, most sincere and civil exchanges he'd had with Anne for quite some time. Tom had to pass her on the way out of the door and they both fumbled, clumsily trying to avoid making contact.

Settling into the back of the cab, Tom felt confused. He wasn't sure why Anne suddenly wanted to talk to him. Her attitude was more placatory than he'd experienced for some time. She'd been keen to know when he'd be back. Was it because she wanted to determine how much time she had to reorganise everything and move Arthur back in as a more permanent fixture? Or was it so they could sit down and have the long overdue, serious talk about their relationship; perhaps ascertain how to make the split least painful for both of them and the children. Or could she even be seeking some sort of reconciliation?

He tried to evaluate the possibilities. The first option would imply she had been coldly calculating how to take advantage of their situation. It would be inconsistent with the confession she made on Saturday, when she'd given the impression she wanted to be open and honest and draw a line in the sand. It would have been more in keeping with what he might have expected from his brother, but Arthur hadn't been there to guide and instruct her and they didn't seem to have parted on particularly good terms last night. Tom thought it improbable that Arthur could have subsequently contacted her to persuade her to act so deviously, and so out of character. Such a strategy would mean all-out war.

The second possibility was the most likely. Anne had probably been thinking about how best to handle their separation and she wanted them to work together to find the most practical solution. Anne was usually pragmatic and it would be a natural way for her to respond, once she'd got over the emotional outbursts.

The chance of Anne wanting a reconciliation couldn't be ruled out, but was the most confusing prospect. Perhaps she would want them to co-habit, to make life seem normal for the children or possibly, there was a chance she wanted more? But would she really want them to return to the way they had been? Tom knew he had no wish to go back to the insufferable relationship they'd shared over the last two or three years. He wanted to maintain his connection with the children, but he couldn't go back to the absence of emotion or warmth he'd experienced from Anne. He'd been walking on eggshells for too long already and the one thing the last few days had taught him was it mustn't go on the same way. The love and closeness they'd shared was intense, but it was a distant memory. He still cared deeply, but wasn't certain how strong his emotional attachment was. The revelations of the past few days, the knowledge of the secret she'd kept from him for years – whether or not she was culpable – was so damaging. Her adultery with Arthur was a further major blow. How could he ever forgive her treachery? Tom had little difficulty believing how cruel and manipulative Arthur had been, but it didn't excuse Anne. She was an intelligent woman with a mind of her own. Perhaps Arthur did take advantage of her weakness, but her behaviour was inexcusable.

Tom's head was beginning to throb again. He popped a couple of painkillers and started to think of the day ahead. It was no less complicated, but not so personally draining.

"You look as if you've got the weight of the world on your shoulders," the driver said, viewing Tom in the rear-view mirror.

"I've got a lot to think about and I've got one hell of a headache," Tom replied dismissively. "Sorry, I don't make very good company," he added.

"Don't worry mate, you don't have to. Will you be alright flying? Where are you going?"

"I'll be fine; I've taken a couple of pills. I'm flying to Glasgow."

"So that'll be BA in Terminal 5?"

"You've got it."

Tom was looking forward to getting back to work and when he thought about it, he was particularly looking forward to Sally's company. His spirits lifted at the prospect.

Glancing back in the mirror and seeing Tom's contented expression, the driver continued. "Those pills worked bloody quickly. You'll need to tell me what they are. Can you get them over the counter or do you need a prescription?"

"It's not the pills," Tom replied with a smile. "I was thinking about someone special." He amazed himself –not only with the thought, but more so, having voiced it to a complete stranger. In the short time he'd known Sally, she'd obviously made a big impression. She was someone special; caring, intelligent, charming, challenging and fun to be with, not to mention drop-dead gorgeous. This was the first time Tom had considered what he truly thought of her and he surprised himself with the strength of his feelings. When he thought about his current feelings for Anne, it was like comparing night and day. Where Sally was bright and radiant, Anne's darkness hid too many secrets.

Tom's thoughts were interrupted by a loud roar as two motorcycles raced up behind them, overtook the taxi, then swerved quickly back into their lane, forcing the taxi driver to brake hard.

"Bloody maniacs, they shouldn't be allowed on the roads!" the driver yelled. "I'm doing seventy-five. They must be travelling over the ton. I hope the police stop them – not that they'd ever be able to catch them."

Tom wiped his brow nervously; he'd broken into a cold sweat. He tried to rationalise. There were thousands of bikes on the road. If he was going to have a panic attack every time he saw one, he'd end up in a mental institution.

"Sorry, mate. I didn't mean to give you a shock, but there was nothing I could have done. Are you okay? You've gone awfully pale. Do you need to see a doctor?" the driver questioned.

"No, just get me to Heathrow in one piece and I'll be fine," Tom said.

The bikers weren't connected, but Tom was reminded of his situation and the warnings he'd received. He thought again about the whisky. Where had it come from? He'd intended to ask Anne about it, but he hadn't expected to see her before he'd left and it was too early to phone her, as it might awaken the children. Tom checked his watch and saw it was a little after five a.m. He was making good progress and should arrive with plenty of time to clear security before the seven ten flight. His scheduled landing was eight thirty, so Anne would be busy getting Jenny to school. That might be the best time to call her on the mobile and ask.

Tom disembarked outside the massive new glass and metal structure and took a series of escalators before he snaked past the automated, self-service check-in machines towards the security area. He stood impassively to have his photograph taken, proceeded through the luggage and personal scanners then descended an escalator to the main concourse. Knowing he was through security, Tom felt more relaxed, realising no bikers were able to get near him and no-one could be carrying a weapon of any type. He purchased a coffee and found a seat in the central cafeteria, observing the busy bar, where even this early in the morning, there were hordes of customers gulping down pints of beer.

Once aboard the plane, Tom saw most of the other passengers were as bleary eyed as he was. They stumbled around grumpily, finding their seats and sorting luggage. To fly so early in the morning meant a middle of the night rise and Tom reckoned they must all be in the same boat, so to speak. *As long as the pilot is wide awake,* he thought. Being early on Monday morning, every seat was taken, the plane filled with commuters who spent their weekends at home. He settled into his seat and closed his eyes. His drowsiness had almost overcome him when he heard his name announced.

Looking up, he saw a stewardess standing over him. "You're Mr. Bishop, aren't you? We identified you from the seat manifest."

"Yes, I'm Tom Bishop."

"I have a message. It was left at the gate. You mustn't have noticed when you boarded." She handed Tom an envelope.

A premonition of dread descended on Tom as he ripped at the opening and saw the familiar chequered letterhead. "Where did this come from? Who sent it? What did he look like?"

"I'm sorry sir, I have no idea. It was handed in at the gate and because you didn't collect it, I brought it for you."

Tom yanked at his belt. "Stop the plane, I need to get off."

"No, sir, I'm afraid that won't be possible. You must sit down or I'll have to call for assistance." She pushed Tom back into his seat.

"Yes, of course," he replied unsteadily, aware of the worried stares from the others around him. He did up his belt then removed the note from the envelope apprehensively.

"After withdrawing to safer territory,
Black Bishop is again advancing.
Does this leave Black's home defences weak?
Are you sure this is what you want?"

Bile rose in his throat. He'd been cavalier about continuing his investigation, believing he was the only one at risk. His determination and bravery weren't in question. But this was a new threat. Black's 'home defences'. What did it mean? Was it a challenge against Global Weekly or was Tom's family being threatened? He thought about the whisky in his house again. Had someone already been there? Tom was trapped on the plane. If he'd picked up the message before boarding he could have changed his mind and turned back, but now he couldn't do anything. The plane had finished queuing and was accelerating down the runway in the process of take-off. He was trapped for another hour or more, and then he'd be in Glasgow, four hundred miles away if his family needed him. He couldn't even use his phone or email until they landed. Tom reached up and pressed the call button. The plane was ascending sharply and it was a couple of minutes before the same stewardess returned, her appearance stern.

"The note you gave me before was a threat against my family. I need to get a message to the police, so they can provide protection. Can you have the pilot contact them?" Tom was agitated, but he tried to give an appearance of calmness, not wanting to seem deranged.

"I'll talk to the captain, but it's his decision. Can I take the note to show him?"

"You can show him, but I need it back," Tom said.

She returned moments later, saying the pilot had made a report, but she knew no more.

Tom resigned himself to sitting it out. He tried closing his eyes again but he wasn't able to settle. He opened his laptop and sat it on the pull-down table. He couldn't concentrate on anything and instead drummed his fingers on the case, not initially realising he was beating time to the noise escaping from his neighbour's iPod. He recollected hearing the radio earlier that morning. Another 'New York Minute' and everything had changed again.

A stewardess came around, distributing breakfast trays and Tom placed his computer under the seat. The aroma of hot food was enough to turn his stomach and although Tom accepted a tray, he didn't open the container.

Once they landed, Tom extracted his bag from the overhead locker then barged past other passengers to be one of the first off the plane. He raced into the building and powered up his mobile. The moment he had a signal, he phoned Anne. "Where did the whisky come from?" he blurted without preamble.

"What? What are you talking about? I'm out in the street at the school. I can barely hear you."

"The whisky, the bottle of White Horse whisky in the kitchen. How did it get there?"

"Arthur brought the whisky round. Why?"

"Where did he get it? He doesn't normally drink blends," Tom demanded.

"Tom, have you gone nuts? What's this about? You're acting very strange. He was given it. He told me he won it in a raffle."

Tom breathed a sigh of relief.

"The funny thing was, he said he didn't remember buying a ticket," Anne continued.

Another tingle of apprehension ran up Tom's spine. A myriad of thoughts and questions ran through his mind. Was the whisky a coincidence? Maybe Arthur really had won a raffle. Why would he bring it to Tom's house and leave it in the kitchen? Was Arthur set up? Or could he even be involved? Who was trying to get to Tom and why? Was his family in danger? Should he be flying straight back to protect them?

He didn't want to take any chances. "I want you to take Jenny out of school, go back home and pack a few essentials and then go to your parents' house in Bristol and stay there for a few days."

"I'm doing no such thing. Tom, you really have gone nuts. Was it that bang on your head? You're scaring me, what's this all about?"

Tom spluttered out a confused ramble of words, trying to explain his fears and misgivings.

Anne's tone was caustic when she spoke again. "I think you really have gone mad. Either that, or this is some elaborate plan to get me to leave the house. Has your lawyer put you up to this?"

"No, it's true. Every word is true. I'm really worried. I want you to be very careful."

"If you were that worried, you wouldn't have gone to Glasgow."

"I didn't know until I was already on the flight!" Tom protested. "I'm going to try to catch the next plane back."

"Don't bother. You'd be wasting your time. I don't think I could handle seeing you now." The line went dead.

Tom slumped into a chair. What should he do? He could catch the next available flight south, but what was the point if Anne wouldn't see him, or believe they might be in danger? He couldn't snatch his own children to take them to safety. If he tried, it would be seen as an attempt to steal them from Anne because of their marital difficulties and he might be breaking the law. There was really nothing he could do. He'd warned Anne and he'd have to hope that she'd be careful and act responsibly, and in the meantime, hope his fears were unfounded.

Chapter 17

Completing the long walk from the arrivals gate, Tom descended the stairs, bypassing the luggage reclaim to enter the main terminal.

He checked for signage to show where to collect a taxi and was surprised to see Ahmed rushing towards him. As always, the young man was bright and enthusiastic.

"What are you doing here?" Tom asked, delighted to be greeted by a friendly face.

"I thought I'd collect you and take you to the meeting, so we could talk on the way. I can let you know what I've found. Sally's coming up by train and won't arrive early enough for a pre-meet, but we can call her if there's anything we all need to know before going in. How's your head now? Are you still in pain? You're looking strained, was it a bad flight?"

Instead of answering Tom gave Ahmed the latest note. "This was handed to me on the plane, otherwise the flight was okay."

Ahmed read and reread the warning. "What do you think it means?" he asked.

"That's what I'm worried about. I don't mind taking risks myself, but if my family are at risk, that's something else entirely. I tried calling Anne to warn her, but she won't believe me."

"It doesn't specifically make a threat to you," Ahmed replied, carefully analysing the words. "The previous warning suggested the bishop was in danger, but this one talks about 'Black's home defences'. That suggests to me that this one's not aimed at you personally."

Although not totally convinced, Tom experienced some relief from Ahmed's interpretation. "If not me, then who?" he questioned.

His deliberations were cut short by his phone ringing and Tom saw Stephan's number displayed. He pressed accept, wanting to bring his boss up to date with the latest events.

"Tom, I wanted to give you a heads up. I've been with the police this morning, something really strange happened. It might not be anything, but I thought it best to warn you."

"The police? Are you okay? What happened?"

"When I went out to my car this morning, it was sitting where I'd left it on the driveway, but the windscreen was smashed. There was a large dead bird lying on the bonnet. It seemed to have flown straight into it, but for some reason, the alarm didn't go off."

Tom rubbed his fingers over his forehead, wincing when he touched the bruising. "A large dead bird? What sort of bird?"

"I don't know. It was a big, black bugger. Maybe a crow or something."

Tom's eyes widened. "You mean a large black crow-like bird – as in a rook?"

"Yes. What do you… Oh shit!"

Tom told Stephan about the latest warning he'd received, and his fears for his family. Although struck by a twinge of guilt for being happy to hear about Stephan's problem, Tom was overcome by relief hearing what sounded like a confirmation of Ahmed's interpretation of the note. If Stephan had been targeted, it was the organisation being threatened, not Tom's family.

"Who the fuck's behind all this?" Stephan pondered aloud. "Whoever it is has some serious amount of power if they can reach you in Glasgow and Manchester, get a message delivered to you on a plane, and attack me as well. I suppose it makes sense – if they're strong enough to take on a big international bank, what right do we have to feel safe?"

"Where to from here?" Tom asked, suspecting Stephan might close them down.

"It doesn't bother me to continue," Stephan replied. "Mind you, I don't have that much to lose. I'm game to keep going, but I'm not going to push you into doing anything you're not comfortable with."

"I don't know about comfortable, but I'm not ready to stop now. I think we must be getting close."

"Okay. I'll go back into the police and re-categorise my report as harassment and I'll tell them to link it to what happened to you in Manchester. They might not have taken it too seriously so far, but we'll see what we can do, because I'm not without influence. You'll probably be hearing from them to get your side of the events, too. I'll see if they'll do something about investigating the bike rider, but I think we've got as much, if not more, chance of getting a result ourselves. I don't have any more than I told you already, but I've got a couple of the lads in the office working on it now. Keep me updated on how you get on and we can talk later."

Stephan disconnected the call and Tom turned back to Ahmed. "Things are hotting up."

"My car's parked in the short stay. It's not far." Ahmed led Tom out the terminal and across a road while Tom brought him up to speed with what was happening in London. Ahmed paid what he considered a ransom to have his ticket validated and within a few minutes, they had left the airport and were speeding along the M8 towards the city.

"You said you'd found out some things?" Tom asked.

"It's nothing earth-shattering, but I did a little bit of checking on the internet; you may know most of it already."

"Go on."

"Well, I've been trying to find out more about 'White Knights'. The term has been used an awful lot. There's an appliance company, they sell dishwashers, fridges, freezers, dryers and the like. They're big and they're all over the place, but I think we can rule them out. The other reference is the business term 'White Knight', which is used to describe a friendly investor, one who'll help out a company facing a hostile takeover bid. Often they'll come in with the company's blessing to make a more acceptable takeover offer."

"Hmmm, that has possibilities if it's someone who views himself as a white knight. It doesn't mean he is one though," Tom said.

"On the same theme, it's a term for someone who rushes to the aid of a female in distress, a signification of chivalry," Ahmed explained. "Then there's a series of computer games, the 'White Knight Chronicles', quite highly rated, they're made for PlayStations, and added to that there's a whole load of companies who use 'White Knight' in their names. There's a national laundry service, a Midlands carpet and upholstery cleaner, an estate agency in Reading, a recruitment agency in Winchester, insurance brokerages, intellectual property consultancies, marketing. The list goes on and on."

"What about couriers?" Tom asked.

"I found some who are locally based. But I didn't see any in Kent, or Manchester for that matter. I noted ones in Fife, Cornwall, and Sussex. None of them used a rearing horse or a chess-like logo that I could see, but I can't claim the research was exhaustive."

Tom leaned his elbow on the windowsill, leaning his head against his fist while he thought. "Maybe not, but you've done well. Good work, Ahmed, thanks."

"It doesn't take us much further though, does it?"

"No, but even so, it was research which had to be done."

A call to Sally confirmed she was on the train and expected to get in on time. Ahmed offered to detour past the station to collect her, it would give them an opportunity to compare notes on what they'd discovered over the weekend before the meeting.

Tom left Ahmed sitting in the car, outside the Union Street entrance to Central Station, while he ascended the stairs, checked for the correct platform and stood at the barrier to await Sally's train. It arrived on schedule and she was one of the first to disembark, alighting from the first carriage. Tom's face lit up on seeing her approach; she looked stunning. He inhaled the subtle scent of her perfume as they exchanged a brief hug before he grabbed her case and led her towards the waiting car.

"We'll need to move, we're due there in a few minutes," Tom warned.

Sally hurried around to the roadside, climbed into the back seat, and reached forward to squeeze Ahmed's shoulders affectionately. Tom slung Sally's case in the boot and dashed back to take the front passenger seat. He'd barely closed the door before Ahmed accelerated into the busy traffic flow.

They soon pulled into the car park of the RNB call centre. Once inside, they were sent directly to the eighth floor. Avril, the PA they'd met on the last occasion, was there to greet them from the elevator and usher them to the same room they'd used before.

The room hadn't changed, except it now also housed a large, two-level document trolley, sitting next to the window. It was stacked high with plain, buff coloured, A4 folders, many of them the thickness of a phone book. There were also jugs of hot tea and coffee, and plates of biscuits.

Before they had time to settle into chairs, the door flew open again and Oliver Matthews breezed in, accompanied by Rachel Young, the Communications Manager, but this time instead of DuPont they were accompanied by a second lady. She was slim and petite and appeared to be aged in her early forties. Her expression was troubled, the worry accentuated by sharp, angular features and a long pointed chin. She appeared to have been roused from her sickbed, her complexion was pale, with deep dark rings around her eyes. She wore no cosmetics or jewellery, further exacerbating her sickly appearance.

"Tom, Sally and Ahmed," Matthews greeted, pumping each of their hands enthusiastically, lingering on Sally's as he had before. "Thank you for coming back. You've already met Rachel, but I'd like to introduce you to Catherine Farnham."

When Tom shook hands with Catherine, he experienced a spark of recognition. He stared at her for a minute, before saying, "Your face is familiar, have we met before?"

Sally immediately quipped, "Now that's an old line…"

Catherine smiled faintly. "No, I don't think we've met before, but you may have seen me at Heathrow this morning. I remember seeing you on the plane."

Tom's skin flushed, remembering the fuss he'd made and knowing how outrageous his behaviour must have seemed to an onlooker. "I can explain," he offered defensively. "It's not what you think."

"What's all this about?" Matthews demanded, his gaze skipping from Tom, to Catherine, and back again.

Tom began hesitantly, he hadn't intended on revealing the details of the threats he's received to Matthews, but under the circumstances, he could see no alternative. Once he started talking, the floodgates opened and he told Matthews and the others about the three written warnings, the attack in Manchester and Stephan's car being vandalized; the real or imagined sightings of bikers and the suspect transactions on his bank and credit accounts.

"That's quite a story. I'm sorry to hear about the business with your bank account. We know enough about you to consider you a safe bet. Perhaps I can set you up a credit card with a small limit, to keep you afloat while this business with your accounts gets sorted out." Matthew's suggested. "Perhaps five hundred pounds? I think I could manage that."

Tom studied the man for a moment, wondering if there was any way this could be an attempt on Matthews part to get him on side and if he should consider it a bribe. Figuring it was acceptable, he decided to accept gratefully. He was limited to his business credit card, and had no funds for incidentals he might need. "Thank you, I'd appreciate it."

Matthews smiled. "That's settled then, I'll get it organized for you." Matthews took a moment to take some personal details from Tom, then sent Rachel out of the room briefly to make the arrangements for Tom's new credit card. Once she'd returned, Matthews turned his attention back to Tom. "Your story explains why I didn't hear from you after your trip to Manchester. I suspected you'd found nothing, or you'd have contacted me," Matthews said.

"Actually, what we found was very similar to here. A document had been sent from the local banking centre to the newspaper. The paper treated it as a whistle-blower situation and released an article, and the result rocked the bank's share price."

"You've done very well. Moving on; the first item on my agenda today is Catherine and what happened with the email she appears to have sent. Catherine's been good enough to fly up here for this meeting, and once we've talked everything through with her she'll be free to go back South."

"To be more accurate, you provided the ticket and ordered me to be in Glasgow for this meeting," Catherine stated. Despite her fragile demeanour, she straightened her back and lifted her chin defiantly.

"Well, yes," Matthews replied. "You're a senior employee of this Bank and I asked you to attend this meeting, so we can try to get to the bottom of a problem you're involved in. It's in your own best interest."

"A senior employee who's currently under suspension," Catherine replied tersely.

"You're not under suspension. You're enjoying a fully paid leave of absence to enable the problem to be properly investigated. You've retained your seniority and your benefits and it will stay that way unless we discover a disciplinary issue."

Catherine shook her head. "That wasn't the message given to the media. I'm the sacrificial lamb."

Matthew's frowned, leaning forward in his chair and glaring at Catherine. "Now that's enough. If you have a grievance, you can take it up with me personally. This is neither the time nor place to discuss this, and certainly not in the presence of outsiders."

Catherine began to cry. "Of course, you're right. I'm sorry. This has all been so upsetting. I've given my life to the bank and I've done nothing wrong."

Matthew's face revealed some compassion. "Okay, Catherine, that's what we're hoping to prove. Now let's all sit down so we can make a start." Matthews produced the copy of Catherine's email and placed it on the table in front of her. "What can you tell me about this?"

Catherine took her time and examined the copy carefully. "It looks authentic and the trace codes show it's been sent from my desktop machine. It has my location on it. If someone was signed into my account from a different machine, this code would have been different," she said, pointing. "Also, if it had come from my Blackberry, it would have been totally different. The circulation list is one of my standard lists so that part is right, but the content's all wrong."

"What do you mean?" Sally asked.

"First of all, I would never have made comments like that. Even if I thought them, I'd never have put them in writing. I might have discussed these issues with management, but only in private and nothing would have been recorded. I didn't get to management position I'm in by being stupid. But it's not only that. The whole style of how it's written, it's not me. It's too flowery. Look at any correspondence that I've ever sent and you'll see what I mean."

"But if it was done from your machine?" Ahmed said. "You'd have had to be out of the room. Unless..."

"What?" Matthews asked.

"Unless the machine was hacked into from the outside, or even the server was hacked, to give the impression it came from Catherine's machine," Ahmed continued.

"Could that be done?" Catherine asked, "And if it was, would there be any way to prove it?"

"Didn't you say you couldn't find any traces of it, either in Catherine's sent box or in the inboxes of the supposed recipients?" Ahmed continued.

"Yes, that's true," Rachel confirmed.

"What about the date?" Sally asked. "Were you in your office and working at your machine on that day?"

Catherine examined the paper again. "Yes, I was at work on that date." She examined it more closely. "But wait a minute, the time says 11.40 am. That can't be right. That was the day of Willy Martin's funeral, he was one of my deputies. He took ill and had been off work for months. I attended his funeral, as did most of the office. I'd have been there at the time and there would have been dozens of witnesses to confirm it."

"So if there were very few people about, and your office was empty, anyone might have gone in and used your machine without you knowing?" Sally asked.

"Yes... except my door would have been locked and anyone breaking in would have needed to know my sign-on codes," Catherine replied. Her demeanour was more confident now she had been given an opportunity to fight back.

"Could you have left your machine on accidentally, so that they didn't need to sign in?" Rachel asked.

Catherine stared back at her with narrowed eyes. "Certainly not, I would never be so careless. In any event, after five minutes of non-use the machine goes into hibernation and you need to re-enter your codes to unlock it. What's more, it doesn't explain how there was no recording of the email in any of the machines. Only someone who was expert in computers could set that up."

"One thing we now know for sure –you didn't send the rogue email," Matthews said.

"Thank God for that," Catherine exclaimed. "Will I be able to get back to work now?"

"I'm afraid not," Matthews replied. "We need to find out what's behind all of this, and until we do, we don't want to reveal that we're onto anything. I'm afraid you'll need to stay away from work, on paid leave, for a little while longer."

Catherine smiled. "At least now I might enjoy the break. Up until now, I've been worried sick that I'd be sacked."

Matthews returned her smile. "You can relax knowing you're much safer now, but this can't go beyond these four walls. I can't stress how important this is. I need you to continue giving the impression you're still worried sick. That's all we need from you for now, so you can go home, but please, call me directly if there's anything you need to talk about."

Catherine happily picked up her handbag and walked towards the door, making a visible effort to school her expression back to its previous anxiousness, before going out in public.

"I didn't want to discuss any of this in front of Catherine," Matthews said, once the door had closed. "We've been doing our own research and

I'm going to give you access to it. As well as our own people, we've brought in consultants, specialist forensic accountants from one of the big four. We've been trying to identify all the former customers who maybe harbour a grudge. We have groups of the files pulled so you can look through them. The first batch is on the trolley over there. I'm going to set some rules, however. We're working together on this and any access we're giving you is totally confidential and not for use on anything other than this enquiry. We're sailing close to the wind on privacy rules and data protection here, so you either comply with my demands, or I can't let you near them. You can use a notebook and make your own records, but you're not allowed to copy, scan or photograph anything we make available. We can allow you the use of this room to do your work, but as a security measure, I'll ask you to leave your phones and computers with Avril whenever you're working here. I'll also want one of my people in the room with you at all times. Before you see anything, or I tell you anything more, I need to know these conditions are acceptable and I also want you to sign a confidentiality agreement."

"Wait a minute, we're reporters, we need to be able to write up and publish what we find," Tom protested.

"That's been allowed for in the agreement. I'm not being unreasonable – you can do what you like with anything you source from elsewhere, but you can't use anything you've discovered from what we show you without our consent," Matthews continued. "There's something else, in view of what you've told me, I can help you all with your personal finances."Looking at Tom, he added"As your cards and accounts are blocked, I can set you up with something right away. But the other thing is I'll introduce you all to our special executive banking service. It's normally only for high net worth individuals, but I can swing it for you. There's no real cost to the bank and it will give you special facilities, better rates, lower charges and a whole range of free and discounted services, banking, insurance and general. I can have the facility set up in a matter of minutes and I can provide you with temporary cards until your official ones come through."

For a moment Tom was speechless while he considered the offer. He glanced across at Sally and Ahmed's to gauge their reaction before replying bluntly, "It's an amazing offer, but I'm sorry, we're not for sale. We're in the midst of an investigation into RNB. There's no way we can receive a whole load of benefits we're not entitled to. It would destroy our credibility as independent reporters and it would put a question mark over our integrity forevermore. Yeah, if it's possible for me to have an account with a temporary card set up quickly then I'd appreciate it, but only if it's on normal commercial terms." Having dealt with their personal circumstances, Tom addressed the business issues. "We're not authorised to sign a confidentiality agreement, not without running it past our boss first. We understand your concerns and we want access to the information, but we'll also need to run it past our legal people."

"I see what you mean and I respect you for it," Matthews replied. He handed Tom a sheet of paper "For the basic account, if you can fill out this standard form now, then I'll get it processed and you'll be up and running before you leave the building."

"You can actually do that?" Ahmed asked, clearly impressed.

"Yes I can." Matthews was smiling, relishing Ahmed's unrestrained admiration.

Tom quickly completed the form and Matthews arranged for Avril to submit it for processing.

"For the confidentiality agreement, we can email it to your people now, so that you can get started."

Tom nodded. "I'll call my boss now, tell him it's coming and he'll ensure it's prioritised. We won't be able to start right away, however. We've got a flight booked out of Prestwick this afternoon to check out another angle and won't be back for a couple of days. That's probably beneficial, should allow plenty of time to get the approval sorted out."

"Where are you flying to?" Matthews questioned.

"We're going to Barcelona," Sally said, while Tom put through the call.

Tom finished his call and turned back to Matthews. "I know you can't give details yet, but can you tell us anything about the nature of the information you do have for us?"

Matthews nodded. As he spoke, his eyes leered over Sally as they had on their previous meeting. "We've tried to consider anyone who might have a grouse against the Bank and we've pulled all their files. It's an extensive list. The first thing we identified was ex-employees and then all receiverships and liquidations, any company where an Administrator has been appointed, and all personal sequestrations. It's not that we're particularly aggressive, but because of the size of our organisation there's a big list and of course, it goes international as well. We've cut it down to the last three years, because we imagine that the events which have caused this situation would be relatively recent. Onto that, we've added individuals and companies where we've closed their accounts or told them to take their business away. That happens for a host of reasons. Sometimes it's because of a change in our policies regarding who we want to deal with, and at other times because we've become unhappy with how the account is being operated. We've added customers to the list who have left us after expressing a serious grievance and there's a further list we're working on where we still have the client – in some shape or form – but we've significantly altered the relationship; maybe cut their facilities or forced them to reconfigure their assets. These usually result from us taking action after becoming aware of a serious breach of covenants. Finally, we've compiled a list of individuals and companies who have suffered, because we've called in a guarantee. It's strange, but some people are relaxed about granting a guarantee on their business or to a relative or a friend, never believing there's any chance of it being called in. The silly buggers don't seem to understand the very reason we've asked for it is because the original borrower doesn't have enough security of their own to justify their loan. Then, when the inevitable happens, they get upset and blame us for their misfortune, instead of taking it up with the party they'd given the guarantee for or realising it was their own bloody stupid fault."

Sally felt her skin crawl from Matthews lecherous inspection and her opinion of the man wasn't improved hearing him berate people who'd suffered major losses at the hands of the bank. She understood all banks had to be clinical in their dealings and it was true; often it was the client who had engineered their own downfall – but nevertheless, Matthews approach seemed callous. There was no doubt he had a strong grasp of the numbers, but he seemed incapable of seeing beyond the figures to the multitudes of people whose lives had been affected by the Bank's actions. Worse still, rather than being incapable, perhaps he was untouched by the personal consequences, even relishing others' demise as an exemplification of his power.

"What about your insurance customers? I thought the bank owned a number of insurance companies, providing risk cover as well as investment," Ahmed asked.

"You're right," Matthews replied. "I hadn't even considered them. There must be a load of customers who've been upset when their claims were rejected, or the value of their pensions and investments haven't achieved their expectations. I'll get onto that as well."

"When we last spoke, you mentioned checking disgruntled employees and the potential of stock market manipulation," Tom queried.

"Yes, I did. Any issues we have with current employees are wholly internal. We're checking into them, but I can't give you access to those files. I doubt we'll find anything there, because this whole scam is far too large and sophisticated. That criterion also rules out the vast majority of the contents of the previous lists I mentioned. As for a trading fraud, that's far more complicated. Our shares aren't only traded on the London exchange. There's Wall Street, the Bourse, the Nikkei and the Hang Seng, plus a whole load of smaller exchanges. Anyone in London or New York with a computer, or for that matter in Damascus or Kabul, could arrange a large number of small transactions, which on their own, wouldn't be suspicious – but the aggregate affect would be quite substantial. A more sophisticated investor with access to multiple accounts in multiple names could make serious money, if he had foreknowledge of a price shift. In fact, their own series of transactions might cause some movement in itself. We've checked and there was abnormally high speculation in the Bank's shares falling immediately before each of the revelations. Not enough to be blatantly obvious, but enough to be suspicious. We've submitted a confidential report to the Bank of England, but it's unlikely they'll be able to do much or find out more than we already have."

"So it might be entirely financially motivated?" Ahmed asked.

"It may all be an unfortunate coincidence, but I doubt it. I do think it may be financial," Matthews replied. "But even if it is, then why us? Perhaps we're an easy target, or maybe we've been selected for a personal reason. So we believe it's worth doing all the research."

Tom checked his watch. "We'll need to make a move if we're going to catch our flight." He handed Matthews a sheet of notepaper. "Here's the email address to send the agreement to. If something can be worked out, we should be back here on Wednesday."

"Excellent," Matthews said. He glanced at his watch. "I'll check on your new card." He made a quick telephone call and spoke for a couple of minutes before he disconnected. "All done. You can pick up the new card and PIN number downstairs at Reception. Give it a couple of hours before you use it though, to make sure we get it activated. As I said, I can only give you a five-hundred-pound limit, but it will be better than nothing."

Chapter 18

"Matthews was amazing," Ahmed enthused on the way to the train station. "He'd arranged all that information since we met on Friday and organised some credit for you to be going on with."

"Amazingly crass, is what I'd say. Every time the smug bastard looked in my direction, I felt he was undressing me with his eyes," Sally replied.

Tom nodded cautiously. "I agree with your appraisal of Matthews, Sally. Much as setting up the account has been a good help to me, I'm sure he was trying to play a fast one. Yes, he'd gotten lots of information together, but I'm not sure I trust him. He's a control freak. He wants to have us under his thumb. If we'd accepted what he'd offered then we'd have lost all our independence, anything we've done or do in the future would be tainted. As it is, he's done me a favour in providing a bank account and credit facility, but the only unusual part there was the speed so I don't consider it a problem. Giving us access to those files would be fantastic if it works out, but it's not likely to happen, not with the confidentiality agreement he showed us. I doubt it's as simple and open as Matthews suggested. I only caught sight of one or two of the paragraphs, but my first impression was that it's pretty onerous. We'll have to leave it up to Stephan. He'll get our lawyers onto it and hopefully, they'll be able to negotiate something acceptable. Either that or we won't be playing ball. I'm glad we were already booked to fly to Spain or it would have given RNB an unfair advantage in any negotiations. We'd have been standing about waiting for it to be resolved, and the pressure would have been on our lawyers to make concessions. As it is now, they have free rein to negotiate without being under any such influence."

"You're right, I hadn't thought about all that," Ahmed agreed.

Tom smiled at him. "Sometimes it pays to be a cynic."

No sooner had the train left Central Station than there was a flash of lightning, followed by a dull rumble of thunder. Although it was the middle of the day, there was little light outside and they heard a steady patter of rain hitting the carriage roof.

"It might be a bumpy take-off, providing we do get off at all. I hope we don't get delayed," Tom said. He glanced at Sally and noticed her colour had drained and there was a glow of perspiration on her brow.

"I don't like it," she replied nervously.

"Are you okay? You look a bit fragile," Tom asked.

"I lied to you last week," Sally confessed. "I didn't have an ear infection. I don't like flying at the best of times. I have to, of course, or I couldn't do my job, but I don't like it and I always have to take Valium before I board. I can just about handle it normally, but when it's stormy like this, I get really nervous."

"I wouldn't have pegged you as being afraid of flying," Ahmed said.

"I'm not afraid of flying, I'm afraid of crashing," Sally replied, forcing an artificial grin.

"But that's completely irrational," Ahmed replied. "Statistics I've read show that flying is the safest form of transport. You've got more chance of being killed or injured on a train, or in a car."

Sally smiled wryly. "Thank you, Ahmed. That makes me feel so much better, when we're sitting on a train on our way to the airport. Besides, I think you'll find that walking is the safest form of transport." She shook her head. "I'll be okay. I wouldn't miss this trip for anything. Don't worry, I won't try to open the emergency door mid-flight. I'll just be a bit anxious, that's all."

"At least you'll have us for company and reassurance," Tom offered.

"*That* prospect gives me so much confidence." Sally retorted.

By the time they reached Prestwick, heavy rain was lashing the platform. Collecting their luggage, they hurried under cover and ascended the escalator to take the enclosed walkway across to the terminal.

Noting there was only a smattering of shops and eating places, Tom suggested they went through security first to see if there was more variety in the departure lounge.

Clearing security, they discovered the main departure lounge was similar to the outer terminal. It was clean and airy with a high ceiling, but the décor and furnishings were old and worn. The central area was filled by rows of clinical metal seats, but besides the duty free, the only vendor was a WH Smith bookshop and newsagent, and for food, there was a cafeteria, a coffee shop and a bar/restaurant.

Tom looked about, disappointed. "I was hoping for a decent lunch before we flew. Let's see what the menus look like." After a quick scan of alternatives, they decided they wanted to stock up on calories before the journey and opted for fish and chips from the bar, tempering their excess with bottles of spring water.

Waiting for their food to arrive, Sally went for a walk to explore, returning a couple of minutes later. "Did you see the presentation on the wall over there? This airport claims the distinction of being the only place in Britain where Elvis ever visited. It was in 1960, while he was serving in the American forces and his plane touched down here on its way from Germany back to the States." Sally was bubbling with enthusiasm.

"Yeah, I think I remember reading about it. I've never been that much of a fan. I can't under-stand the popularity for all these impersonators. I suppose he was before my time and I'm more into rock music," Tom said, sounding fairly dis-interested. "I'm pleased you're happy about it. It seems to have made your day."

"It's nothing to do with the music, you dolt. Don't you see? Elvis Presley, he was the 'King'."

Tom absorbed the information before exclaim-ing, "Sally, you're a genius! Stephan's surname is Presley. That's the link! He must be the 'Black King' referred to in the warnings."

"It's another clue solved," Sally replied. "We don't know any more about who's behind this, but we've got a slightly better idea about how his mind works."

They toasted their small success by clinking their cups of water together, then heard loud cheering from nearby.

Tom spun around on his chair to discover a procession of elves walking by. "What the hell!" Tom exclaimed.

The three sat open-mouthed, staring as twenty young men, all dressed in bright green tunics and tights and wearing pixie hats, approached the bar with a declared intention to drink it dry before their departure. Their raucous laughter filled the entire hall. For anyone who hadn't guessed their purpose, it was explained by a label attached to each of their backs declaring they were members of 'Andy's Stag Party.'

"Please don't let them be on our flight," Sally whispered.

Ahmed studied the departure screen. "There's a flight about an hour after ours, going to Derry, maybe that explains the costumes. Perhaps they're leprechauns."

Any optimism they retained was deflated when the assembled revellers burst into a poor attempt at a chorus of the Queen song, 'Barcelona'.

Although he was disturbed by the volume of noise from the party-makers, Tom saw a silver lining – it was providing a distraction for Sally from her fear of the imminent flight.

Finishing their meal, Tom, Sally and Ahmed found seats in the relative quiet at the far side of the lounge. Tom took the opportunity to call Stephan and advise him of the Presley link.

"I should have realised it myself," Stephan replied. "Everyone called me 'Elvis' when I was growing up. It never occurred to me that there was a connection. Tell Sally she was bloody clever to figure it out."

"I will," Tom agreed, glancing down at Sally and offering her a reassuring smile.

Stephan continued. "Listen, I was talking to my friend Philippe in Barcelona and there are a couple of things to note. He'd arranged for the reporter involved in the story to be available to talk to you when you got there but since then, the guy's been sent out on an assignment and he's not been in the office since. Speak to Philippe when you get there and see what's planned now. The reporter's name is Abdon."

"

"It name doesn't sound Spanish, or even French for that matter."

"No, I asked exactly the same question. It's Catalan, apparently. You need to remember there's a strong Catalan independence movement, so be careful what you say if you don't want to create an international incident."

"Noted."

"The second thing is there are roadworks on the main highway from the airport into the city, and its creating major delays. Normally, the best way in is by taxi, but you'd be better to take the train instead. You'll be arriving at El Prat, Terminal 2. All you have to do is go out the front doors, there's an enclosed bridge to take you over the road. Once in the station, there are two platforms, but they're both the same, operating a shuttle service into the city every half hour or so. Go to whichever one has a train in it first. The journey only takes about thirty minutes and you get off at Sants, that's the main station. From there, take a cab to the paper."

"Sounds good. How are you after this morning's episode?" Tom asked.

"I'm bloody annoyed. I lost more than three hours this morning, trying to sort out the repair for my car and then with the police. I want to get the bastards responsible, even more now than I did before. But some good news, the legal department are already a good way through the agreement and working out terms."

Their conversation finished just as the flight was called and Tom, Sally and Ahmed moved forward to board.

Thinking it best if Sally didn't travel in an exit seat, Tom selected a row about a third of the way back. On his suggestion, Ahmed took the window seat, with Sally in the middle and Tom in the aisle.

"You've had your Valium?" Tom queried.

"Oh yes, I took it early so the effects would kick in long before I had to board. The taxiing and then take off are the worst parts," she replied.

As the plane filled, Tom was disappointed to see most of the elves found seats in rows close by.

When the engines fired up and the plane began to manoeuvre towards the runway, Sally extended her hands and grasped Ahmed and Tom's, holding on with a vice like grip. Her grasp grew even tighter as the plane accelerated down the runway and the wheels lifted away from the tarmac.

Buffeted by strong winds, the plane vibrated profusely and lurched from side to side. Sally's face was chalk-white and perspiration ran from her brow.

"Are you okay?" he enquired.

"No," she blurted, then threw both her arms around Tom's shoulders and pulled him close.

He held her, feeling her body trembling. Much as he regretted her discomfort, he had to admit to enjoying the sensation of her body close to his. He continued the hug as the plane approached cruising altitude and began to level out.

Sally was beginning to relax when the plane rocked as it was hit with turbulence. There was a loud noise and some shaking, accompanied by yelps and shrieking from some of the more inebriated stag party passengers.

Sally buried her head on Tom's shoulder and held on tightly. He cradled her head in one hand while the other stroked her back reassuringly, occasionally whispering comforting words in her ear. Her breaths were coming in deep gasps and as a result, her breasts heaved against his chest. His head was close to hers and he pressed his lips to her hair above her brow. Much as he was sympathetic for Sally, this was the closest female contact he'd had for some considerable time and Tom was enjoying the sensation, growing mildly aroused. Out the corner of his eye, Tom spotted

Ahmed, wedged into the corner of his seat. He seemed embarrassed by the display of affection between Tom and Sally and tried to cover for it by showing great fascination in the contents of the in-flight magazine.

Once clear of the storm, the plane stabilised and settled into a smooth pattern of flight. The pilot made an announcement, apologising for the discomfort and he advised that he expected plain sailing for the rest of the journey. A whoop went up from the stag party, amidst simultaneous yells and beckoning the stewardess to bring the drinks trolley.

To Tom's disappointment, Sally prised her head off his chest. "I think I'm okay now. Thank you for taking care of me."

"Anytime," Tom replied. "I can honestly say it's the first time I've enjoyed turbulence on a flight." He grinned mischievously. "I'm hoping the pilot's wrong and there might be some more before we reach Barcelona."

"You really are a cruel bastard sometimes, Tom Bishop. Do you know that?" Sally said, but she tempered her words with a bright grin.

Tom smiled back, admitting to himself that though his words had been spoken in jest, they'd held a strong foundation of truth.

"We haven't had time to talk properly yet. You haven't told me what happened with your sister," Tom asked.

Sally's face took on a wearied look. "There's not much to tell really. I tried several times, calling her to apologise and I sent a text, but she wouldn't pick up or answer. I followed your suggestion and went to my Mum's house. I stayed with her the last two nights. I didn't call in advance, I just arrived. She was pleased to see me although she seemed unsure at first. When I explained what had happened she was okay about it, but I don't know whether she really believed me until the police phoned and then came round to take my statement. Afterwards she was all sweetness and light. She helped me to get through to everyone Liz had invited over and it all worked okay, but not with Liz herself. She either wasn't home or wasn't answering; not even my Mum's calls and her mobile went straight to voicemail.

"She's always been a stroppy cow and when we were growing up she'd go into sulks for weeks when she didn't get her own way. She's not stupid. In fact, she's probably a lot smarter than me, but she never makes the effort to do anything she doesn't want to and always tries to take the easy way out. She could have gone to Uni and made her own career. She was brilliant at languages, but instead she left school at sixteen to work in a supermarket. A year later she was pregnant and managed to get her own council house. Since then she's lived off the system. We're of a different mind-set."

Tom nodded.

"She always resented what I had, but she could have been the same if she'd only been prepared to work for it. As you can probably judge, we've never really got on."

"Another case of sibling rivalry?" Tom said.

"More like a barrel load than a case," Sally replied. "But on that subject, whatever happened with your brother? The last I heard you couldn't get hold of either him or Anne. So tell me what happened to you at the weekend."

Tom's smile faded. "I don't want to go into details. As far as I'm concerned, I don't have a brother anymore. Arthur doesn't exist. As for Anne, I'm pretty sure our marriage is over. I learned some unwelcome truths and none of it can be brushed under the carpet. I've spoken to a lawyer about handling divorce proceedings. What it boils down to, is that I'm a single man again." Tom forced a brief smile, then turned away.

Sally said nothing, only placed her fingers on his arm in a comforting gesture. He turned his wrist to grasp her hand and gently squeezed.

The remainder of the journey passed without event. Towards the end, Tom talked inanely to distract Sally's attention from the incredible scenery outside as they crossed low over the Pyrenees. Ahmed's eyes were glued to the window. When the plane made its final approach, they sat as they had for take-off, Sally gripping their hands anxiously. Moments later, the plane touched down.

After disembarking and walking for what felt like an eternity, they found the train station. They followed a procession of passengers onto the crowded platform and then, when the train pulled in, fought their way on board to secure the last available seats. Many passengers were standing but it wasn't too crowded by the time they got underway.

They were 'entertained' by a busker attempting to play an accordion. As he came collecting between numbers, Tom extracted a few euros from his wallet before replacing it in his trouser pocket. He thought no more about it. But when they arrived at Sants and Tom was standing in line behind Sally and Ahmed, waiting to alight, he felt a warmth and slight sensation of movement on his leg. His hand reflexively patted at his thigh, fortunate to be in time to contact the hand of a young lady as it was being withdrawn from his pocket. Shocked at being caught, she pulled back quickly and ran off heading for a different door. It took a moment for Tom to realise he'd foiled a pickpocket and only found voice to shout, "Stop, Thief" when it was already too late.

Hearing his call, Sally and Ahmed turned back, "What is it? Who was it? What happened? Did they get anything?" they queried competing to fire their questions.

"That girl, she's gone now. I almost caught her. She had her hand deep in my trouser pocket," Tom replied.

"Are you sure she wasn't only being friendly?" Ahmed chuckled.

"I'm certain it was my wallet and not my family jewels she was after," Tom said.

"Did she get anything?" Sally asked.

"She almost did, but she let go when I tried to grab her," Tom answered.

"I know what's happened," Ahmed said. "When you opened your wallet to give the busker money, she's watched where you put your wallet and when you were standing in the crowded queue she'll have thought you were easy prey. It might be she even follows the busker around seeking out targets and possibly they even work together."

"Should we go to the police? Do you want to report it?" Sally said.

"No, she's gone already. Besides, I think we've had enough of the police recently and here there's the added language problem."

Chapter 19

With tension heightened by the pickpocketing incident,, the three reporters walked through the massive concourse of Sants station, following directions to locate an exit with a taxi rank.

Tom spied an ATM. "Wait a minute, I want to check this new card and see if it's been activated yet. I need some cash." Tom extracted the card from his wallet, slotted it into the machine, and keyed in the four-digit PIN.

"That's strange," he said. "Matthews said there'd be a limit of five hundred pounds on the card, but this machine says I can withdraw up to a thousand euros. I'd better phone the bank and check." Tom took the card from the machine, checked for the phone number on the back, and called the banking centre to query his account details.

"The evil bastard," he muttered when he'd disconnected the call. "He's set me up!"

"What is it Tom?" Sally questioned.

"This is meant to be a brand new account with a zero balance and a five-hundred-pound credit facility, but I asked them to check the balance and there's been ten thousand pounds lodged in the account since it was opened. Matthews is trying to bribe me! Unbelievable!"

Tom dialled the direct mobile number he had for Matthews; it was answered on the third ring. Before Matthews had time to identify himself, Tom burst into a furious tirade. "What the fuck do you think you're up to? Do you think I'm some sort of idiot? I don't want your fucking money! Maybe you think you can go through your cosy little life buying people, but I'm not for fucking sale! You can't buy me, Matthews! And to prove it, I'm going to bury you for trying!"

Sally rested a gentle hand on Tom's shoulder, "Steady on," she whispered. "If you want to get anywhere, you should give him a chance to explain."

Matthews spoke from the other end of the line. "Tom, I've got no idea what you're talking about, but don't go making threats against me, particularly ones you're not in any position to carry out. If you'd like to calm down and tell me what you're on about, we can see what's happened."

Still battling with his temper, Tom allowed Sally to take the phone and explain about the money in his account, but then she held the phone so that Tom would be able to overhear Matthews response.

"Tell Tom I'll forgive him for his outburst, but he'd better not make a habit of it. I won't abide anyone talking to me like that. I can understand what he thought, but I swear on everything I hold dear, it wasn't me. I don't know how the money got into his account. It's got me worried. The account was only set up a few hours ago and hardly anyone knew about it. So how did they find out? Who can be behind this? And how on earth can they have known about the account and lodged that sort of money into it? We have strict money laundering laws and it's not easy to move money around without it being traceable. Leave this with me and I'll see what I can find out. In the meantime, tell Tom not to use the account. I'll try to work out something else."

Sally rang off and explained what Matthews had said to Ahmed, then looked up into Tom's eyes. "I don't like the man and I definitely wouldn't trust him, but I think he was being truthful. He sounded genuinely shocked to me."

"But if it wasn't him, who could it be?" Tom demanded. "How many other people knew about the account? There are very few possibilities. Other than us, there was only Matthews, Rachel Young and whoever set it up."

"There'd have been other people involved in creating the card and the account," Ahmed contributed. "Someone must have been monitoring what was going on, tracing anything where your details cropped up."

"Aren't you getting a bit '1984'? Is Big Brother watching everything?" Tom said scornfully.

"Is it really so inconceivable with today's technology? Is it less likely than it being Matthews? What does he stand to gain?" Ahmed demanded.

Tom rubbed his fingers against his temples tiredly. "I really don't know. If it is someone or something so powerful, what chance have we got of breaking it down? And if we do, what chance have we got of surviving the fallout?"

On that sober note, they silently located a taxi to take them to the newspaper offices.

It only took a few minutes for their taxi to arrive at a large glass and metal building which towered skywards. Walking into the reception, Tom used his vague smattering of Spanish to announce who they were and who they wanted to see.

Much to Ahmed and Sally's amusement, in perfect English and with no detectable accent, the receptionist advised them they were expected and directed them to Philippe's office. He came out to welcome them when they arrived. He was a dapper man, slim and of average height, clean-shaven with thin blonde hair which rolled down to his shoulders. He was dressed in a loose fitting, cream coloured, linen suit and open necked shirt. With a casual and comforting approach, he ushered them into his office where stylish armchairs were set up in front of the large desk, piled high with files which almost obscured his computer monitor.

"Stephan asked me to take good care of you, so before we begin can I get you some coffee, or would you prefer..." He beckoned towards a row of filing cabinets. On top were four tumblers and a bottle of Carlos I, Spanish brandy. Next to them was a large glass ashtray holding the stubs of three cigars, as well as an extinguished, half-smoked one. The ashtray was positioned immediately below a sign proclaiming 'Prohibito fumar'.

They declined the proffered hospitality, accepting some filtered water.

Philippe began. "I'm very sorry, but I have some bad news for you. Abdon is not here. I'd expected him back in time to meet you, but he has had an accident. He was assigned a story this morning which shouldn't have taken long. He was sent up to Ceret, across the border, in France. He was working on a story about bull-fighting. The traditional type, where the bulls are killed, has been banned here in Catalonia, but it's still allowed in France."

"Really? I thought the other side of the border was Catalonia too?" Sally asked.

"Yes, historically that is true, but in modern terms, Catalonia stretches to the border and the area that's now situated in France, we now refer to as Northern Catalonia. Northern Catalonia is technically in a different country and comes under French, not Spanish laws. On a regional basis, they have different administration and different rules. In cultural terms we are all Catalan, but it's more complicated than that."

"I see," Sally replied unconvincingly.

"Getting back to Abdon; he finished what he was doing this morning but went to visit his cousin, who lives in Collioure, on his way home. He'd intended to return after lunch. However, I'm afraid he had a mishap. He slipped getting out of his car at his cousin's home and sprained his ankle. He's unable to drive for a few days. I'm sorry you have had a wasted journey."

"Are you not able to help us?" Tom said, sounding frustrated.

"Of course, I'll tell you everything I know, but it isn't much. You really need to speak to Abdon and unfortunately, he has the file with him, as he was planning to read it to reacquaint himself with the details before he met with you."

"Could we travel to Collioure to visit him?" Sally asked.

"I'm sure that could be arranged, but if you're using public transport, it's not an easy place to get to from here. You'd be best to hire a car, if you're happy to drive."

"I don't see why not," Tom replied. He glanced at Ahmed. "Would you be happy to drive?"

Ahmed grinned. "Sure."

"Did you bring your driving licence? You'll need it to hire a vehicle," Philippe asked. Ahmed nodded, patting his pocket. "I never travel without it."

Philippe smiled, and glanced at his watch. "It's late. There's no point travelling up there tonight, you'd never find accommodation if you did. I suggest you spend the night in Barcelona and set off in the morning when you're fresh."

Tom inclined his head. "Thank you. You've been most helpful. Can I ask you one more thing? Will you phone Abdon and set up a meeting with us for tomorrow morning?"

Philippe agreed, calling Abdon immediately. "It's all arranged. I've set it up for noon, to give you plenty of time to get there. He's going to make a booking for lunch at Didier's restaurant. It's at the front, overlooking the harbour. You can't miss it."

"That's great, thank you very much. Can you suggest a good hotel for us to stay at?"

"I can get you a good deal with the Ayre Rosellon; I have a friend there. It's four star and well located next to Sagrada Familia. It has wonderful views."

"Sounds excellent. We'd better book in for two nights," Tom said.

Philippe picked up his phone again. "Will that be three rooms?"

"Yes, it will," Sally replied immediately.

A few minutes later, Phillipe disconnected the call and looked up at them and smiled. "All organised. I'm leaving to go home now, I can drop you there. It's on my way."

By the time they'd checked in, deposited their luggage and met up again in reception, it was already nine o'clock.

"Is anyone hungry? Personally, I'm still quite bagged up after the fried lunch. I want to eat something, but it'll need to be something light," Sally suggested.

"I'm the same," Tom said. "I wouldn't mind a walk to get some fresh air. We had a really early start and we've been cooped up all day. Perhaps we'll see something to eat that appeals while we're out."

"I can always eat, but I can't say I'm starving," Ahmed said. "Some fresh air would be good though."

Walking through the front doors, they were awestruck as they craned their necks to peer up at the enormous, looming structure of Gaudi's famous creation. They approached it and walked around the perimeter. Sally read aloud a sign she discovered, explaining how construction of the as-yet-incomplete church had begun in 1882 and it was still only twenty-five percent finished by the time of Gaudi's death in 1926.

Turning away, Tom was attracted to an on-street churro stand which he found irresistible, and they each treated themselves to a bag.

Only halfway through, Tom doubted the wisdom of their purchase, not only had they consumed even more fried food, this time it was sugar-coated as well. They found an open convenience store and purchased water and colas to wash away the greasy aftertaste.

No sooner had they turned back towards their hotel, Tom's mobile rang. The display revealed Matthews' direct number.

Matthews wasted no time coming to the point, "Tom, I've been working on this since we last spoke and I have some good news and some bad news."

"Hit me with the bad news first."

"I've been trying to research what happened to your account. I was able to trace the money coming in – that was the easy part. It was transferred from the current account of one of our octogenarian customers living in Salford. I can't give you his name, but there's no chance he was involved, as he's been in hospital for the past month or more and he's at death's door. At the same time as the money came out of his account, an identical amount went in, so anyone who examined his finances wouldn't see anything wrong, or at worst think there'd been a bank error and it had been corrected. Tracing how the money came to him was more complex, but we've tied it down to an international transfer from a division of an American-owned bank, located in Cyprus. We're trying to see if they can tell us anything, but so far we haven't had a lot of cooperation and I don't expect much. It's a bank known to specialise in international trading with the Middle East, and they don't have the same level of corporate governance as we have. So I'm afraid, it's a dead end."

Tom raised an eyebrow. "Okay, so what's the good news?"

Matthews paused for a moment. "This is going to sound a bit complicated, and to be honest, it's not entirely legal, so I want to keep this between you and me. Don't even let Sally and Ahmed know."

Tom was immediately suspicious. He didn't trust Matthews and wasn't comfortable with his suggestion of keeping secrets from Sally and Ahmed. "Let me know what you're planning, and I'll think about it." He took a few steps away from the others, so that he could talk privately.

"I want to help you with your finances, but it's not easy. I've closed down the account we set up for you and transferred the balance to a suspense account, so it's not linked to you in any way. I've been trying to think of a way you can have an account, without risk of anyone tampering with it.

To be honest, I got the idea from whoever tapped into the one we set up today."

"What's the idea?"

"Okay. Step one; we set up another new account, but this time we use a variation of your name and a different address. I've checked all your data and saw your middle name is Edward, so we can set it up as Edward Bishop or Edward T. Bishop and use your work address. You'll be able to use the account to receive your salary, but otherwise it shouldn't have any links to you. I'd go so far as to recommend you having your salary paid by cheque, so there isn't any record of the account at Global."

"Okay," Tom said slowly.

"Step two; we set up a second account, let's say in the name Tom Edward, again at a linked, but false address so it's not directly associated with you. I'll arrange for you to have cards attached to this account. Following this I can create a mechanism so that whenever money is paid into your first account, it will automatically transfer straight out and into an overseas account, and an identical sum will be deposited from abroad *into* the second account."

"I'm sorry, I'm really not following," Tom admitted.

Matthews voice remained patient. "It's all rather convoluted, but it will give you working capital and it should be almost impossible to trace. It's important you don't do anything to link the new card to you, or else you'll be back to where you started – or worse. Don't use it in any hotels or restaurants where people could see you making a purchase. Don't use it for mail order purchases where it can trace you back to your address. Ideally, only use it to withdraw cash and only do that in places where you're not being watched. Cash is almost untraceable and you can use it to make purchases or Fedex payments. The most important thing, as I said at the beginning, is that I want no-one else to know about it, so there's no chance of the information leaking out."

"It sounds incredibly complicated," Tom muttered.

"It is," Matthews replied, "and I'm really running rings around the money laundering laws, which is another reason I don't want anyone to know. I could get into huge trouble for doing this.

Do you want me to set it up? I can do the ground-work and finish it off when you get back to Glasgow."

"I don't know," Tom began doubtfully. He thought for a moment longer. "Wait – yes I suppose so," Tom replied.

Matthews voice was dry when he responded. "You don't sound too enthusiastic. This is for you, Tom, I don't need to do any of this."

"I'm sorry. I'm very tired and it's all rather confusing. I really appreciate what you're doing. It's kind and thoughtful of you. Yes, please go ahead."

"Don't think it's only out of kindness. I can see what you've done and the chances you're taking. I reckon I need your help if RNB is ever going to solve this mystery and turn things around. So we're in this together. You scratch my back, and I scratch yours. We don't need to like it, but I think we need to play on the same side and work to-gether if we're going to have any chance of suc-cess."

"You're right, I guess. Go ahead and set it up."

Tom ended the call and saw Sally and Ahmed watching him expectantly. "That was Matthews.

He's been trying to trace where the money came from that went into my account, but he's reached a dead end."

"And that's it?" Sally asked, sounding dubious. "You seemed to be talking for a long time. What else is he doing?"

"That's it," Tom replied with a shrug. "He spoke about different checks he can make and how he'll try everything possible to get to the bottom of it, but he wasn't hopeful." Tom felt guilty about lying, but he saw some merit in what Matthews had said and what he'd asked of him. The less people who knew what was being proposed, the better.

Sally appeared sceptical, but she said nothing more.

"I need to get some sleep before I fall over," Tom said, thinking it might be best to get back to the hotel and hopefully, by morning, Sally and Ahmed would have forgotten about his conversation with Matthews.

They detoured briefly at the hotel to speak to the night porter, and put in place arrangements for a car hire in the morning and then retired to their rooms.

Tom collapsed into bed, so tired he didn't have the energy to undress. Despite his exhaustion, he wasn't able to sleep at first. The day's developments continued to roll through his mind, and he wondered again whether he'd been wrong to accept Matthews' offer of help.

Pondering the dilemma, he decided that even if he couldn't tell Sally and Ahmed, he needed to make some sort of record of the arrangement, in case Matthews was setting up an elaborate trap. He got up and pulled a pad of paper from his bag, then made detailed notes of what had happened and what was planned with the accounts. He sealed the information into an envelope, then placed the envelope in a second envelope addressed to Bernard Carter, his new lawyer. He put a note inside explaining that the inner envelope should only be opened in the event of his death or in case of some significant accident or emergency.

Purged of his worries, Tom finally fell into a deep sleep.

Chapter 20

Tom, Sally and Ahmed rose early, raring to go. They breakfasted on fresh breads, cold meats and cheeses, washed down with fruit juice and rich dark coffee, then went to locate their car. All the arrangements had been made and a four door Ford Fiesta was sitting at the front of the hotel.

Ahmed was nervous about driving at first, taking his time to acclimatise to driving on the right. He grumbled, more than once, about adjusting to changing gears with his right hand without losing control of the steering. Traffic was heavy and slow moving, which proved to be a blessing, allowing Ahmed more time to manoeuvre and change lanes.

Once onto the main route out of the city, they see-sawed between fast bursts of speed on clearer stretches and crawling nose to tail at other times. Ahmed grew more confident and comfortable, but Tom showed signs of extreme tension at the many motor bikes which weaved in and out of the traffic. He tried to convince himself that he was being over-sensitive, but couldn't stop himself from breaking out in a cold sweat every time a biker paused, leaning on their car when they were stopped at traffic lights.

He was relieved once they'd cleared the city limits and were able to proceed at high speed along the AP-7 toll motorway north.

"I've never been to the Costa Brava, but I recognise so many of the place names I see on the road signs," Ahmed commented. "There's Sitges; isn't that where they hold an international horror film festival?"

"Yes, it is," Tom answered. "And if you stay on this road for about another four hundred kilometres, you'll come to Cannes, which is even better known for movies."

They chatted as they made progress northwards. Passing Figueres, Ahmed remarked on a sign depicting the Salvador Dali museum. "I'd like to go there, if we only had time. I really love his work."

"Yes, and speaking of work, that's what we're here for," Tom said. "I'm afraid we don't have time for sightseeing. But if you're interested, Dali grew up in this area and spent a lot of time in a small coastal town not far from here. It's called Cadaques. It's beautiful and it's worth a visit if you ever have the opportunity."

"You seem to know a lot about these things," Ahmed pointed out.

"I'm no expert, but I've got an interest in art. Many artists have visited or worked in these parts, particularly in the Pyrenees, because the air is so clear and the light is good. Picasso, Chagall, Miro, Matisse and many more. As you're from Glasgow, you might be interested to know Rennie Mackintosh spent time here as well. I read somewhere that there's a Mackintosh museum in Port Vendres, only a couple of miles from Collioure. It's linked to the Mackintosh museum in Glasgow."

As their conversation continued, Tom became aware of Sally's extended silence. She was normally so bubbly and to remain quiet was unlike her.

"Are you feeling alright? You're very quiet." Tom enquired.

Sally turned from staring out the window. "I'm fine," Sally replied. "I don't have anything to say. I know you're keeping something from me and consequently, I don't really feel like chatting."

Tom suffered a stabbing pain in his stomach. What could he say? He hadn't been comfortable keeping secrets and now he was being challenged, he had no viable defence. *Why on earth had he listened to Matthews?* he thought. He'd never liked or trusted the man and his earlier concerns were being justified. It was the first time he'd followed Matthews' advice; now it was driving a wedge between him and Sally. But Matthews' request had made sense, too. Was this situation engineered by Matthews, to cause trouble?

"You're right. I have kept something from you. Matthews talked through a formula he's devised, to give me an operational bank account without it being at risk of being tampered with. It's nothing whatsoever to do with the enquiry and he swore me to secrecy. I can't say I fully understand what he was talking about, but even so, I'm not meant to say to anything to any-one. I'm sorry, I should have explained before." Tom felt better, even though his response had still been quite cryptic, to keep the details se-cret. He turned to Sally, staring earnestly into her eyes. "Honestly, that's all there is to it."

"Why didn't you say so before?" she asked.

"I don't know. He said to tell no-one, and I fol-lowed his instruction."

"Since when did Matthews set the rules?" Sally vented angrily, but at least she seemed to be re-suming her normal attitude.

"Do you forgive me?" Tom asked sheepishly.

"How could I ever stay angry with you?" Sally asked, although her lips remained pursed.

Clearly excited, Ahmed interrupted, "That sign says we're approaching the border. Do you have your passports ready?" The last stretch had been a steady ascent into the foothills of the Pyrenees and he eased back on the accelerator as the terrain became more craggy and moun-tainous with sensational views.

"Only one kilometre to go," Tom said, pointing to another sign.

They drove past a line of low buildings and continued forward, then the road began to descend steeply.

"That's really odd, we should have been there by now," Ahmed said, sounding puzzled.

"We are there," Tom replied with a grin. "We've already crossed into France. Look, the road-signs are in French, not Spanish."

"But how can that be?" Ahmed asked. "There was no frontier."

"It's very relaxed now, it's all European Community. The buildings we passed a while ago are for the border control, but they only stop people and do checks when there's someone they're looking for, perhaps suspected traffickers or ETA terrorists," Sally explained.

"I thought ETA was the Basque separatists. Isn't the Basque region on the opposite side of the country, at the Atlantic?" Tom asked.

"They are, but that doesn't mean they don't travel and transport weapons at this side. I've heard of a number of successful raids in this region," Sally continued.

"Well, I'm getting quite an education on this trip. They say travel broadens the mind and I'm beginning to understand the justification. Having knowledgeable company helps of course," Ahmed added. "Oh look, the satnav's telling me to take the next exit. A town called Le Boulou."

"I knew it wasn't far into France, but I didn't realise it was so close to the border," Tom said.

After leaving the motorway, they proceeded towards the coast, following the robotic instructions from the satnav. Already late morning, the temperature was rising and the sky was a faultless, clear blue. Before long the Mediterranean came into view with the horizon becoming indistinct. There was a lack of clarity where the sky stopped and the sea began.

The road took them through the hills, where they passed a number of interesting terraced vineyards. With some reluctance, they resisted the temptation to view or sample on the way at the many roadside shops and bodegas.

Arriving in Collioure, Ahmed followed signs for the town centre, looking for parking facilities as he went. They passed no spaces and Ahmed was verging on panic, squeezing through narrow gaps between carelessly parked vehicles before reaching a small square, near the harbour, in the shadow of a castle. All spaces in the square itself were occupied, but there was a parking sign and a barrier in the corner. Seeing no alternative, he thought he'd give it a try and drove up a steep slope to a large area of undeveloped, hilly ground, which was partly tarmacked. It was almost entirely covered by a haphazard matrix of deposited vehicles, giving the impression they'd been abandoned, rather than parked. After driving around for several minutes, Tom spotted a small, triangular shaped space, which he thought was capable of housing the Fiesta, wedged between two much larger vehicles. With Tom's assistance to guide him and with the mirrors turned in, Ahmed succeeded in parking their car.

They had arrived early, which gave them half an hour to walk along the sea wall, examine battlements and explore the town. Tom found it quaint and appealing, his attention drawn to the many shops and galleries and the artists trying to capture the picturesque scenery.

Shortly before noon, they returned to the harbour area seeking the restaurant. They had little difficulty finding it and were shown to a table close to the windows with views overlooking the sea. Recognising Abdon wasn't a problem because they saw a young man hobbling in their direction. He was carrying a small briefcase in his left hand and his right arm was wrapped around a crutch, providing support. He was looking around at other diners, until his glance settled on them and his face broke into a broad smile. "You must be the English?" he checked.

"Yes and you're obviously Abdon," Tom replied, standing and extending his right hand in greeting before realising Abdon needed to balance on his crutch and wasn't able to immediately respond. Abdon dropped his case onto a vacant chair and used his left hand as a more casual acknowledgement.

Sally followed suit, but as Ahmed offered his hand, he added, "I'm Scottish, actually."

"Ah yes, I understand the difference." Abdon displayed an amused expression and placed his hand over his heart. "We in Catalonia are fighting for our independence, too."

Ahmed jumped forward to help move the case and position the chair, before Abdon sat down to join them.

"Have you had a chance to study the menu yet? I can recommend the *Moule Frite*. It's a house speciality and the mussels are always fresh."

"I'd love to, but I'm allergic to shellfish," Sally replied.

"I don't eat them either," Ahmed added.

"Would it bother you if we have them?" Tom asked politely.

"Perfectly okay," Sally replied with a cheeky grin. "As long as you know you won't be able to kiss me."

Tom hesitated, uncertain how to react. He was pleased when his embarrassment was covered by the waiter arriving with menus.

The choice was extensive and Abdon ordered the mussels, but Tom and Sally instead decided on *Magret de Canard avec Banyols*, grilled duck breast served in a delicious thick sauce made with a locally produced fortified wine. Ahmed opted for *Rosada* with salad. Fresh bread, a jug of water and a litre size carafe of house red were all deposited on the table. The food was delicious and the company affable, although Ahmed was disappointed to find salad meant only a variety of different lettuce leaves. They all partook of a cheese course, followed by dessert. It was only when coffees were brought to the table that the conversation turned to business and Abdon's article concerning RNB.

"Can you tell us how you sourced your story?" Tom asked.

"I am not a financial specialist, but over the last few years I have presented many stories on the economy and on the precarious state of the banking industry. I don't write from the financial angle, but instead where it's matters of human interest – maybe that's why I was chosen."

"Could you please explain?" Sally asked.

"I didn't research the story; it was given to me. Obviously, I checked the authenticity, but I can't claim credit for making the discovery."

"Exactly what was the discovery, and how did you find out?"

"I received a letter, well an envelope, to be more precise. It was addressed to me, but it contained only one sheet of paper, a photocopy of the minutes of a meeting."

"Go on, please," Tom urged, his excitement rising.

"The list of attendees had been obscured, but the report discussed waiving the bank's procedures for dealing with defaulting clients. In particular, it discussed mortgage arrears. The normal procedure was to go through the stages of warning letters and when that failed, to repossess the property and use an agent to sell or auction it to recover the bank's debt."

"Yes, that sounds fairly normal," Ahmed said. "It's what happens in the U.K."

"Exactly. What the minutes said though, was that the normal policy should not be followed. Gentle coaxing to make payments would continue, but they were placing a moratorium on taking any action to repossess, even when no payments at all were being made."

"Did it say why?" Sally asked.

"There were loads of technical statistics quoted, about the number of unsold properties and the fall in house prices, and some details of losses incurred on sales, where the bank was not able to recover the outstanding debt. There were also figures about the costs of keeping custody of empty properties."

"And you checked all of this?" Tom asked.

"Of course, I did everything I could to check it. A number of officials were prepared to confide background information, but nobody would make any formal statement. I found out that all banks have been suffering. The economy and the property market in Spain have been dire. The level of arrears and doubtful debt is measured in multimillions— no, billions would be more accurate. If the banks were to repossess every property they were entitled to, then it would put even more pressure on the market and would lead to total collapse."

"Was this information new?" Tom probed.

"Not entirely. For some time, banks have been making arrangements with clients to reduce their payments, so they'd cover their ongoing interest and make a small contribution towards repayment. But the aspect suggested in this minute implied that even if the client was making no payment, the bank would turn a blind eye. It meant the arrears would be growing, not lessening. Even more damning, was the suggestion that the level of doubtful debt was not being properly accounted for, or disclosed in the bank's official returns."

"And this was the basis of your article?" Tom asked.

"Yes. Haven't you read it?" Abdon questioned.

Tom shook his head. "My Spanish isn't good enough to follow the exact meaning. When I heard about it, I arranged for an English translation, but a literal translation can often lose many of the subtler inferences. That's why we wanted to speak to you personally."

"My original article was factual and discussed the state of the economy and the housing market. It touched on the precarious state of the banking industry, with a particular focus on RNB Espana, as that's where the original information came from. Within days, it had been picked up by all the other papers in Spain and even the internationals. Some of the articles questioned why anyone should pay their mortgage? They came close to advising everyone to stop making any payments to the banks and of course, RNB were highlighted for special treatment. Of course, the banks denied the strategy. They claimed they would always pursue all debt, albeit they allowed themselves room for manoeuvring to make payment arrangements. Some of the reporting was irresponsible, as it prompted the banks to make a knee-jerk reaction and in the following weeks, there were an unprecedented number of repossessions."

Tom nodded, absorbing the information. "And it's not only about money, people's lives have been turned upside down. Do you have the minute?"

"Yes. It wasn't an original, but I've run you a copy of it, if it's any use to you."

"Did you get anywhere, tracing who sent it?" Sally enquired.

"It was a local delivery, but I don't know any more than that. I asked questions at the local banking centre, and from the reactions, I'm fairly certain it came from there, but there's no evidence."

"What do you mean by reactions?" Sally questioned.

"Nothing I can put my finger on. I don't even know how to describe it, but when I spoke to staff, there was an odd kind of defensiveness. Perhaps it was nothing. Maybe it was because they objected to the bank's strategy and they were pleased it had been exposed. I really don't know."

All business taken care of, Tom called for *'l'addition'* and settled the bill using his Global card. They left the restaurant together, slowly walking back to the small square.

"So, I guess you're on to something pretty big?" Abdon questioned.

"We really don't know anything for sure yet, but there's been a sequence of events which seem suspicious and we're trying to identify a pattern to discover the extent."

"Well, if I turn out to have been part of your jigsaw, make sure you give me a mention and an acknowledgement. I need all the recognition I can get if I'm going to get anywhere in this business."

"Can we give you a lift anywhere?" Tom offered.

"No thank you. I'm not going far." Abdon hobbled off into the distance while Tom, Sally and Ahmed climbed the hillside back to their car.

Arriving back at the hotel, they deposited the car with the rental company. Once Ahmed realised they were early enough, he convinced Tom and Sally to join him on a city tour from one of the companies operating close-by. He was joyful to find out they had an English language guide on board.

It was a whistle-stop excursion only lasting two hours. In that short space of time they were whisked around the city and given an external impression of the Olympic Village, the Neu Camp, beach area and the harbour, taking in a sighting of three cruise ships in port. They were also driven through the centre of town, providing views of the cathedral, *La Pedrera*, *Casa Batilo*, the Gothic Quarter and various other points of interest. After arriving back at *Sagrada Familia* they were invited to take a walk up the hill to examine the *Guell Park*, where they had the opportunity to enjoy more of Gaudi's designs and creations. Ahmed was enthralled by the tour and the opportunity to learn more about the city. Sally and Tom both enjoyed the experience, but were distracted by the investigation and frustrated by the hiatus resulting from their travel arrangements.

It was already late evening by the time the three were ready to step out to dinner and they were surprised to find many of the eating places filling up with local people newly arriving. They took a gentle stroll through the city and found an attractive restaurant, serving traditional fare. Over a most enjoyable meal, provided with ample servings of house wine, they discussed the similarities of the three incidents they'd examined. In all three, a provincial reporter was supplied with information to generate an article which would prove embarrassing and costly to RNB. In each case, the article was relatively innocuous, but kicked off a media frenzy which resulted in a severe blip in RNB's share price and market position. They found they were all in agreement. They wanted access to Matthews' papers, to try to determine who had a motive – hoping to discover who was behind the plot and how they'd enacted their strategy.

They ambled back to the hotel and Tom suggested a brandy as a nightcap, in part at least, to mark the success of their visit. Sally was quick to accept the offer.

"I'll give it a miss, if you don't mind," Ahmed said. "I'm going to my room to phone Morag. I haven't spoken to her since we got here. She'll be impressed that I've been driving in Spain *and* France."

"No problem. Off you go," Tom agreed, secretly pleased for the opportunity of some private time with Sally.

After enjoying two generously proportioned brandies, they decided to call it a night and made their way, rather unsteadily, towards the elevators.

"I think, even with his crutch, Abdon was able to walk a straighter line than you're doing now," Sally said with a giggle.

"You're hardly one to talk," Tom replied, guiding Sally around furniture.

They entered the lift and when the doors closed, Tom plucked up the courage to ask the question he'd been thinking about all through their nightcap. "What about that kiss you promised me?"

"What kiss was that?" Sally replied, sounding slightly bewildered.

"When I didn't order the mussels at lunch," Tom replied.

"I don't remember making any promises, but obviously I need to be more careful how I word things, so you don't take me too literally."

Despite her words of protest, Sally showed no resistance when Tom pulled her towards him and lowered his face to meet hers, their mouths meeting and their lips parting to consummate a passionate embrace. Their bodies pressed against each other, Sally's petite frame was enveloped by Tom's. They only parted to gulp air when the elevator stopped, reaching their floor.

Stepping out onto the landing, Tom noticed another guest was standing a distance away in the corridor, depositing a room service tray outside his door.

"Now that was nice, but you're a married man, Tom Bishop. I'll wish you a good night and see you in the morning," she whispered. She pecked him gently on the cheek before half-walking, half-staggering towards her room.

Tom watched her go, regretful about their parting. He had thoroughly enjoyed their embrace and didn't want their coupling to end – didn't want it to stop there, truth be told. He was simultaneously euphoric at the physical contact he'd enjoyed and frustrated because he wanted more. For a moment, he thought about rushing after her, to assertively impose himself into her room or maybe invite her back to his, but he didn't know how she'd react and didn't want to risk embarrassment or rejection. Tom savoured the taste of Sally's lips, the fragrance of the alcohol from her breath mixed with her alluring perfume. He stood watching her find her room and access the door. His heart sank when she turned, blew him a kiss and vanished inside. Although he craved more, seeking the intimacy of a deeper and more sexual connection, deep down he knew it would be wrong. It wasn't the right time. Sally had said as much and Tom knew he had plenty of issues to settle at home. He had more than enough problems to solve, without the added complications of a new relationship. Tom sombrely padded back to his room, thinking of what might have been. Contemplating that he must quickly resolve his position with Anne, his head cleared and he felt very sober. He had to consider what would be best for the future.

Chapter 21

Tom, Sally and Ahmed had another early rise, breakfasting at seven, as their flight was due to leave mid-morning. Tom found he was apprehensive as he headed downstairs, not knowing how Sally might react after their encounter the previous evening. To his surprise, her attitude was no different to normal. It was as if nothing had happened between them. He was relieved there was no tension but he was also disappointed, as he'd hoped the seed had been planted for a greater intimacy between them. He felt like a nervous schoolboy with a crush, too frightened to ask for a first date.

Their journey was a reversal of the one they'd taken two days before. Walking through security they sensed an absence of any urgency. When Sally bleeped, walking through the metal detector, no-one stopped or frisked her. They reached the departure hub for their flight to discover that the other planes leaving from their area were destined for Moscow, St Petersburg and Islamabad.

Ahmed excused himself, wanting to look at the shops hoping to buy a souvenir to take for Morag.

"I'll need to get something for the kids, too," Tom said, "but first I'll call Stephan and update him."

After giving Stephan a brief report, Tom asked, "Have the legal boys come to an agreement yet? We can't wait to examine the information in Glasgow and see what we can find."

"They have, but it took a while," Stephan replied. "As you might have expected, they did their usual arguing over the finest of details until the last minute. When the whole thing was on the verge of collapse, they found a solution at twenty minutes past midnight. Matthews has got a copy for you to sign, but I'll email one directly to you, so you can check what he gives to you is the agreed version. The research on the Honda is almost complete; I'll email that to you as well. For security reasons, I won't send any of it to your normal email address. Instead, I'll send it to that Gmail account we spoke about at the weekend. You remember how to access it?"

"Yes, I do." Stephan was obviously being particularly guarded, in case the phones were tapped. There was no Gmail account; their agreed web account was on Outlook. He wondered if he'd admitted too much in his own report. "Are you okay, Stephan? No more unusual incidents?"

"Don't worry about me, my boy. You've got enough to do taking care of yourself and the delightful Sally, not to mention Ahmed. I can take care of myself."

As Tom disconnected the phone call, he suffered a sharp jab in the ribs from Sally. He was about to protest when he saw she was indicating the row of chairs in front of them.

Sitting in the seats were three middle-aged women. They had eastern European complexions and were enjoying a snack. A quick glance at their baggage tags showed a destination unfamiliar to Tom. The woman in the middle was holding an open Tupperware container on her lap, which contained several pieces of fresh fruit.

Her hands were slightly above the container and she was peeling a peach, using a filleting knife with a six-inch long blade. The gleaming stainless steel drew Tom's eye.

"How the hell did she get that through security?" Tom whispered.

"That's precisely what I'd like to know!" Sally replied. "I'm going to find an official."

They scanned the surrounding area, but the only person wearing a security-related uniform was at one of the gates behind a glass door. Sally marched across and beckoned him forward.

Sally tried to explain, but his only reaction was to shrug and turn away, so she suspected he didn't understand English. She scanned the area again but couldn't see anyone who looked remotely official. Seeing the duty-free shop and knowing all their staff would be multi-lingual, she approached a sales assistant for advice.

When she explained what they'd seen, the girl immediately scoffed. "No, don't be ridiculous. Nobody can bring a knife through here." When Sally insisted, the girl reluctantly agreed to go with her to the police centre. They went back through passport control, walking to the designated police area and pressed the reception bell. When the issue was explained, the receptionist gave a similar response, but when Sally challenged her, she pressed a second button to call out a duty officer. No response ensued and the receptionist disappeared for a few seconds. When she returned, talking in Spanish with accompanying arm gestures for Sally's benefit, she explained there were no police available because it was a meal break.

Sally laughed at first, thinking it was a joke. When she asked the duty-free girl if it was actually the case and Barcelona airport had no active police security when it was a meal break, the response was silence, followed by yet another shrug.

Believing her time was being wasted by this audacious foreigner, the police receptionist showed great hesitancy to do more, but Sally persisted and she agreed to locate a security officer. As chance would have it, the only one she found was the first person Sally had tried to speak to. With much shaking of heads and shrugging and throwing arms in the air, the whole entourage returned to where Tom and

Ahmed were sitting, who confirmed the offending lady was still there with her knife now packed away.

Reluctantly, the security man approached the lady and in rapid fire Spanish, ran off a load of statements and questions. The lady looked up at him and lifted her arms in the universal 'I do not understand' gesture. The duty free lady attempted to communicate with her, trying English, French and German but received a similar response. The receptionist suddenly snapped her fingers, indicating she had an idea. Beckoning for the others to stay where they were, she dashed off to one of the cleaners nearby, who was clearing debris into a large waste trolley. The two returned, the cleaner dragging her trolley along behind her. This time the cleaner rattled off some words to the now-bemused lady and the result was the same. The cleaner tried again in what seemed to be a second language.

"Ah! Dah!" The lady responded gleefully, nodding her head. She pulled out her bag, lifted the lid from the container and raised the offending weapon high in the air. Everyone jumped back a pace or two and the receptionist turned to Sally in amazement, offering her a thumbs-up sign. The weapon was freely handed over by the lady and given to the cleaner to dispose of in her cleaning trolley, then everyone dispersed amidst jovial and enthusiastic chattering. The woman sat down with the rest of her party, while Sally remained standing, staring open-mouthed at the entire circus. "I can't believe what happened!" Sally said to Tom and Ahmed. "They didn't even question her, or check in her bag or take her and the rest of her luggage back through the scanners! If she was able to bring the knife through here, who's to say she didn't have a machine gun in there as well?"

"She didn't seem like a terrorist, but then, who knows what a terrorist looks like these days?" Tom said in agreement.

"She might have been genuinely harmless, but looking at some of the strange characters waiting to board flights, I think there's a real risk one of them could have removed the knife from her and used it," Ahmed said.

"And you wonder why I'm nervous about flying?" Sally demanded.

"How can this happen?" Tom asked. "Barcelona must be one of the busiest airports in Europe." He stopped suddenly, thinking for a minute before he continued. "Terrorism! That might be it. Do you think the RNB sabotage could be economic terrorism?"

"What do you mean? Talk me through it?" Sally replied, staring intently at Tom.

"Maybe times are changing and terrorists are no longer craving headlines from hijacking and blowing up buildings. Perhaps they're becoming more sophisticated and instead of going after human targets, they're trying to create financial chaos?" Tom said slowly.

"But aren't terrorists mainly driven by a desire for media coverage? They create these atrocities to publicise their cause. The individual killings don't do them any good. It's the publicity they want," Ahmed replied. Their flight was called, and the three stood up, walking toward the boarding gate.

"I don't think it's that simple," Tom suggested. "The term 'terrorist' is a label, not a definition. One man's terrorist is another man's freedom fighter. The term has been applied to anything from political persuasion, to mass murder. It's not only Al-Qaeda – anyone who uses extreme measures to either achieve or publicise their objectives can fit the label."

"Go on," Ahmed prompted.

"Well, if someone has an agenda against the RNB, or maybe against all banks – or globalisation, or even western democracy – and they're prepared to take significant unorthodox action to further their agenda, is that not terrorism?" Tom explained.

"Now you're playing with semantics." Sally replied. They settled into their seats on the plane, and Sally buckled her belt tightly around her waist.

"That's only one aspect. Look on it another way. If a terrorist blows up a building and kills, let's say a hundred people, then what's the effect? The hundred people and their relatives and friends are significantly affected and there would no doubt be howls of public outrage, but does it really go much further? If it takes place in Iraq or anywhere else in the Middle East, it barely gets a mention in the western media, and after a few days it's completely forgotten. If it happens in the West, there'll be more coverage and post mortems of what went wrong, who's to blame. Everyone will be appalled and up in arms. There will be calls for vengeance and there might even be a ripple in the stock market, but once again, apart from those directly affected, it all gets forgotten in no time. Now, by contrast, if an organisation like RNB was targeted – to such an extent as to cause its demise – then the effect would be profound. We're not talking about hundreds of people, but thousand or perhaps even hundreds of thousands of people – all the staff, their families, all the account holders who'd stand to lose their jobs, their life savings or their pensions. Then there's the knock-on effect for other companies. It would upset the whole market, might even cause a crash. The effects could spread worldwide. How long would it take to forget that? The perpetrators may choose to stay anonymous, or they might relish the publicity – who knows?"

Ahmed adjusted the air over his seat. "If the motive is really to cause chaos, wouldn't there be easier, quicker and more effective ways to do it?" he asked.

"Maybe so," Tom replied. "But this has been done without any physical intervention and there's no obvious threat for the security services to pick up on. Perhaps whoever's behind this is prepared to be patient, so they can cause maximum damage and achieve their desired result without being traced."

As the plane taxied and rolled down the runway, each analysed the theory, attaching their own spin and they agreed that they all considered it a feasible proposition.

"What other possibilities might there be?" Ahmed questioned.

Tom listed items on his fingers. "First of all, it could all be coincidence. There might be a series of major faux pas made by RNB, which has given rise to their own problems. That was one of the theories I considered at first, but I think we can discount it now. A series of screw ups would be a coincidence, but to suggest the revelation of each one was sent to a local newspaper by a different whistle-blower, stretches the imagination too far. There's the Glasgow case, where Farnham's email can't be traced anywhere and she has an alibi for when it was sent, and that's a killer. It proves someone set it up. So I'm confident we can discard this theory entirely.

"Next, there's the prospect that someone had a grouse against RNB and this is their way of taking revenge. We can't discount it, but it needs to be someone with a lot of power and influence. It's more than a disgruntled employee, or someone who feels they've been overcharged or wrongly had their credit restricted. It would need to be someone really senior, or someone with a big business, but even if that were so, they'd need to have the resources to know about everything going on. They'd need to be able to trace people and accounts and they'd have to have the computer skills, or control over people who had the necessary skills to hack into RNB's secure systems."

Raising his hand to show a third finger, Tom continued. "Then there's the chance that the whole thing is financially driven. As Ahmed suggested before, some devious bastard who's been playing the market, selling short on RNB shares, controlling and knowing when the next revelation will make the shares tumble." He held up a fourth finger. "And fourth, what we've been debating – premeditated, economic terrorism."

"Of course it might not all come down to a single cause – there might be elements of two or more of the possibilities involved," Ahmed pointed out.

"Absolutely – more than likely, in fact. There's more we need to consider as well. What's been going on hasn't been rational. It's not someone simply trying to meet one of the objectives we've discussed." Tom shook his head. "No, I think it's someone playing a game."

"A game?" Sally repeated.

"All this business of the warning letters, for one thing. Why has he done that?"

"To try to warn us off," Ahmed responded immediately.

"No, I don't think so," Tom said. "The person behind this knows everything that's been going on. He's been able to hack into the Bank's computer system. He's probably been able to tap into phones. He's known where we've been and what we've been researching and he's sent messages to me, or taken action, in various parts of the country. To do that takes a hell of a lot of contacts and money, and an enormous amount of power. Now someone with so much power could have stopped us, or squashed us – even killed us – at any time they liked, and no-one would have been any the wiser. He didn't though; he sent us messages instead, and watched us panic. Even the messages were cryptic, another game. That's why I'm suggesting he was playing with us. In fact, I don't think the messages were intended to frighten us off. He didn't need to, or if he did, there were easier and more effective ways. No, I think the messages were designed to keep us hooked, to stop our attention from wavering in case we went on to another story. He wanted us to follow what he'd been doing. He wants us to write it up. He wants us to tell the world how clever he's been. He gets some perverse pleasure from playing with people's lives. He's a puppet-master, and we've become some of his toys."

"But if that's the case, who is he and why is he doing it?" Sally demanded.

"We don't know who, but I suspect we might find out soon. I suspect though, it won't be until he wants us to."

"Do you really think that? Are you truly that much of a defeatist?" Sally snapped.

Tom shook his head. "No, not really. I'm just thinking aloud. If I didn't think we could make a difference, there'd be no point going on. However, I don't think we should underestimate what we're up against and we need to track this down and do it fast – before he wants us to. We're a good team. Working together, we can crack anything."

"A bit like the Three Musketeers," Ahmed agreed. "All for one and one for all."

"Let's not go there," Sally replied darkly. "That could make Matthews D'Artagnan – and I don't want to even think about that prospect."

It was sometime before Sally realised their conversation had been so absorbing and intense she hadn't noticed the plane had taken off and was already well into its flight-path.

Although the plane landed smoothly at Prestwick, heavy rain started falling almost as soon as it touched down and all the passengers became drenched on the short walk down the stairs and into the terminal.

Once through passport control, Tom, Sally and Ahmed detoured to the toilets to dry off and change into fresh clothes, before reassembling and proceeding to the station for the next train into Glasgow.

Only once aboard, Tom remembered he hadn't bought a gift for his children. He'd meant to buy something at the airport in Barcelona, but he'd been distracted, first by the call to Stephan and then by the knife incident and it had totally slipped his mind. Forgetting to buy the gift brought his own failings into focus. Tom grew pensive, thinking about his domestic circumstances. He couldn't get his head around what had been happening or what he really wanted, and as his thoughts descended into a turmoil of confusion, a series of random ideas plagued his mind, undulating between contrition at his own inattentive behaviour, to anger at Anne's betrayal and fury at Arthur's opportunism.

He craved being part of a physical relationship but he was uncertain whether he or Anne would be willing to make the concessions required to make a reconciliation possible. A formal separation would be simpler and would give them both a clean start. But that would create its own complications, particularly with the children. If he never saw Arthur again, it would be too soon and Tom was firmly convinced he never wanted Arthur near his children.

He recalled Anne saying they needed to talk, but that had been more than two days ago and their only other conversation had been his panicked phone call from Glasgow airport. She'd thought he was demented and maybe she was right, at that point in time, anyway. Tom thought about how frantic he'd been and ready to jump on the next flight back to London. After he'd heard from Stephan and realised the threat wasn't personal, he'd relaxed, but he hadn't explained that to Anne.

Tom lifted his phone to call her, but stopped. What could he say? How could he explain? What was he hoping to achieve, anyway?

Try as he might, Tom couldn't pinpoint when it had started to go wrong. He remembered nothing but happy times up until Colin's birth. However, from what Anne had revealed at the weekend the heaviest load she'd been carrying through her pregnancy had been psychological, and not physical. How could he have been un-aware of her anguish? As much as he wanted to claim the moral high ground, to assert extra rights as the injured party, he had to accept he wasn't blameless. He racked his brain for ideas, inspiration: but he couldn't think of a plan. There was no perfect formula. Tom made up his mind to phone Anne, to explain everything to her as soon as he got an opportunity to call in private. He felt he owed her that much.

Chapter 22

"Tom? Tom! Are you planning to stay there all day?" Sally said, sounding impatient.

"What?" He saw Sally and Ahmed standing over him. He'd been so deep in thought, he hadn't realised the train had arrived at Glasgow Central and most of the passengers had already disembarked.

"Give me a minute." Tom rushed to collect his belongings and followed them out of the carriage. Once on the platform, he straightened his clothing and buttoned his jacket to give him some protection from the colder conditions.

"We can take a cab directly to RNB's office, it's early enough to get some work done," Ahmed suggested.

They were shown in to the same meeting room they'd visited previously. This time there were three trolleys sitting against the wall, loaded with files. A member of the bank's staff was waiting for them. "Hi, I'm Philip McKeown. Call me Phil. I've been asked to stay in the room while you're working here. I have my own work to get on with, so I won't be a bother. Now before I can let you begin, I have an agreement you each need to sign and then I'll ask you to give me all your cases, computers, mobile phones, cameras and any other recording or imaging devices you might have. They'll be left outside with Avril, so you can have access to them whenever you need, but they can't be brought into this room. You can use the terminals which we've set up over there and you can access the internet or your email if you require to do so."

"Sounds good," Tom replied. "But first I have to go online to check the agreement with the version my company's legal department have approved. Can I print it out?"

"Certainly," Phil replied. "The printer is outside, in the room next to where Avril sits, so you'll have to go and collect it after you print."

"We can live with that. I'll download our copy. But while it's printing, is there an empty office

I can use? I'd like to make a call. It's a private family matter." He avoided Sally's startled gaze.

"Of course. I'm under orders to stay here with the files, but if you ask Avril, I'm sure she'll be able to sort you out."

Tom arranged for the files to be printed, then requested the use of a room from Avril. Once alone, he dialled Anne's mobile but it went straight to voicemail. He left a message, telling her he was back in Glasgow and that he'd call back later. He added an apology for his previous call, saying, quite truthfully, there had been a problem on Monday, but he thought it had settled down now.

He, collected the agreement plus half a dozen sheets printed with names, addresses and categories then returned to the meeting room.

After conducting a detailed check, they were satisfied that the agreement Phil had supplied was identical to Tom's copy, Tom, Sally and Ahmed each signed their names to the contract.

There's something else I'd like to add to our original arrangement," Tom said. "Something I have a hunch about. I'd like to interview some members of the RNB's staff and the sooner the better. Will I need to speak to Oliver Matthews, if I want to set it up?"

Both Sally and Ahmed shot questioning glances.

"Give me the details and I'll check with him. It might take a while. I know he's tied up in meetings all afternoon."

While Phil was making the call, Sally nudged Tom. "What the hell's this about?" she spat.

"Trust me. Something occurred to me that I'd like to check out. Please just play along.

Although she said no more Sally's frown betrayed her doubts while Ahmed's eyes darted between them wondering what he might be missing.

Tom was pleasantly surprised when Matthews not only agreed to the request, but said the interviews could be conducted in the meeting room with Phil present.

"Great, when can we set that up?"

Phil checked his watch "Now if you'd like – all three of the people you've asked to interview are presently on site."

While Phil was organising the interviewees, Tom turned to Sally and Ahmed who both looked stunned by this turn of events. "I promise, it will all come clear soon. I'm not keeping anything from you, I give you my word."

"What's it all about," Sally hissed.

"It just occurred to me; we knew from the frank stamp that someone in this building must have been involved, but I have this hunch it not only came from this building, but from someone in that specific department. While the thought was live in my head, I wanted to play it. I'm sorry, I'd have said sooner if I'd thought, but the idea only came to me a minute ago.

"We're meant to be a team," Ahmed said.

"We are," Tom reassured. "I didn't plan this, but I'm used to working on my own and using my instincts and I thought it too good an opportunity to miss. Please, give it a chance and follow my lead."

Several minutes later, Doreen Alder entered the room. She was the alleged recipient in Glasgow of the email from Farnham. She sat down to answer Tom's questions and although visibly uncomfortable, she answered competently and confidently, explaining how her systems and administration worked and adamant in denying she had ever seen the offending email.

She left the office and a couple of minutes later her assistant, Patricia Burrows knocked and entered. She cautiously moved inside, reached towards a chair, then looked at them apprehensively, as if expecting an introduction.

"Why did you do it?" Tom demanded, speaking bluntly and giving her no chance to settle.

Patricia jumped. Her hand sprang back from the chair as if she'd received an electric shock. "Do what?" she asked. "I haven't done anything."

"Don't lie! We know it was you; we have the evidence proving it! Let's not waste any more time. We want to hear your side of the story, before we decide what action to take."

Patricia started to shake uncontrollably. Her already pale face bleached to the colour of parchment and tears streamed down her cheeks. "How did you find out?" she whispered.

Tom exchanged a glance with Sally and Ahmed. He felt triumphant, but concealed his excitement. He needed to maintain an emotionless, professional demeanour if he was going to get the most advantage from this.

"How we found out doesn't matter. What's important is that we know. Now, will you please answer my questions? I think you'd better sit down."

Patricia slithered onto a chair miserably. "I didn't mean to cause any trouble. I didn't want to do it, but I was forced."

"How were you forced?" Tom demanded.

"I need this job, I'm a widow. My husband died over a year ago and I have two teenage children. When I was younger, I had a responsible position in junior management, but I gave it up eighteen years ago to raise my kids. After Tony died, I had to go back to work, because we needed the money. My experience was out of date and the only work the agency found me was administration with an insurance company. After six months, a position came up here and I transferred across. It's a much better job with more responsibility and I make more money. I was delighted, and so was the agency. A few weeks after I left the last company, a fraud was discovered in the department I used to work in. I had nothing to do with it and I knew nothing about it, but when I heard, I was scared that if RNB found out they'd end my contract and I couldn't afford for that to happen."

"Go on," Tom prompted.

Patricia's story came out in a breathless monologue, "I received a call. I don't know who it was. He said he needed my help, he told me someone at RNB had been acting improperly and he needed my help to sort it. He said there would be an email sent to Doreen and that I was to intercept it and destroy it, but first I had to take a copy and send it to Charlie McMillan. I didn't understand what it was about or why he wanted me to do it. I tried to argue with him and said I didn't want to do it, but he told me if I didn't do as he said, my connection to the fraud would be made public and I could wave goodbye to my job." Patricia covered her face with her hands. "I'm so sorry! I didn't mean to cause any harm. I didn't want anyone to get hurt! I only wanted to hold onto my job."

Tom and Sally's eyes met. He gave her a nod and she placed a reassuring arm around the woman's shoulder. "Can you tell us about the man who phoned you? Do you have any idea where the call came from or was there anything you can remember about his voice? Maybe he had an accent?"

"I can still hear his voice in my head. There was nothing special about his tone. He spoke slowly and clearly and he had an English accent – south of England, I think."

"What about the email?" Tom questioned.

"He told me when it would come in. I was to download it, take a print and then delete it from the inbox. I glanced at it, but I didn't read it properly. I just wanted it to be over. He promised he'd leave me alone if I did what he said and he kept his promise. I haven't heard from him since."

"One last question," Sally added. "Did anyone else at RNB know about this?"

"Not that I'm aware of; I didn't tell anyone. But I thought the man was from RNB. How else could he have sent me the email on the internal system?"

"Thank you, Patricia. I think that will be all for now," Tom said, now revealing a little more kindness in his voice. "But we may need to speak to you again about it. In the meantime, you must keep all of this confidential. It's important that nobody knows what you've told us."

After Patricia left, Tom told Phil to let the third girl go, because they wouldn't need to talk to her.

"How on earth did you work it out?" Ahmed asked. "You seemed to know exactly how to get her to confess."

"It was all luck," Tom replied modestly. "When she walked in, she was already in a panic and I could see she had something to hide, although I didn't know what. I was hoping it would give us a lead and it turned out to be the jackpot."

"Absolutely brilliant, I'm learning so much," Ahmed said, his face beaming.

"Let's keep it in perspective," Tom warned. "We now know it's a set up. We know how it was carried out here, but we're no closer to knowing who's behind it."

"It's a major step forward," Sally's voice was fired with enthusiasm.

"Mr. Matthews will want to know," Phil said. "You'd better call him.""

"You can tell him yourself if you'd like. It might win you some Brownie points," Tom suggested affably.

"Should we get stuck into the files now?" Ahmed asked.

"I don't know about you two, but I'm bushed. What do you say to putting in an hour or so, we can sort the files into the priorities we've set ready to hit the ground running in the morning, and then we call it a night?" Tom suggested.

"Sounds good to me," Sally replied.

"Me too," Ahmed echoed.

"We need a system," Sally said. We need some sort of database. We can list everybody and every company and put a risk ranking against them then we can cross check to see if the same individual or company recurs in more than one file."

"Run that past me again," Tom asked.

Sally explained in more detail what she had in mind and they all agreed it would be a sensible approach.

"I have the email from Stephan, with the research on the Honda owners," Tom said, "can you include a section for them as well?"

Sally went to work preparing her system while Tom and Ahmed made a start arranging the files.

Before they had time to make much of an impression, the door burst open and Matthews entered. "Bloody marvellous!" he enthused, wasting no time on preamble. "I'm normally a good judge of character and I made no mistake with you lot. You've already achieved more than I'd hoped for and you've barely started. We now know Farnham was innocent and Doreen Alder had nothing to do with it either. The Bank should be almost totally vindicated. We ought to string up this Burrows woman, hang her out to dry. We can go public about it being a conspiracy and then win back some of the Bank's credibility."

"I don't think that would be a good idea. It's too soon," Tom warned. "Going public might absolve the Bank of culpability with the insurance story, but it wouldn't take long for an astute reporter to reveal the weaknesses in the Bank's security system that allowed it to happen. The damage it might do will most likely outweigh any good. Also, we don't really want whoever's behind this to know what we have. We've got a better chance of finding out more if he doesn't realise we're getting closer."

"You're right, of course." Matthews said, "but what am I supposed to do about her?"

"It's not a good idea to fire her. Your safest option is to keep her employed," Tom advised.

"I can't risk keeping her in a position of re-sponsibility. She's betrayed us once; I can't risk her doing it again – it would be my own neck on the line if I did. I'll need to have her transferred to a position where she's not privy to anything and can't do us any more harm." He frowned, rubbing his hand across the back of his neck. "It really irks me that we need to keep employing her after what she's done. She's cost us millions."

"I understand, but it's the best solution in the short term," Tom said. "I'd wager there will have been something similar happening at each of the other locations. I don't have time to go back and check them out. Do you think your people can handle it?"

"I'm sure they can, now you've shown them the way. That said, if we're going to keep the lid on this, I can't tell them what you've found. And if they discover anything, we don't want it to go public straight away. I do have one or two trusted friends in the audit department and I can rely on their discretion. I'll put them onto it." Matthews turned to leave but he stopped mid pace and called Tom over. He spoke in a conspir-atorial whisper. "What we talked about before,

I'll have everything set up by tomorrow morning. Come to my office when you have a moment. Avril can show you the way." He stopped for a moment, leant forward his lips almost touching Tom's ear, before adding, "I'd wager Avril can teach you quite a few things." Matthews slipped out through the doorway, but then poked his head back through. "I forgot to ask, have you been following today's news?"

"No, we were travelling for a large part of the day, and we don't have our computers or phones to take messages or follow what's happening," Sally replied, quite pointedly.

Ignoring the implied barb, Matthews spoke again. "Smedleys shares have collapsed, they're almost in free-fall. They're one of our biggest banking competitors in the UK. I wish them no harm, but it's nice for it to be happening to someone else for a change." Despite his words, Matthews seemed to be relishing the ill fortune of his rivals.

Tom froze. "What was the cause?"

"There's nothing official, it seems to be driven by rumours of major losses in one of their over-seas subsidiaries. There's been a social networking campaign and it's gathered a head of steam. Smedleys have played it down, but not effectively enough."

"I don't like it," Tom said. "It's too close to what's happened to you. Of course, it may be a total coincidence and I can understand your relief that it's someone else suffering the grief this time, but if it's the same person behind it, you can't sit too comfortably. Even if you're not targeted, you're going to suffer the ripple effects."

"You may be right, but after the last two or three months, I'll take whatever good news I can get." The door clicked shut and Matthews was gone.

"Let's call it a night," Sally suggested. "I think I'll make a much better job of this when I'm fresh."

"Okay, but give me a few minutes. Before we leave, I want to try another call." Tom slipped out, found a private room and dialled Anne's number again.

"Tom, I'm glad you've called, but I only have a few minutes. I've got to pick Jenny up from her friend's house and I don't want to be late."

"Did you get my message?"

"Yes. I won't claim to have understood it, but I got it."

"Can I talk? Are you alone?"

"I have Colin with me, but he's having a nap at the moment."

Tom barely restrained a sigh. "You know what I mean."

"Arthur isn't here, if that's what you're asking. He won't be back either."

"Oh," Tom said, uncertain how to react.

"It was a mistake, Tom, a really bad mistake. I told you what happened. I was weak and I was vulnerable. Arthur was there to help me. At least, that's what I believed at the time. I'm not blaming him. I should have known better, but I let him convince me not to let you know what had happened and it all developed from there. It's over now, I've told him so. It could never have worked out. It should never have happened."

"But it did," Tom heard himself saying. He hadn't intended to let the words slip out; he didn't want to fight.

He heard the heaviness in Anne's voice, the intermittent sobs she was trying to cover up. "Yes, it did and I'm sorry, but as much as I'd like to, I can't turn the clock back."

"And would you really like to?" Tom asked quietly.

"Yes." It was a barely audible whisper.

"And how will it be?"

"I don't know, Tom. It's up to you, too. You called me on Monday, screaming to take the kids and run away and then I didn't hear from you again for two days. I can't live like that. I know I've made mistakes and I'm truly sorry, but I can't go through the rest of my life with you punishing me at every opportunity."

"I wasn't trying to punish you. When I called, I really thought there might be danger to you and the children. I called because I cared. It's a long story."

"And what changed? You left me like that, not knowing what to think."

"I should have called back to explain. It was wrong of me. I'm sorry."

"But you were too busy, I guess." There was a long pause at the other end of the line. "And you're with some gorgeous new girlfriend you're besotted with, from what Arthur said."

Tom gritted his teeth. "Arthur's trying to make trouble. Nothing has happened between Sally and me. We only work together and there're three of us on the team."

"You're not telling me everything, are you? I can tell." She sighed heavily. "But don't, I'm not asking. I've no right."

"I've told you the truth."

"What do you want for us, Tom?"

Tom took a minute to assemble his thoughts. "I'd like to go back to how it used to be. By that I mean before Colin. Don't misunderstand me; I love him dearly – but if we're going to get back together, I want us to have the relationship we had before he was born. I can't go back to the way it's been for the last few years."

"I can't either, Tom, but I can't make any promises. I don't know what I'm capable of and I don't know what you're capable of either. I'm not even sure I know who you are anymore. Maybe we need to take some time apart, a few weeks possibly, to get our heads together then perhaps we can try—"

"Is that what you want?"

"I'm not sure what I want, but right now I need to go. I can't keep Jenny waiting. We can talk better face to face when you get back. When will that be?"

"I'm not sure, but I think I'll be able to come home at the weekend."

"Okay, goodbye 'til then," she said, and the line went dead.

Tom was aware of Sally's appraising gaze when he shuffled back into the meeting room. His conversation with Anne had resolved nothing, and if anything, he was more confused than he'd been before he made the call. His sentiment was more of disappointment than anger, but he couldn't see any clear route forward and any prospect of reconciliation seemed a good distance away. He realised Anne must be going through similar turmoil, but his sympathy was limited as he still felt their problems were largely of her making. Anyway, any potential resolution was deferred now until they could meet and talk properly at the weekend. No doubt it would be easier if Arthur was no longer an issue and his influence had been severed. Tom's bond with Anne was still strong, further cemented by the children, but whether it was strong enough to over-come their past difficulties and the recent reve-lations, only time would tell.

"What's going on, Tom?" Sally probed, her expression stern.

"I'm trying to make arrangements to see the children," he lied unconvincingly, then, with manufactured enthusiasm, he added "All ready to go?"

"All set, Ahmed replied cheerfully. "You're booked in at the Radisson again, so at least you'll know your way around."

"Will you join us for dinner?" Sally asked.

"Thanks, sounds great," Ahmed replied. "Morag's working a back shift so I'd enjoy the company, but I'll make it an early night so I have a chance to see her when she gets off."

"No problems. I can understand you being desperate to get home after three days away. Tom and I will go and check in and get cleaned up. I want to pick up a bottle at Tesco on the way round. Let's say we meet up in an hour's time. Ahmed, how about you book something to sur-prise us? You did really well last time."

Chapter 23

The team's mood was jovial. They were happy with their progress, and the bottle of Cava split between Sally and Tom raised their spirits even further. After his conversation with Anne, Tom had suffered a bout of melancholy, but his mood had improved. Being in Sally's company was enough to jolly him along and the celebratory atmosphere was an added lift.

"We'll need to get going," Ahmed announced. "They might not hold the table if we're late."

"Okay, where are we going?" Sally asked.

"A new restaurant I've not been to before, but it's popular and the reviews were good. I looked on '5pm', but as I was booking so late there wasn't an awful lot to choose from. It's a five-minute walk from here, near George Square."

They arrived at the restaurant and cast their eyes over the palatial setting. The building was more than a hundred years old, constructed from red sandstone with carved statues decorating the outside. It had been built in the days when Glasgow had enjoyed great wealth and opulence. Inside, the room was massive with high ceilings and ornate cornicing. Large crystal chandeliers hung down from the ceiling at regular intervals.

They walked to the concierge's desk and Ahmed provided his booking reference. An elderly man, dressed in a penguin suit guided them to their table, one of very few unoccupied. Already late, and having eaten little since breakfast, they were all ravenous. They quickly scanned the menu and placed their orders and Tom perused the wine list. "I'm going to order a bottle of wine from the Languedoc, as a reminder of our trip. It's priced at more than five times what we paid for it in Collioure, but who cares? Global can afford to take care of us." Tom grinned.

Their meals were served and while the food was beautifully prepared and immaculately presented, Tom professed to being disappointed by the small portions, the *nouvelle cuisine* taking up only a small section of their plates.

"Do you think this is the night to try those deep fried Mars bars?" Ahmed joked. "It might be required to take my calorie count up to an acceptable level." He wiped his lips with his napkin and got to his feet. "Joking aside, I'll pass on dessert – I want to get home. I take it you'll be okay finding your way back to the hotel?"

Agreeing to meet at RNB the following morning, Ahmed departed, leaving Tom and Sally to sample the cheesecake, with a coffee and liqueur to finish. After paying the bill, they took a slow walk back to the hotel, admiring some of Glasgow's finer architecture on the way.

Emerging from the elevator on their floor, they walked to Sally's door and she slotted her card in the lock. Tom placed an arm around her shoulder. "Is it time for my reward?" he asked quietly.

Sally glanced up at him, her gaze curious. "What do you mean?"

"I didn't order shellfish again. Doesn't that earn me something?"

Sally grinned and Tom, interpreting this as acceptance, spun her towards him for their lips to meet. He held her head in one hand, kissing her, his tongue probing. His other hand held her

441

firmly, enjoying the sensation of her soft, warm skin against his body.

Sally eased back and pressed a kiss to Tom's cheek then reached for the door handle. "Good night Tom."

His face fell. "Can't I come in?"

"No, Tom, not tonight." Before he had time to protest, she was through the door and it closed.

Tom stared at the solid timber frame. He was stunned, not having expected the evening to end so abruptly. He trudged back to his own room and tried to slam the door to release some tension, but he was deprived of even that small satisfaction when the door closer took control and gently and slowly clicked it shut.

Tom paced up and down in his room, taking account of his own feelings. A few short hours before, he'd shared an earnest conversation with Anne, contemplating whether they had a future. Then only minutes ago, he'd made a clumsy pass at Sally and been rejected. Although he hadn't told Sally about his conversation with Anne, she was astute enough to know what was going on. Of course she hadn't wanted to be a second choice. Tom had no justification for thinking she was romantically interested in him, at any rate. Yes, they'd shared a drunken snog the previous evening, but it was no reason to believe she was ready to hop into bed with him and not for what she would no doubt perceive as being a one-night stand.

Tom had been so wrapped up in his own feelings, he hadn't truly considered what Sally must have been thinking. They'd known each other for little over a week. In that short space of time, they'd been more than work colleagues, they'd become close friends. Tom considered her physically attractive and he imagined she felt similarly about him. Following his lengthy period of abstinence, Tom had almost become asexual. Sally had been the catalyst to making him more aware and now he lusted after her. He craved physical contact and he enjoyed her company, but in all honesty, he didn't know if he was ready for another serious relationship. Was he ready to turn his back on Anne and embark on a new and real partnership so soon? Tom thought it was a genuine possibility, but he didn't know if it was for real or because he only craving company and a physical connection. Perhaps Sally saw through him, quite possibly knew him better than he knew himself. Of course, she didn't want a sleazy affair with a married man.

He valued Sally's friendship and hoped his behaviour hadn't damaged it. He considered the evening and questioned whether he might blame drinking too much for his gaucheness. It was a credible excuse, but Tom knew better. He was tired and drained, knowing the last few days had caused a great strain both physically and emotionally. He needed to sleep, but didn't feel ready. Instead he stripped off, letting his clothes lie where they fell, then walked into the en-suite, turned on the taps in the shower and immersed himself under the warm jets. He considered turning the thermostat down to cold, but chickened out. Instead he emerged, roughly towelled himself dry, used the remote to switch on the television and climbed under the duvet.

Some current affairs programme came on screen and Tom half-heartedly followed a panel discussion about the day's news, focusing on Smedleys' problems and debating the dire state of the banking industry as a whole following RNB's repeated troubles.

At 2.00am, Tom drowsily opened his eyes to a loud buzzing noise. He had no idea how long ago, but the station he'd been watching had closed down for the night and the screen was filled with fuzzy dots. He reached for the remote, switched off and tossed and turned for ages before being able to drift back into a fitful sleep.

* * *

Once again, Tom found he was apprehensive about Sally's reaction when he descended to the dining room the following morning. Although it seemed a lifetime away, he remembered his panic attack from the previous week at the same location and he was determined to stay calm and act normally.

Sally was already seated in the restaurant and offered him a warm welcome. He was relieved to discover she clearly hadn't found his behaviour unacceptable. Seeing the debris on her table, Tom wondered at the size of her appetite, finding it surprising someone of her height and slight build was able to devour so much food. Although not seeking to compete, Tom scoffed a full cooked breakfast, accompanied by several slices of toast and marmalade while Sally kept him company, drinking tea, perusing the morning papers and talking over their planned strategy for the day.

They met Ahmed in RNB's foyer. Phil greeted them and opened the room. Sally and Ahmed went to work on developing a database to track the information they discovered, while Tom made an inventory of the files so he could extract data for inclusion.

Around mid-morning Tom excused himself and went to visit Avril to ask for directions to Matthews office, leaving the others deeply engrossed in their tasks. She'd just started to explain how to get there, when they heard ringing coming from the side of her desk.

"That's one of your phones," Avril said. "It's the second time it's rung. The first was only a few minutes ago, but it stopped after four or five rings. I was going to come and tell you." As she was talking, Avril fished out the phone and passed it to Tom.

Even though it wasn't his phone, he pressed accept and lifted it to his ear. He could always pass a message on to one of the others.

He was about to speak when the incoming voice beat him to the draw. "Are you there, Barbara?"

Tom frowned. "I'm sorry, I think you must have a wrong number, this is Sally Ferguson's phone."

"And who might you be? And why are you answering her phone?" The voice demanded.

"If you've dialled a wrong number, why should it make a difference who I am?" Tom replied, growing irritated with the woman's attitude.

"I didn't dial a wrong number. Barbara is my sister."

"I told you, this isn't Barbara's phone. You've got a wrong number," Tom said, intending to disconnect the call.

"It *is* the right number, Barbara *is* Sally. She changed her name years ago when she had a Moslem boyfriend and converted to Islam, but I've always known her as Barbara and I'm not going to change what I call her now."

"What?" Tom swallowed. "Tell me that again."

447

The voice grew shrill. "I want to know who I'm speaking to, and why you're answering my sister's phone?"

"I'm Tom, Tom Bishop and I work with Sally. She'd left her phone behind and I picked up when I heard it ring. But—"

"Tom and Barbara? Like in 'The Good Life'? Hmm, as a child Barbara always wanted that type of lifestyle. Listen I've got to head out. Tell her I called." The line went dead.

Tom stood stock-still, holding the phone against his ear and trying to assess the possible implications. Sally wasn't who he'd imagined she was. In fact, she wasn't even Sally, if the caller was to be believed. Tom ran it all through in his head, remembering various titbits she'd told him about herself. She'd been deceiving him all along. What's more, she'd converted to Islam, she'd worked with the army and she'd been to Afghanistan. Could it all be a coincidence? It seemed unlikely. Only the previous day, they'd been debating the possibility of this whole business being economic terrorism. Could that really be the cause and was it possible - Sally – or Barbara, or whoever she was – could perhaps be involved? After the revelations of the last week anything was possible, and Tom's head was filled with anger and confusion.

Avril was mystified when Tom returned the phone, and strode towards the meeting room.

"Don't you want to see Mr. Matthews?" she called.

"It can wait," Tom replied brusquely, as he marched forward, throwing open the door. "I think you've some explaining to do," he yelled at Sally.

All heads turned from what they were doing, their expressions shocked.

Tom continued, his arms crossed over his chest. "Who the hell are you really, Sally? Or should I call you *Barbara*?"

Ahmed and Phil's gaze moved to Sally.

She was clearly stunned, but maintained her composure. "What's your problem? I've got nothing to hide!"

"Except who you really are, apparently."

"You *know* who I am. We've worked together for the past week. You know about me, my work, my family," she said defensively. "Why are you attacking me?"

"So what's in a name?" Tom asked wryly. "What else haven't you told us?"

"Calm down, Tom! You're making something out of nothing. My name at birth *was* Barbara. When I was at uni, I fell in love with a boy called Aarif, or at least, I thought I did. His family were Moslem and wouldn't accept me, so I converted to Islam. I was given the name Salimah."

"That's my sister's name; it means safe and healthy," Ahmed pointed out.

"Safe for who?" Tom spat.

Sally ignored them both. "I was in the early stages of building my career as a journalist and I shortened it to Sally for my writing. That was how I became known. I began to build a reputation, so I didn't want to change my name back again. That's all there was to it."

"And Aarif?" Ahmed asked.

"It didn't last. We were different people; it wasn't the religion and he didn't really follow the faith anyway. I'd only converted, because I thought it would make us closer. I was prepared to give it a try, but I don't really follow any religion. We drifted apart, and the only part that stuck was the name. I went back to drinking alcohol and eating bacon, as you've already witnessed. I haven't been hiding anything. It never seemed important and I had no reason to say anything. For umpteen years, everyone has known me as Sally. It's on my passport and all my official papers – my degree even. It's only my family who still refer to me as Barbara." She looked up at Tom, her eyes holding a question. "How did you find out?"

"I was talking to Avril and your phone rang. You forgot to switch it off. She said it had rung a few minutes earlier and she hadn't got to it in time, so I answered, in case it was something important."

She arched an eyebrow. "And was it?"

"I don't know. I didn't get as far as asking. It was your sister calling, she said to let you know."

"Thank you, thank you very much for telling me," Sally said frostily and stomped out of the door.

Tom turned to Ahmed and raised his hands in supplication. "What was I meant to think?"

"I don't know, but her story sounds credible to me," Ahmed replied. He turned back to his screen, making it clear he didn't want to be

pulled into the middle of a dispute. Phil too, bus-
ied himself with his own work, keeping his head
down and appearing to be completely engrossed
in what he was doing.

Tom contemplated what Sally had said; was
her explanation believable? Could it all be coincidence? Her religion was of no consequence,
but what else might she be concealing. Might
this beautiful young lady, who he'd spent the last
week lusting over, really be involved in such a
heinous plot? Tom remembered their embraces.
He imagined the sweet taste of her kiss, the smell
of her hair and the sensation of her breasts heav-
ing against his chest as they had when she'd
been terrified on the Barcelona flight. Surely this
divine creature wasn't part of a terrorist movement? On reflection though, was he really a good
judge of character? Brilliant and accomplished
reporter perhaps, but did he really know people? He'd lived with Anne for the last three years
without having the first clue about the real cause
of her anguish. He never suspected anything
about her developing relationship with Arthur.
Maybe he was a sucker for a pretty face, not to

mention full breasts and perfectly formed, if petite, tanned legs.

A few moments later, Sally strode back into the room, heading in the direction of her terminal.

"Peace?" Tom offered, extending a placatory hand.

"We're in this deep – I suppose we have to keep working together," she replied, her voice cold. She returned the gesture, but their fingers only met for an instant, the corners of her mouth raised in a resigned half grimace.

"I'm sorry. How are things with your sister?" Tom asked. He wanted to appear conciliatory, but he still wasn't comfortable with Sally's explanation.

"She's good. We don't get on much. At best, we tolerate each other."

Tom wondered if her words were only about her sister.

They returned to their tasks, and as the day wore on they progressed, amassing mountains of data and structuring it in the way they'd planned. Each mentioned particularly interesting cases to each other, wanting to ensure they were all aware of any person or company considered to have a particular reason for a grievance or any exceptional power, skill or aptitude which singled them out as potential candidates to have masterminded the scheme. Their concentration focused on their work, leaving little opportunity for interaction. Shortly after 5.00pm, they heard a knock on the door. Avril stood in the entrance and she spoke to Phil. "I'm about to finish up for the night. I've locked our guests' phones and computers in the closet. Here's one of the keys, so you can get them out when they leave. Oh, and I've got a delivery for Mr. Bishop. A courier handed this into reception about twenty minutes ago." Avril handed Phil an envelope.

Overhearing the exchange, Tom leapt to his feet. "What delivery? Who was the courier? What did he look like? What was he wearing?"

Avril took a nervous step back. "I don't know anything about it. Betty from reception called to say it was there and she was sending it up. I didn't know I was meant to ask anything else. She finished at five, so she'll be away home by now, but if you like, I can ask her in the morning to see if she knows any more. Stan only brought it to me a couple of minutes ago. Did I do something wrong?"

"No, no, everything's fine, thanks," Sally responded. "Now you go off home."

Before the door had closed, Tom snatched the envelope from Phil, ripped it open and spread the contents onto the table. Sally and Ahmed crowded in, leaning over his shoulder as he read from the familiar, chequered letterhead paper.

'Check mate
The King is Dead. Long live the King.
Elvis has left the building.
Another game?'

Tom paled. "The King is dead. Oh my God! Stephan! Quick, get me my phone," he demanded.

"I can't let you have your phone in here," Phil protested.

"I don't give a fuck where I get to use it, get it now. In fact, get all our belongings," Tom demanded.

"There's no need—" Phil began, but seeing the fierce expression on Tom's face and supportive body language from Sally and Ahmed, he relented and led them out to the closet. The moment he unlocked the door, they barged past him, recovering equipment and switching it on.

Tom groaned. "Shit, I've got three missed calls on my new phone and another three from Stephan, as well as two from the office on the other one. There's a text from the office, too."

"I'm the same, I think," Sally said.

"I've got a voicemail on mine," Ahmed said.

Tom grew increasingly frustrated as he tried to make contact with someone from the office. "No answer from Stephan's office phone or mobile. The text is from Andrews, the editor-in-chief. I'm summonsed to see him in his office on Monday morning at nine. He's invited me to bring a work colleague or union representative along. What the hell is this? It sounds like a disciplinary interview," Tom said. "There's something else. He says my company credit card has been temporarily suspended."

"My text is from Andrews, telling me to be in the London office on Monday morning too," Sally said.

"I've been told I'm off the job. I've got to report back to my normal duties tomorrow," Ahmed added dismally.

Tom was transfixed, staring at his screen. His mouth was half open and his hand shook.

"What's happened to Stephan? Do you think the message was literal when it said 'The King is dead'? Have you got any other means of contacting him? Is there anyone else in the office you can ask?" Sally questioned.

"I don't think he can really be dead, after all he sent the texts and the note said he'd 'left the building', which suggests he wasn't taken out. But I'd really like to speak to him to be sure he's okay and see what he can tell us. I'm sure I have a home number for him. Let me try." Tom forced himself to concentrate and regain his composure, but even so, it took several attempts before he found Stephan's number and made the call. It went straight to voicemail. Tom called the general office number. The phone was answered by one of the features' assistants.

"I'm trying to find Stephan; can you tell me what's happened to him?" Tom asked.

"Sorry, I can't help you. He was called to a meeting early this afternoon. He returned an hour ago, went into his room and came back out five minutes later carrying a large bag. He took it out to the elevator and he hasn't been seen since."

Tom disconnected the call and collapsed into a chair, feeling relieved. "He was alive and well about an hour ago, although putting two and two together, he might not work for Global anymore."

"Where does that leave us?" Sally questioned.

"I really don't have a clue," Tom admitted. "And I'm in even deeper shit. I only have about seven pounds and a couple of euros in my pocket. I don't have any other money. My credit cards don't work and now the company one's been cancelled. God knows how I'll settle the hotel bill, or get back to London."

"Wasn't Matthews going to help out?" Sally asked. She bit her tongue when she remembered Phil was there and showing great interest in their conversation. She gave Tom a warning glance.

Tom correctly interpreted the gesture. "There was nothing he could do. I want to have a private word with him anyway, so I can let him know

458

about our time restrictions. Can you give him a call, Phil, and see if he's able to see me right now?"

While Phil was busy, Sally quietly spoke to Tom. "What can we do now?"

"I reckon we need to keep going. We need to see how far we can get by close of business to-morrow. There's no telling what will happen next week. What's more, there'll only be the two of us since Ahmed's been recalled."

Ahmed shook his head firmly. "No way! You don't get rid of me that easily. I've come this far with you, I'm not going to let you down. I can always go back to my job next week."

"We can't ask you to do that, Ahmed. You might be putting your career at risk," Sally warned.

"You're not asking me, I'm offering and I'm not taking no for an answer. Besides, what career are you talking about? All I was doing at the paper was goferin' and making tea. This last week has been *real* journalism. It's the reason I wanted to get into this business in the first place. I'm due holidays, I'll phone in to say I'm claiming one and I'll go back on Monday. That's unless you can find something better for me?"

"If it was within my power, I'd do it in a heartbeat," Tom replied, "but as things stand at the moment, I'm not confident I'll have a job myself come Monday. I don't know what sort of problem Stephan has, but we seem to be caught up in the same thing and I'm sure it must be related to this story. If we're up against the same person who had the power to bring RNB to its knees, then we have a serious problem. We need to speak to Stephan to find out."

The words were hardly out of his mouth when Tom's mobile rang and the caller ID screen showed it was a withheld number. He tentatively pressed accept and was relieved to hear a familiar voice.

"Tom, it's me. I'm using a payphone. Don't say anything which identifies who you're talking to, as you might be being watched or listened to. Are you okay?"

Tom eyes darted to check if Phil was in earshot before grimly responding, "I've been better."

"As I'd expect. Listen carefully. Word isn't officially out yet, but I've been suspended from

Global. There were a whole load of revelations regarding my misdeeds over a period of years sent to Andrews. The most recent suggests I've been overindulging you, and accepting spurious expense claims. Worst was allowing you to use your company card for private expenses. The two hundred quid cash I advanced you was targeted for particular scrutiny, because I didn't have a mandate to recover it. Of course, I've been ordered not to have any contact with you, so this call is another transgression."

"Who sent it?" Tom questioned.

"You know better than to ask. Anyway, Andrews may be seen as a 'Young Turk', trying to bring the business into the twenty-first century using all the right buzz words to impress the board, but he's a really sound guy. I had a private meeting with him last night that no-one knows about. He told me what was coming and I explained what we've been working on. He has to be seen to be going through the motions, firstly for his own protection, and secondly, so the enemy think their plan is working. Consequently, I was dragged in for a disciplinary interview this afternoon and as of now, I'm officially suspended, pending further enquiries. Andrews has brought in a team from our external auditors to carry out those enquiries, so we have some time to work with. As for you, you're being called back for the same treatment on Monday and Sally's going to be cautioned and sent back to Oz."

"I see. So we can't all meet again after the weekend?" Tom suggested surreptitiously. He saw Sally and Ahmed's puzzled expressions and shook his head, signalling them to stay quiet and he'd explain later.

"That's about the sum of it. Keep trying my mobile and home numbers every so often from your company phone, to make it seem like you haven't heard from me and you're still trying. I won't answer, because they could be being monitored. I'll send you a new number you can get me on later, once I sort it out. I'll go now and we can talk tonight."

Tom lowered the phone from his ear and placed it back in his pocket. "What was that about?" Phil asked curiously.

"A family matter. Listen, we think we'll need to work late tonight. Any chance we can order in some sandwiches?" Tom suggested.

Phil looked unconvinced but was wary of asking more. "It's a bit late, but I'll see what I can do. I might be able to send someone around to M&S and see if they have anything left. In the meantime, Mr. Matthews is still in his office. He said he's leaving in half an hour, but he'll see you if you go now."

Chapter 24

Arriving at Matthews' office Tom was invited in as if he was an old friend.

Tom let Matthews treat him to a further elaborate explanation of the system devised to enable Tom to have banking facilities and was given a new credit card under a pseudonym which he'd be able to use immediately.

Matthews was smug about what he'd put together, but again swore Tom to secrecy on the whole process.

The mood became far more serious after Tom advised him of the new developments at Global. Although circumspect with the details, Tom gave Matthews an indication of the problems he was now facing, and he explained his requirement to work late so they could take their research as far as possible before the weekend.

Matthews seemed sympathetic. "If it's any consolation, Tom; if you can't resolve your problems with Global then you'll have a job to walk into at RNB. Your first task would be to complete your investigation into this mess. After that, I can't think yet what we'd get you to do, but I've no doubt we can utilise someone with your talents and we'll undoubtedly pay more than you're getting at the moment."

"I reckon your primary motive is to stop me writing any more stories about bankers' bonuses?" Tom joked. He had no wish to work for the bank, but the idea of having a safety net was reassuring.

Apologetic for rushing away and profuse in his gratitude to Matthews for his help, Tom returned to the meeting room to assist Sally and Ahmed.

The work was detailed and laborious. Already beyond 9pm, Tom, Sally and Ahmed had read through so many files they were barely able to focus and Phil had checked his watch for the umpteenth time, making it apparent he wanted to go home.

"I think we have to call it a night," Tom announced. "We need to be fresh enough to understand what we're reading or we could miss something important."

They collected their equipment and Tom saw he'd received a text, sent from a new number by Stephan. The message was brief: **'Call me when you have a chance'**.

They split up at the front of the building, Ahmed and Phil heading toward their respective homes and Tom and Sally returned to the Radisson. They collected their keys and made their way tiredly up to their floor.

"See you in the morning," Sally announced quietly, before disappearing into her room. Tom stood for a moment, dog tired, but even so, regretful he hadn't received as much as the now customary peck on the cheek. Although not completely comfortable with the issue of Sally's identity, he accepted she wasn't a threat and regretted his explosive behaviour. He recognised that she hadn't forgiven his accusation. He felt bereft, missing their recent intimacy. Tom entered his own room and collapsed onto the bed. He intended to steal a couple of moment's relaxation before calling Stephan, but his eyes closed and he was sound asleep within seconds.

Tom and Sally breakfasted early. Sally wasn't unfriendly but her conversation lacked her usual warmth.

Tom felt uncomfortable. "I'm sorry about what I said yesterday. I was already stressed and on edge when your sister's call came in and I over-reacted. Can we put it behind us.

Sally shrugged. "I guess; we've a lot more to concern ourselves with."

They used the hotel's speedy checkout, key drop off. Tom hoped the pre-registration of the company card would work and pick up his bill. They arrived at RNB shortly after eight o'clock, meeting up with Ahmed, then all three paced the floor impatiently, until a quarter to nine, waiting for Phil to turn up with the key to give them access to the meeting room.

They beavered into the files as they had on the previous day.

Already approaching midday, tension in the room was growing to fever pitch as everyone realised their time was running short. Tom feared they wouldn't finish in time, and could feel his panic growing. He was relieved when Sally suggested a new approach. "I think the remaining files will all be low risk," she said. "Why don't we try to re-sort the database at this point, see if we can identify any prime suspects?"

Glancing over at Ahmed to gauge his reaction, Tom saw his nod of agreement. He pushed back his chair, relieved to have a new plan to try. "Yep, let's do that."

"Will you need the files any longer?" Phil asked, sounding hopeful.

Tom's gaze met Sally's in an unspoken question and she answered. "No, I don't think we will, thank you."

Obviously relieved at the prospect of escape, Phil arranged for the trolleys of files to be removed from the room and the minute they'd been collected, he slipped away, clearly happy to no longer be serving as their nursemaid.

Sally collected the thick wad of paper they'd created from their database at the printer outside and returned to the meeting room so the three colleagues could scan the results. Sitting together at the table, they each took a section and began to work through the information they'd collated.

"I've got an Anchor Maritime Group," Sally suggested. "Went bust earlier this year."

Tom and Ahmed shook their heads.

"Cargo Automotive? A big guarantee claim."Ahmed asked.

"Nope," Tom replied glumly. "How about 'Kaiser Domestics?"

They continued for some time without success, each listing some of their high risk entries until Sally announced, "What do you know about Select Personnel Services.

"That's one I listed too," Ahmed replied. He leafed through some papers before reading aloud, "Their problems date back to about two years ago; the bank pulled their overdraft, claiming Select had failed to disclose any of the required information and were in breach of covenants. There was some aggressive correspondence in the file. Select were furious, saying they'd take all their business elsewhere. I think they threatened to sue and claimed the bank had harmed their whole viability – and they'd make them pay."

"So just your average, dissatisfied customer?" Tom chuckled. "Let's check them out. Google them and we'll do a search on Companies House."

Ahmed tapped out some words on his keyboard and paused for a moment before he began to read information from his screen. "They were liquidated over a year ago. It was a stand-alone company, a recruitment consultancy and employment agency. The file reveals that not long after the bank called in their overdraft, they went to the wall. Their assets and business were sold on for next to nothing and they went down with over two million in debts; mainly to contract employees. Here's the ironic part – they specialised in the financial sector and I.T."

Sally extracted more information from her terminal. "There's an ongoing enquiry about wrongful trading, but it's expected to be closed without any penalties."

"What about the directors and owners?" Tom questioned.

"I've got two directors," Ahmed replied. "There's a Carlos Perez and a Clive Sommers. Each owned five percent of the share capital."

"Is there any other information on either of them?"

"I don't see any other directorships noted on the Companies Register. Perez is listed as a Colombian national though," Ahmed continued.

"I don't see anything significant on Google," Sally said. "Sommers is on LinkedIn, but there hasn't been any activity on his account for two or three years."

Tom leaned back in his chair, tapping a pencil in a quick rhythm on the table. "Is there any information on who held the other ninety percent?"

Ahmed scanned the results on his screen for another few minutes, and Tom's heartbeat sped up, hoping for something useful. "Yes, it was one shareholder and held personally, so he must be considered a shadow director as he had a controlling interest," Ahmed announced excitedly.

"What's his name?" Tom demanded.

Another long silence seemed interminable. "It's Leroy, Francis Leroy," Ahmed replied.

"That sounds familiar, where have I heard it before?" Tom said pensively. He was certain he'd heard the name recently, and tried to rack his brain as to where it might have been. Was it related to the story, or something completely un-connected to their investigation?

"I've heard it too," Sally announced. "I'm sure I entered it, in its own right, on the database for some reason. Give me a second." She punched swiftly at the keyboard, leaning closer to the screen as she studied the results. "Here it is. Yes, I remember this now, it was on Stephan's list. Francis Leroy is one of the people who owns a Honda Goldwing GL 1800!" she announced triumphantly.

"Bingo!" Tom shouted, throwing his arms in the air with glee.

Ahmed slumped back in his chair, his eyes wide. "Good God, that's it. Don't you see?"

"What?" Tom and Sally asked simultaneously.

"It's the name – Leroy, don't either of you speak French? LE - ROI! L.E. R.O.I." spelling out the words. "It means the king," Ahmed replied.

Tom smacked his head in frustration. "Damn, how could I not have seen it before? Stephan mentioned the name to me days ago. He was one of the first ones listed, because he was based in Kent. I should have realised at the time. He's our man, he must be. What else do you have on him?"

Ahmed continued to scan his screen for a minute before he spoke. "There's a lot. He's a serial entrepreneur. I have him listed as owning a significant holding in at least twenty companies."

"I've got some biographical notes," Sally added. "Leroy's not his real name. He's Iranian. He was born Mohammed Asad in Tehran in 1964. He was a chess master and highly rated, believed to have the ability to achieve International Grandmaster status. He came to Britain in 1990 and he's been here ever since. He must have had a shed-load of money, because he bought and sold different businesses and started up or invested in plenty more. There's no mention of chess after he arrived. He changed his name in 1992."

"He owns the majority stake in two different investment companies. There might be more, there's quite a maze with companies owning shares in other companies," Ahmed continued. "It may be very difficult to establish what he really owns overall, when it's spread through different holdings and there might be offshore interests as well."

"Let's see what we can find out," Tom suggested.

They went to work, toiling for a considerable period of time, trying to establish the true extent of Leroy's share ownership amassed over various nominee holdings.

Ahmed tabulated the results and stared at his screen in disbelief.

"What is it?" Tom demanded.

Ahmed hesitated for a minute before he spoke slowly. "This can't be right. According to my figures, he's effectively a majority shareholder of Headcount. It's massive. As you must know, its one of this country's biggest companies, a specialist agency for employment, outsourcing and contract staff. It's the one I worked through when I was employed at RNB. It supplies staff to nearly every large company in the country, as well as the police, fire service and NHS – even the military. There's nothing they're not into. Not only that, it's multinational. It's in every developed country across the globe. It must be one of the most powerful organisations in the world and he must be a billionaire. We knew someone with loads of clout was behind all of this, but the level of power he must have is beyond my imagination."

Sally collapsed into a chair, "Oh nooooo!" she wailed.

"What is it?" Tom asked. "Are you okay?"

Sally was holding her head in her hands. "It's all my fault," she moaned.

"What's all your fault? What are you talking about?" Tom demanded.

"When I was trying to get a job in Australia, I registered with Headcount! They found me the job with Global. I started on a temporary contract and they charged out my time. They paid me a much lower rate than they were being paid, but they did everything and supplied everything, all my travel passes and equipment. I was given a Headcount computer and mobile. When I was promoted to the Sydney lead, it was still processed through them. I have to provide regular and comprehensive reports of what I'm doing. They know where I am and what I'm working on at any given point in time. If Leroy's been aware I've been working on investigating his scam, he's no doubt been keeping a close eye on what I've been doing. That must be how he's been able to follow us every step of the way. For all I know, he might have my equipment bugged! I think I must be the mole, I'm so sorry," Sally burst into floods of tears. "You were right to doubt me, but not for the reasons you thought."

Tom was beside her in an instant, placing an arm around her shoulder. "It's not your fault," he soothed.

Sally turned and buried her head in his shoulder, her tears soaking into his shirt.

"This man has more control than most heads of state," Ahmed said. "He runs a business which has its fingers into practically every level of every major organisation. He has the ability to see and hear everything that's going on. He's got more power than God."

Through great sobs, Sally's muffled voice was barely audible. "Our only advantage is he doesn't know we're on to him, yet. All our conversations concerning him have been when the equipment's been locked away." She pulled away from Tom, leaving a blotchy stain from tears and running mascara. "We need to think carefully about what we do now. We only have a small window of opportunity to move on this."

"What can we do? This man is untouchable. He owns everything, or at least, controls everything. He probably knows what's going through our heads, before we do," Ahmed said, clearly awestruck.

Tom shook his head. "Sally's right. He doesn't know that we know. We could publish everything we have on him and take him down. We could go to the police, the Serious Fraud Office, Special Branch – whatever."

"But what could we actually do that is going to hurt him?" Sally protested. "Yes, we know it's him, but what hard evidence do we have of him committing a crime or even being involved in one? We know he's blackmailed bank staff, but we have no proof, and if it came down to it, we're talking about one person's word against another's, with Leroy's likely to have more credibility. There's no evidence to implicate him in your assault, or the attack on Stephan. Possibly, we might connect him to hacking or insider trading offences, but to do so, we'd need to gather more evidence and that would require a lot of investigation and research. Time's against us. We don't have a hope of learning what we'd need to make an accusation which would stick. We could wing it and go to print without the necessary corroboration, but think through the consequences." Sally glanced from Tom to Ahmed and back again. "Headcount is so big and powerful; he might be able to block the story. Even if it did get out, look what would happen. They have staff in important positions everywhere. If Headcount was called to task in a significant way, it would freeze up the entire country. Everything would come to a standstill and the economy would crash. It would create the biggest recession the western world has ever seen. The impact could be catastrophic. Without western support and logistics, managed by Headcount controlled personnel, there might be widespread famine in large parts of Africa. Are you sure you want to be responsible for causing all of that? True, we'd most likely become the most famous journalists since 'Watergate', but would that be enough for you? The expression, 'Publish and be damned' might have become a bit of a cliché, but it could well apply here. Could you live with the consequences, having it all on your conscience?"

"Surely you're not suggesting we let him away with it," Tom replied.

"We can't defeat him, but we have to be able to do something," Sally suggested.

"We're only pawns in his chess game," Tom said. "But a pawn can still threaten a king and in the right circumstances, a pawn might even win a game."

"You're flattering yourself, Tom. We're not even pawns, "Ahmed said morosely. "You said it yourself the other day, before we even knew what we were up against – whoever was powerful enough to have taken on the RNB could have wiped us out at will. He was only ever toying with us for his own amusement. This isn't a chess game, it's more like a computer game. He has the controller and he's relieving his boredom. He could wipe us out, or switch us off at any time. We continue as long as he's prepared to tolerate us. We're only pixels on his screen. We either go public with what we have and accept the consequences, or we have to walk away."

Tom waved a hand in denial. "No, you're wrong. We're more than that. We can't allow ourselves to be so defeatist, or we might as well lie down and die. Maybe we're not in the same league, but perhaps we can stop him from getting everything his own way, even stymie some of his plans. But we can't afford any mistakes, we're going to have to learn everything we can about him and we'll also need help, though there's hardly anyone we can trust."

"You've got something in mind, I can tell. Is this one of your hunches?" Sally demanded.

"I don't know. It's a real long shot, but from everything we've seen so far, Leroy likes to play games – but he does it covertly. Perhaps he has something to hide, or else he relishes his own privacy. Either way, there might be a weakness to try and exploit."

Ahmed's expression brightened. "What can I do?"

"I want you to both work at finding out everything you can about Leroy, both past and present. Anything you can discover about his days in Iran, how he accumulated his wealth and what he's done since. Search for information on family, friends, colleagues, mentors and anyone else who's had anything to do with him. Oh, and get me his phone number."

"And what are you going to do?" Sally asked.

"First, I'm going to have a chat with our Mr. Matthews. I've had some doubts about him and I can't say I like the guy, but we're on the same side and we need all the help and support we can muster. When it comes to power and influence, he may be dwarfed by Leroy, but he's certainly no lightweight. After that, I'm planning to speak to Stephan. I'll go out of the building and find a landline somewhere, so I can use it to call him securely."

"What's your plan?" Ahmed asked.

"Wait and see," Tom replied. "I don't know if we have much chance, but it's worth a try."

Before they were able to ask anything further, Tom was out of the door.

* * *

"What have you got?" Tom asked without preamble, when he returned more than an hour later.

"Quite a bit," Sally announced, sounding pleased. "Including Leroy's phone numbers."

Tom scanned through the notes Sally and Ahmed had prepared. "Perfect," he declared. He picked up the phone and dialled the number Ahmed had obtained for Leroy's home. "I'd like to speak to Mr. Leroy," he said when the call was answered.

"Who's calling?" a very proper, male voice repled.

"This is Tom Bishop from Global Weekly."

"Is he expecting your call?" the voice, when it responded sounded suspicious.

"I wouldn't think he'd be expecting me."

"Mr. Leroy doesn't speak to journalists."

"He'll want to talk to me, go ahead and ask him."

There was a pause for a couple of minutes before Tom heard a clunk as the phone receiver was picked up and he heard a man's voice, well-spoken and revealing a gentle accent. "I don't believe I know you Mr Bishop."

Tom glanced at Sally before he responded. "Oh, I think you know me very well, but perhaps what's more important, is that my associates and I now know you, Mr. Leroy – or should I call you *Asad*?"

Tom heard deep, rhythmic breathing, but little else for a few long seconds. He was tempted to speak again, but decided against it, judging it would be better to wait for a reply from Leroy. From the corner of his eye, Tom saw Sally and Ahmed's faces, their expressions strained, frantically trying to gauge Leroy's half of the conversation.

When Leroy did speak, Tom thought he detected satisfaction in the man's voice. "Mr. Bishop, it seems I have underestimated you and your associates. It is a long time since I have met a competitor who would dare to resist me. I think we would make good friends. Now, why have you called me?"

"For starters, an explanation would be nice," Tom snapped.

Leroy's voice sounded amused. "An explanation? Of what?"

"All this tinkering with share prices, why do you do it? You certainly don't need the money."

"You are right. The money means nothing to me. At one time, it was important, but no longer.

I am in the position where I can do what I want, when I want, and no-one can stop me. So I ask you – where is the challenge? You see my friend, for amusement, I test myself to see what I'm able to achieve. When I was younger and poorer, I applied my strategies on the chess board, but I believe you have worked that out already. Now it is more interesting to play my games with real people and businesses and countries." Leroy paused for a moment, as though considering his next words. "When I used to win a game of chess, I relished the look of disappointment and frustration in my opponent's eyes. It was deeply satisfying, and that moment of success is what drove me on to becoming more successful. Now when I win a game – and I always win my games – I can enjoy the headlines and the news reports talking about the consequences and achieve my satisfaction in that way."

Tom couldn't believe the audacity of the man, his willingness to tamper with people's lives merely to amuse himself. "Well this is one game you've lost."

Leroy laughed. "I think not, but I'll humour you. Tell me what you would like? You want money – no?"

"It's not your money I'm after."

"No? Then what?"

"There are many things. First, my friends and I and would like our lives back. We want you to stop interfering with us. We want you to stop interfering with the stock market and making artificial market changes and we want you to stop interfering with the RNB."

Leroy's voice was hard when he spoke again. "I will do what I like with the RNB. They are my enemy. They hurt my friends and through this act, they hurt me. They have shown no respect."

Tom gripped the phone a little more firmly. "You asked what I wanted and I've told you. Another thing – you will sell your shareholding in Headcount. We're going to be reasonable with you. You can do it in the open market and sell it over time in tranches, so you'll realise its true value and not upset its trading; but you will do it."

This time, Leroy laughed loudly and Tom could imagine him, sitting in his mansion and thinking he had everything, and everyone under his control. When he spoke, his voice was filled with amusement. "Mr. Bishop, I hadn't appreciated how talented you are! You really are a very funny man. You should be on stage or television. Do you have an agent? I'm sure I could arrange someone to represent you."

Tom's voice was dry when he responded. "I'm sure you appreciate this is no laughing matter, Mr. Leroy. I've told you what I want, and I would like your solemn promise you're going to deliver."

"No, Mr. Bishop. Because you amuse me, I will not become angry. To show what a fair man I am, I will even give you two million pounds, so that you and your friends will go away. You can do what you like with the money as long as I never hear from you again."

"I've already said I don't want your money," Tom responded firmly, even though his heart was racing.

Leroy sounded surprised. "What's wrong? Is two million not enough? You must be a greedy man. But no matter, I am wealthy, I can afford more. Five maybe?"

"For the third time – I don't want your money. I won't tell you again. You're going to do as I ask, or face the consequences."

"Come, come, Mr. Bishop. I am growing tired of you and your demands. You are in danger of annoying me, and I assure you, that is a very, very dangerous thing to do. Why on earth would I care what you want from me?"

"Perhaps because deep down, you're worried about what I know. Maybe because you think I might know something that you don't want the whole world to know."

"You know nothing. Do you think it is important that I changed my name? Do you think that matters? It isn't a secret. I don't care what you know, Mr. Bishop. Leave me alone or I warn you – I will snuff you out like a candle."

"I know a little bit more about you than that. Yes, you were born Mohammed Asad. I also know you grew up in Iran, and you were recognised as a genius at an early age. Your ability for playing chess was nurtured and you enjoyed the patronage of the Shah. I know that everything seemed to go quiet for you after the Shah was deposed, up until you turned up in London in 1990 with a few million pounds in your back pocket." Tom paused, placing extra emphasis on his last sentence. "I'm sure that must have been a very interesting time for you."

Leroy's voice, when he replied, was positively icy. "This is scandalous; you cannot say these things. I assure you, Mr. Bishop – I won't let you."

"In actual fact, I think most people would consider it even more scandalous if they learned of your activities while you were gathering your wealth, before coming to Britain. I doubt there are many who know the real truth and frankly, I'm sure you'd prefer to keep it that way. I've discovered some of the people you left behind and they've told me they would be extremely interested in renewing their acquaintance with you. I didn't get the impression it was for friendly reasons." Tom paused to gulp in a breath before continuing. Perspiration was running down his brow and trickling down his spine. He caught a glimpse of Sally and Ahmed who were watching him in open-mouthed shock. "I know those acquaintances, in particular – and I'd guess plenty of other people – would love to know where and who you are now and discover just how rich and powerful you've become. What's more, I'm sure Companies House would like to have a more accurate recording of your direct and indirect shareholdings and I'm confident there will be many organisations who'll be more discerning in future when they subcontract their business."

Leroy started to splutter, his clear diction fraying and his perfectly modulated voice becoming heavy, guttural and deeply accented. "You cannot do this! I am immune from your threats, Bishop! Nothing you can say will ever get out, do you hear me? You will not live to cause me hurt."

In comparison, Tom's voice grew calmer and colder. "I suggest you stop threatening me now. I forgot to mention that I'm recording this call. A small error not to mention it before now, but I'm sure the authorities would overlook the data protection oversight if the need arose. I accept that the recording can't be used in court, but I doubt that will become necessary. There's always 'YouTube', though. What do you think?"

The silence at the end of the line was telling, and Tom continued, giving Ahmed and Sally a sombre nod. "I've made a detailed account of all the facts behind what I've told you, and copies of all the evidence has been lodged in a number of strategic places. If anything happens to me, or any of my team, or our families, everything will become public knowledge. It will be released to every major television station and newspaper and for good measure, it'll be posted on Facebook and Twitter, providing an immediate readership of several million people. So I don't think your power and control has a chance of silencing it, no matter how hard you might try. In fact, I think it would be impossible to block. Now just to recap; I gave you a list of demands which need to be met if this is going to stay under wraps. Do we have a deal? The clock is ticking."

There was a pause of several seconds before Leroy replied, his voice cold. "It will take some time to organise."

"Of course, I would expect it would. I'll call you back in twenty-four hours and you can advise me of your progress and the planned timetable for completing the arrangements."

Tom's hand was shaking when he dropped the phone back onto the rest and his whole body began to tremble uncontrollably. He drew in great gulps of air and staggered back towards a chair.

Sally guided him into a seated position before he collapsed and knelt beside him, gripping his arm.

"Did I hear you right? Where did you get all that from?" Ahmed demanded.

"He bought it," was all Tom could manage. He leaned forward in the chair, dropping his head into his hands while he struggled to regain his composure.

"Where did you get all the extra information from?" Sally questioned. "We found out about his childhood and his dealings since he came to the UK, but how did you discover all that other stuff?"

"I didn't," Tom admitted. "I've got no idea what he did before he arrived in the UK, but I guessed there had to be something shady involved, otherwise how could he have become so wealthy so quickly and in such a dangerous part of the world?"

"You made it up?" Sally got up on her feet, staring down at Tom in complete disbelief.

"What happened with Matthews and Stephan?" Ahmed questioned. "How did you manage to set up this security plan? What information have you planted, and how did you manage to do it so quickly?"

Tom broke into a broad smile and shook his head. "Matthews wasn't available; he was out visiting one of the branches. I did speak to Stephan and told him about what we had. We talked about whether we should go ahead and publish. You know, 'the public's right to know' argument – and then we considered the alternatives. Stephan was going to lodge some documents for disclosure in the event of our demise, but at this point in time, nothing has been arranged. The social networking angle came from him. Leroy might think he has the power to silence TV and the newspapers. He couldn't be totally confident, but he might have roughed out the threat. But even he would know he couldn't silence the internet. He couldn't take that chance."

"Are you telling me this was all a bluff?" Ahmed asked, his voice filled with wonder.

"Yeah. I guess it was." Tom staggered to his feet, but he was instantly bowled over by Sally as she threw her arms around him, showering him in kisses, Ahmed was drawn into the embrace and they shared a triumphant group hug.

"You must be quite a chess player yourself," Ahmed suggested.

"I've never played the game in my life," Tom replied, "but I was thinking I should maybe take up poker."

"I think perhaps it's time for that bottle of Bolly?" Sally suggested.

"I think you could be right," Tom replied.

"I want in on the celebration too." Ahmed said.

"We should celebrate now, because we still might not have a job to go to after Monday," Sally said.

Tom's eyes sparkled when he replied. "You may be right, but I have a hunch…"

All three burst into fits of laughter.

Epilogue

The party was in full swing and everyone was enjoying the event. In the short space of time since Rex Del Mundo set up home in the area, his regular soirees had become legendary. Anyone who was anyone needed to be there, to be noticed. Any politician, dignitary or would-be celebrity would cut off their left arm to be offered an invitation, to be seen in Rex Del Mundo's company. Every sycophant wanted to be there – seeking favours, money or hoping to improve their own recognition, if only as a result of association.

Rex despised them all, but they served a purpose. They were at his beck and call whenever he wanted anything, whenever he needed to cut through some red tape. Rex was a facade, the real man went to great pains to preserve his own anonymity. His guests knew he was very rich and powerful, but no one knew who he really was; or cared, for that matter. Who he was and how he'd come by his wealth were unimportant. All anyone ever knew about Rex Del Mundo was that he was there and his money and power knew no limits.

As was his custom early in the proceedings, Rex excused himself, leaving the gathering to enjoy and even abuse his hospitality. He slipped along the corridor to his study, firmly closing and locking the door behind him. The room was vast, with one wall completely filled with screens and monitors. Another one was fully glazed revealing a magnificent, uninterrupted view overlooking sparkling clean sands and the Caribbean Sea. Arriving with adequate funds to buy anything and anyone he wanted, Rex had purchased a secure, formidable and palatial mansion, on the Yukatan Peninsula, a short drive from Cancun airport.

Rex sat down at his desk, allowing the luxurious deep leather of the chair to envelop him. He switched on his computer, simultaneously activating the bank of screens. He quickly apprised himself of the performance of his business interests and investments.

Contemplating what had brought him here, Rex acknowledged he'd learned his lesson. He was confident he wouldn't be so complacent, or get caught dozing ever again. He'd complied with the demands and divested himself of his majority holding in Headcount, although he still retained a sizable interest. Since that time, he'd gone on to make several important and strategic investments, but more importantly, he's taken all the necessary steps to cover his tracks. His previous portfolio had been accumulated as he was growing in strength, before he had the power, knowledge and contacts to effectively make his activity untraceable. This time, he'd been more careful. The matrix of trusts and nominees laced through a maze of companies and individuals, mainly in offshore territories, would be impenetrable to a team of forensic accountants working full time on the task for a year. Rex had also made sure there was no-one left from the old days, nobody who was still alive who knew his past and had any grudge to bear. More importantly, great care had been taken to ensure there were no visible links from his previous life to who he was now. Having no family or friends made the task easier, but turning his back on his beautiful house, his fleet of vehicles and his art treasures had saddened him greatly. He'd been sloppy last time and regarded the loss as his punishment. On reflection, he owed a debt of gratitude to the reporter for providing him with a reality check. That's why he hadn't crushed him. Rex was now stronger, wiser and able to withstand any challenge. He'd learned his lessons. Now he was ready for a new game.

He checked the latest information he'd received. He had controlling interests in all the necessary organisations. The bait had been taken by all the right people, some accepting the career opportunity of a lifetime.

Arthur Bishop was gainfully employed – for the first time in his life – and was coping remarkably well. It was just reward for the assistance he had given, albeit unknowingly, in the past.

Sally had been lured with a peach of a job, as news lead for a small, but growing independent news channel. Ahmed too, had migrated to London, so the intrepid trio could re-establish themselves as a team. Rex knew they'd maintained frequent contact; he'd stockpiled the evidence to confirm it.

As for Tom Bishop – so far, he'd spurned any of the job offers presented to him. He'd been seeking to maintain some level of stability, while focussing more of his attention on a vain attempt to restore domestic bliss with his wife. He'd had some limited success, but his home life remained strained.

Bishop was wasting his time. Rex knew this for a fact, but he was prepared to be patient and allow the man to come to the same conclusion himself. A helping hand might need to be given, undetectably of course, to ensure the result, and Tom Bishop would be none the wiser and ready for the next phase.

Having no obvious beneficiaries, Rex was now considering how he should bequest his vast wealth. Charitable foundations had never appealed to him and apparent immortality through the dedication of buildings didn't excite him. Instead, he wanted to find a worthy successor. He had his first choice of contender in mind, but first, many challenges had to be overcome.

Most of the preparations had been put in place. The fun was almost ready to begin.

End

Dear reader,

We hope you enjoyed reading *Source*. Please take a moment to leave a review, even if it's a short one. Your opinion is important to us.

Discover more books by Zach Abrams at https://www.nextchapter.pub/authors/zach-abrams-scottish-mystery-crime-author-glasgow

Want to know when one of our books is free or discounted? Join the newsletter at http://eepurl.com/bqqB3H

Best regards,

Zach Abrams and the Next Chapter Team

About the Author

After a successful career in business and finance, Zach Abrams has relatively recently started writing fiction.

His first novel 'Ring Fenced' was published in November 2011 and this is a crime story with a difference as the underlying theme is obsession tinged with power, control and how they are used and abused.

This novel was followed by a collaboration with Elly Grant to produce 'Twists and Turns' a book of short stories and flash fiction.

Zach's second novel 'Made a Killing' was the first of a series of Alex Warren murder mysteries (published in November 2012) and this has been followed by 'A Measure of Trouble' (August 2013) and 'Written to Death' (February 2015).

Alike his central character in 'Ring Fenced,' (Benjamin Short), Zach Abrams grew up within an orthodox Jewish family. He completed his education in Scotland and went on to a career in business and finance. He is married with two children. He plays no instruments and has an eclectic taste in music, although not as obsessive as Benjamin.

Unlike Benjamin, he does not maintain mistresses, write pornography and (sadly) he does not have ownership of such a wealthy company. He is not a sociopath (at least by his own reckoning) and all versions of his life are aware of and freely communicate with each other. More in keeping with Alex Warren, he and his family reside in the south side of Glasgow.

Source
ISBN: 978-4-86747-958-2 (Large Print)

Published by
Next Chapter
1-60-20 Minami-Otsuka
170-0005 Toshima-Ku, Tokyo
+818035793528
31th May 2021